Praise]

The Grand Duke's Last Chance

"With a single exception, the work of Frank Heller is the best Swedish crime fiction written during the first half of the twentieth century and is still both readable and interesting."
— *John-Henri Holmberg, A Darker Shade of Sweden*

"A first-rate mystery thriller…A novel every one will enjoy"
— *The Sketch*

"A fast-moving story [which]…breaks new ground and is full of thrills."
— *Montrose Standard*

"A story of national bankruptcy, revolution and high adventure in the curious Grand Duchy of Minorca and elsewhere…It is all wildly impossible but none the less amusing on that account."
— *Westminster Gazette*

"Mr Heller has action and to spare to enliven his ingenious plot, but he differs from the merely conventional writer in that the buoyant humour and healthy atmosphere of his pages are their greatest charm."
— *Irish Times*

"A mystery novel of considerable interest"
— *Sheffield Daily Telegraph*

"A clever and irresponsible story of mystery"
— *The Scotsman*

"Let me recommend to you the works of Mr Frank Heller, a Swedish writer of capital mystery tales."
— *Illustrated London News*

The Grand Duke's Last Chance

FRANK HELLER

Translated by Robert Emmons Lee

KABATY PRESS
Published by Kabaty Press, Warsaw
www.kabatypress.com
Introduction Copyright © Mitzi H. Brunsdale 2022

Editing and Project Management by Isobelle Clare Fabian

All rights reserved. No part of this book may be reproduced in any form or by any electronic or mechanical means, including information storage and retrieval systems, without permission in writing from the publisher, except by reviewers, who may quote brief passages in a review. The moral right of the contributors has been asserted.

ISBN: 978-83-964260-8-6 (Paperback)
        978-83-966166-0-9 (Hardcover)
        978-83-964260-9-3 (ePub)
        978-83-966166-1-6 (PDF)

Cover Design © Jennifer Woodhead 2022
Interior Design and Typesetting: Minhajul Islam, ebooklay.com

Table of Contents

Introduction vii

Foreword xvii

I
Among Pines And Palms

1. From which it will be seen that Fortune does not
   always dwell among the High 21

2. In which the reader attends a breakfast and makes
   the acquaintance of a gentleman from Frankfort 35

3. In which St. Urban has an opportunity of
   distinguishing himself 69

4. In which a vessel leaves Minorca 103

II
Kings in Exile

1. In which the reader either meets with two former
   acquaintances or is introduced to a great financier 115

2. In which the reader will realize by what
   thin threads the fate of a nation may hang 127

3. In which the reader finds himself in Paris and
   gets a glimpse of a mysterious young lady 149

4. In which it is seen there are times when the voice
   of the newsboy, even as the voice of the people,
   is the voice of God 173

5. A spring evening in Marseilles 195

III
Midst Rebels and Rogues

1. A March day at sea and what took place there 227

2. Which is the beginning of very adventurous events 247

3. In which we again meet with an old acquaintance,
and in which surprises begin for the Grand Duke 255

4. In which the existence of the Republic of Minorca
seems gravely threatened 269

5. The Grand Duke shall be hung. Long live
the Grand Duke! 283

6. In which the Republic of Minorca's reign of terror
finds its Bonaparte 297

7. In which it is shown that those who escape Scylla have
not necessarily settled their accounts with Charybdis 317

8. In which Mr. Collin attends the most illustrious
wedding of his life 333

IV
The Kingdom, The Power and The Glory

The first and last chapter:
In which Mr. Collin leaves Minorca 349

A Note From The Publisher 369

Introduction

As the 1920s opened, Winston Churchill, writing as Britain's Secretary of State for War, summed up the effects of the First World War: "All the horrors of all the ages were brought together, and not only armies but whole populations were thrust into the midst of them." The war cost nearly 8 million lives on the battlefield and killed an estimated 6.5 million civilians. Britain lost almost a million men; nearly two-thirds of their young officers perished, half of them killed in Europe and the rest so severely damaged they could no longer function in society. France lost 1.5 million soldiers and almost 40,000 civilians. The United States, coming late into the war in 1918, had mobilized nearly 4.5 million soldiers, and almost 54,000 of them died in battle. Germany counted over 2 million military and an estimated 0.5 million civilian deaths; feeling swindled by the armistice agreements, the Germans could not negotiate a peace but had severe terms forced upon them. Exacerbating those bitter losses, the 1918 flu pandemic infected an estimated 500 million people, about one-third of the world's population, and killed about 50 million worldwide. No wonder citizens of the United States, Britain, and Europe embraced postwar escapist urges that made the Twenties roar.

The spirit of the Twenties, which the French called *les années folles* ("the crazy years") celebrated rule-breaking and a headlong pursuit of excitement. "Serious" writers and artists churned out radical rejections of conventional values like duty, patriotism, and marriage. The U.S. stock market soared, and frenzied jazz and Prohibition-promoted bootlegging flourished; women cut their hair, abandoned their corsets, and began to drink in pubs. Cars, phones, films, and labor-saving electrical devices changed domestic lives forever, and one horrified 1919 British observer even claimed that every village chemist was now selling contraceptives. Popular reading material quickly responded to war-weary readers' desire for vicarious thrills with a new mode of fiction and the Golden Age of Mystery Fiction was born.

Flourishing mainly in the 1920s and 1930s, the term "Golden Age of Mystery [or Detective] Fiction" today chiefly refers to the work of British women authors Agatha Christie (whose novels still outsell the Bible), the redoubtable Dorothy L. Sayers, Josephine Tey, and New Zealander Ngaio Marsh. Belgian Georges Simenon wrote his Maigret novels in French, and Americans Raymond Chandler, Dashiell Hammett, and James M. Cain produced their own brash "hard-boiled" variation of popular detective fiction.

The top British Golden Age practitioners subscribed to "rules" codified by Ronald Knox in 1929. Their work usually involved wealthy upper-class characters inhabiting lavish country-house settings or exotic foreign venues and featuring gentlemanly amateur detectives accompanied by Watson-like sidekicks. Dorothy L. Sayers, daughter of a clergyman, craved luxuries she could never have afforded in 1921, so she awarded them to her wealthy sleuth Lord Peter Wimsey. Golden Age "locked room" crimes also employed ingenious methods of murder, like the chess piece Agatha Christie fictionally wired for electricity. Overall, these authors sacrificed character development to puzzle solution. The term "whodunit" defined the genre, which became highly popular with audiences and lucrative for their creators. As mystery historian Bruce F. Murphy has pointed out, too, the "big names" had hordes of imitators, many of them now unreadable.

Frank Heller, a Golden Age author who reads well today, was born in 1886 in Sweden as Martin Gunnar Serner, son of a rural clergyman. He became famous both on the Continent and in the United States for his entertaining mystery novels, though he also produced poetry and travel literature. To finance his education, Serner had to make short-term bank loans that fell due before he finished his studies, forcing him into more loans to repay the first ones, a situation aggravated by his thirst for what Swedish sources delicately describe as "the more cheerful circles of student life." Deciding to leave Sweden in 1912, Serner forged some checks and cashed two at Malmö banks, but when bankers became suspicious of the third, he quickly took a ferry to Copenhagen, proceeding to Hamburg and then to London.

Serner then dramatically departed for Monaco to improve his finances at Monte Carlo's roulette tables. He met a former fellow student from Sweden, Mauricio Jesperson, who put Serner onto an infallible roulette system, and buoyed up by a few minor successes, Serner lost everything. He couldn't even go home because he was a wanted man in Sweden. Destitute, with only a few francs to his name, he cast about for a means of supporting himself. He hit on writing stories, fictionalizing life around the fabled Monte Carlo casino, and before he died in Malmö in 1947, he had become the internationally most successful Swedish entertainment author of his time.

Serner's first short story appeared in *Figaro* in February 1913, where he had just previously published his translation of a poem by the notorious British poet Swinburne. In 1914, under a contract with the Swedish firm Bonniers, he published a short story collection, *The London Adventures of Mr Collin*, now using the pseudonym "Frank Heller." Monte Carlo had been a leading European resort for decades, luring tourists ranging from royalty and movie stars to bumptious well-heeled Americans eager to gape at the lifestyles of the rich and famous. Into this heady milieu, Heller inserted Philip Collin, a lawyer escaping from Swedish authorities and a charming mutation of the "gentleman thief" Raffles, a literary figure introduced by E.R. Hornung in 1898. Raffles paid for his dwelling in a swanky Piccadilly hotel through burglary, which he justified by insisting "we can't all be moralists." He eschewed violence, however, insisting that "violence is a confession of terrible incompetence." In creating Philip Collin, Heller also drew on Maurice Leblanc's Arsène Lupin, a French detective-thief who appeared in sixty pieces of fiction from 1907 to 1941, so popular he won his creator France's Lègion d'Honneur and today appears in a new Netflix series.

Heller's first Philip Collin story collection immediately struck the reading public's fancy, appearing in four editions in its first two years and providing Heller enough income to start the travels he loved all his life. He first went to Paris, where he took several aerial tours with the pioneering French aviator Blériot. Heller spent the First World War in Denmark, living off translations of his work produced by Marie Franzos, a famous translator living in Vienna. Heller's debut in German, *Herrn Filip Collin Abenteur*, was an instant hit, quickly making Heller's stories the rage in Europe. It also allowed Heller to get his Swedish creditors off his back. After the war he went to Rome on a restored Swedish passport and met Annie Kragh, whom he married in 1920, and they built their first villa, "Casa Collina" in Bornholm, then bought Villa St. Yves on the French Riviera.

Philip Collin, who like Heller had abruptly left Sweden to avoid certain claims upon him, solved crimes mostly involving shady international financial transactions. Starting in 1923, translations of Heller's novels began to appear in English in Britain and the United States, both then experiencing financial upsurges, with considerable success. *The Marriage of Yussuf Khan,* appearing in English translation in 1923 and reissued in 2022 as *Beware of Railway-Journeys,* also showcases Heller's penchant for travel and unfamiliar cultures, his hero's clever use of disguises, involved puzzle-plotting, and a *soupçon* of delicious romance. Also published in 1923 in English was one of Heller's first and most popular novels, *The Grand Duke's Finances,* written around 1915 and reissued in 2022 as *The Grand Duke's Last Chance.* It remains Heller's triumphant mélange of an exotic setting, high-rolling financial hanky-panky, and a mysterious *femme fatale* with an intriguing alternative-history past. Central to all this, Philip Collin carries off a huge monetary swindle with exquisite and enviable panache.

Heller set this novel on the small Spanish Balearic Island of Menorca (also called Minorca), little known to outsiders in Heller's day. Since the Middle Ages, Menorca endured several waves of foreigners, from its fifth century conquest by Vandals and the Muslim annexation in 903 to successive invasions by Catholic Spain and the powerful navies of Britain and the United States before its incorporation into today's Spain. The island's apparently bucolic Mediterranean setting posed an unusual backdrop to Heller's complicated plot involving its financially strapped Grand Duke and money-mad foreigners, The intriguingly unfamiliar history and culture encouraged readers to watch a strange mystery with revolutionary overtones unfold, satisfying their curiosity about how bewildering financial finagling can be skillfully accomplished—a mystery in a mysterious setting.

Against this appealing backdrop, Heller's alter ego Philip Collin, with his impeccable manners, his undeniable charm, his ability to avoid physical violence when he can, but use it when he must, and his ease with individuals of many social classes, offers an appealing model of wish-fulfillment in the early 1920s. Collin was fond of claiming that "no one has had such a career as mine," and in this novel, centered on the impecunious Grand Duchy of Menorca, Heller matched Collin with an enigmatic beauty he meets apparently by chance in Paris and brings with him to Menorca, masquerading platonically as his wife.

To pull off this *coup de geste,* Heller took advantage of the literary device of alternative history, a "what if?" divergence from historical fact that allows for amusing or thought-provoking reflection. The deadly pale *femme fatale* who leaped from a car near Paris's Boulevarde des Capucines to whisper "Save me, Monsieur, if you are a gentleman," into Collin's willing ear turns out to be a royal personage indeed, Grand Duchess Olga, the oldest daughter of Nicholas II, Czar of Russia. Heller chivalrously saved her fictionally from being murdered by the Bolsheviks in 1918, using her flamboyant personality to reinforce his tale for lovers of royal escapades. Already as a strong-willed child, Olga Nikolaevna had been considered as her father's heir and contemplated by Britain's Queen Alexandra as a stabilizing mate for her playboy son Edward, Prince of Wales, who eventually abdicated to marry the notorious Mrs. Simpson. Olga's name was also connected to possible matches with the dashing Grand Duke Dmitri Pavlovich of Russia, Crown Prince Carol of Romania, and Crown

Prince Alexander of Serbia, but she stayed single and nursed wounded soldiers during World War I until her own health broke down. Olga's pivotal fictional role in Heller's novel allowed royal watchers plenty of thrills at seeing a thoroughly modern Grand Duchess defy convention to choose the man she loved.

Heller also treated the touchy sub-theme of anti-Semitism common in his time. Historian T.S. Kord in *Lovable Crooks and Loathsome Jews,* 2020, observed that nineteenth-century German criminology began to stress a supposed Jewish tendency toward vice and crime that eventually led to totalitarian anti-Semitic atrocities. In the 1920s, the old stereotype that Jews are good with money accelerated the notion that Jews controlled international banking. Some academics attribute Jewish financial success to the Jewish community's emphasis on learning and literacy, but the unfortunate notion remained, sadly internalized by the general public, that Jews in Central and Western Europe, perhaps three-fourths of them by the late 1800s, engaged in unethical moneylending practices that Christians should reject. That notion underlies Heller's satirical portrayal of German-Jewish financiers. He was by no means alone in doing so; villains in Golden Age mysteries were often victims of anti-Semitic slurs. Dorothy L. Sayers' Lord Peter Wimsey went so far as to disparage two cultures at once by implying that a Scot is likely to be as rapacious a "financial gentleman" as a Jew, and after World War II, Agatha Christie's agent had her publisher quietly remove all anti-Semitic references from reprints of her prewar novels.

Notwithstanding his fun with stereotypes of all kinds, Heller's *The Grand Duke's Finances* enjoyed considerable popular acclaim for its entertainment value, its exotic setting and its gossipy alternative-history romantic motif, swathed in delicious linguistic ironies and sparkling self-deprecating satire. The novel was made into a successful 1924 silent film in Germany, *Die Finanzen des Grossherzogs*, filmed on the lovely Adriatic coast and directed by then-famous F.W. Murnau, his only comedy. Today, traditional morality reels as readily-available contraceptives abound, enhancing easy Internet-promoted hookups; populations around the globe face the aftermath of another deadly pandemic that destroyed millions of lives; and they contemplate the dismaying possibility of yet another worldwide war erupting from an ugly Eastern European conflict. Genteel "entertainment literature" like Heller's can take its readers for a pleasant little while far, far away from horrid realities, for, as the Swedish periodical *Kvällsposten* put it in establishing its Frank Heller Prize in 1981, his literary spirit celebrates tasteful "tension, humor, and a [charming] sense of language."

—Mitzi M. Brunsdale

Foreword

This is an authentic account of the events which took place on the Island of Minorca during February and March, 1910, now laid before the public with the permission of those concerned. The reports brought out by the newspapers at the time were so thoroughly distorted or absolutely incorrect that they need not be considered.

For this reason we have not turned to the press for the details we have gathered together. Our principal source of information has been a former member of the Stockholm bar, Philip Collin, whose name should not yet have faded from the memory of the general public, especially that part of it to which money was owed at the time of his departure from Sweden in the year 1904. We have related elsewhere Mr. Collin's experiences up to 1910; but without some mention of his connection with the Grand Duchy of Minorca, those accounts would be absolutely incomplete.

"No one," Mr. Collin was in the habit of saying, "has had such a career as mine." And, leaving everything else out of consideration, surely it was a strange play of destiny that he, a humble son from the foot of the Brunkeberg ridge in Stockholm, should be called upon to rescue Minorca's ancient throne! Principalities, like books, are the foot-balls of Fate!

But we will let the story speak for itself.

—Frank Heller

BOOK ONE

Among Pines and Palms

CHAPTER 1

From Which It Will Be Seen That Fortune Does Not Always Dwell Among the High

Señor Esteban Paqueno belonged to an old Minorcan family, which had become prominent in the history of the Duchy as early as the sixteenth century. Generation after generation of his forefathers had served the princes of the House of Ramiros, usually as soldiers or courtiers, at times as diplomats; always in return for the barest pittance. Thus it happened that Señor Esteban had served the grand-ducal House of Ramiros for three generations, under Ramon XIX, Luis XI, and Ramon XX. Since 1876 he had managed on their behalf the finances of the Duchy, an unenviable post, to tell the truth, demanding of its possessor the cunning of the serpent, the stubbornness of the mule and the forgiving temperament of a saint. Perhaps Señor Paqueno lacked a good deal of the first of these attributes, but if so he made amends through a superabundance of the other two. No matter how desperate the case might seem, he never gave up;

with indomitable perseverance he continued to bombard the shady financial concerns of Europe with proposals for loans and apologetic letters. In the year 1910 there was not a man in Europe who knew its usurers and economic sharks like Señor Paqueno. And at the same time there was no one whose tastes were further from such things than Señor Paqueno; as the days went by and he half-mechanically attended to his routine correspondence, he dreamed of a little white-plastered cell in a remote Jesuit monastery in Spain; his eyes saw the long stone-flagged corridors, and the flowering garden in front, and his ears were caressed by the profound quietness reigning between those bare walls. For, long ago, Señor Paqueno had received his education in that monastery and it was the dream of his life to return there. But as he kept dreaming, the years went by in an eternal fight keeping the affairs of the Duchy alive, a fight which Señor Esteban now carried on less out of interest for his country than for the sake of his young master. For Don Ramon XX had taken complete possession of the fund of devotion Señor Paqueno had inherited from his forefathers. For Don Ramon's sake he expended year after year in correspondence with all the usurers of the Continent, while his dream of the Jesuit college in Barcelona faded further and further away.

Don Ramon accepted Señor Paqueno's devotion in the same manner as most of the other events in his life, with an inexhaustible good humor, and as something which was as it should be. To brood over life and its problems struck him as absolutely meaningless; he himself was a man without deeper feelings, with a rather good education and a thorough conviction of the vanity of all things. The absurd position he held in the midst of the twentieth century as absolute ruler of a country entirely lacking in resources, constantly catered to his ideas of life and his bantering humor. After his first few years on the throne, his attempts at "ruling" became more and more infrequent, and in the year 1910 he had long since confined himself to trying, with Señor Esteban's help, to keep the machinery going. And, as he rightly remarked, that was no sinecure.

On one fine morning in February Señor Paqueno greeted the entrance of his master with a more than usually troubled air. There was an expression of grave earnestness in his eyes behind the gold-rimmed glasses and a nervousness in his bearing which immediately had the customary effect of increasing the Grand Duke's good humor. After greeting him with a wave of his cigar, he stuck his hands into his trouser pockets, looked at Señor Paqueno with eyes half-closed, and said:

"Did you sleep well, Paqueno?"

"Yes, thank you. And Your Highness?"

As a matter of fact, Señor Paqueno had spent a miserable night, but it would never have entered his head to confess it before he had convinced himself as to how his master had slept.

"Capitally, Paqueno; a man with affairs in such a state as mine always sleeps well."

"Your Highness is joking. Affairs in a bad state are not considered an aid to sleep."

The Grand Duke gave a hearty laugh.

"That depends entirely upon how bad they really are. If they are as bad as mine, that is to say, absolutely hopeless, a person sleeps excellently if he is normal. There was only one occasion when I slept poorly, and that was a couple of years ago when I was hoping for better times. Well, what was there in the mail today?"

Señor Paqueno's face again assumed the gloomy expression it had borne at the time of the Grand Duke's entrance. He drew out some letters from a portfolio.

"About the same as usual, Your Highness. About the same... There is a letter from Altenstein of Cadiz."

"And what does the worthy Altenstein say?"

"That the interest for 1908 must be paid; otherwise he must appeal to the Spanish Government."

"The interest for 1908? What year is this?"

"1910, Your Highness, but the interest for 1908 has not been paid yet."

"That I can well imagine. I thought you meant 1898."

"No, Your Highness; Altenstein received his interest up to and including 1907 last year."

"As early as last year! Paqueno, I am sorry that I have to find fault with an old retainer like you, but you really must be more careful in our affairs. The interest up to and including 1907 as early as 1909—you can see the results of indulging one's creditors. On account of your mistake,

Altenstein of Cadiz has already formed an absolutely false impression of our capabilities which can bring about very unpleasant consequences for us."

"Your Highness, I am overwhelmed with contrition; I will only mention in my defence that this man Altenstein seemed to be a fellow whom we should handle carefully."

"You mean that we might be able to borrow more there?"

"No, Your Highness. I mean that he is a dangerous fellow, an unscrupulous fellow, and that he has already proved it through the difficulties he caused the Spanish Government last year."

"But my dear Paqueno, that does not affect us. Spain is in a bad condition but only a person out of his head would compare their state of affairs with ours. And Spain is a big realm, while we are protected through our diminutive size, exactly like the bacilli. Well?"

Señor Paqueno drew out another letter from the portfolio, and said: "There is also a letter from Thomson and French in Rome."

"Really! And what do Thomson and French in Rome have to say?"

"That it is impossible for them to wait any longer for the 1900 and 1901 interest on their loan of 1900. Half of the loan should be paid by now. Unless something is done they say they must sell the security or. . ."

"What is the security, Paqueno?"

"The island of Iviza, Your Highness, and all its resources. . . or start diplomatic proceedings."

"That's all right, Paqueno. The interest for 1900 and 1901—and now it is only 1910! Modern business haste, Paqueno! If my late lamented father ever heard such strangulation methods mentioned by the bankers! Who is the next?"

"Viviani, Your Highness, in Marseilles. Perhaps Your Highness remembers he is the one who has the salt taxes as security for a loan. He writes in, complaining that these yield too little. . ."

"The Italian rogue! Upon my word, I wish this were 1510 instead of 1910, then I would teach him what complaining is."

"Not content with complaining, Your Highness, he even has the audacity to burst into accusations; he insists that our figures are open to question and that he has been enticed into a more than dubious enterprise."

"The rogue! The shameless rogue! A dubious enterprise from which he reaps fifteen per cent if he does one. Write to him that if he doesn't look out I will issue a grand-ducal decree making the use of salt in Minorca punishable by death. Then he can look out for his security!"

"Your Highness is in good humor. Rest assured I will handle Viviani as he deserves. I am not afraid of Thomson and French either; it is a fine old firm and will listen to reason. We can put off Altenstein too with the argument that Your Highness just brought up. His insistency is due only to immature judgment."

Señor Paqueno stopped a moment and nervously polished his glasses. Then he resumed with a shamefaced look at the Grand Duke:

"Unfortunately, there is also a letter from Semjon Marcowitz. Your Highness remembers our affair with Marcowitz of Paris?"

"Anyway Marcowitz of Paris does not seem to have forgotten it. I must admit that it has escaped my mind."

"Oh, Your Highness, Semjon Marcowitz!. . ."

"Yes, Paqueno, Semjon Marcowitz!"

"Your Highness remembers 1908."

"Why not, Paqueno? That was only two years ago. I am at present thirty-five, and up to now there has been no case of mental imbecility in my family earlier than forty. Well?"

Señor Paqueno sighed at the Grand Duke's joking. In a dejected voice he continued, constantly pausing as though to give the Grand Duke opportunity to interrupt:

"If Your Highness remembers 1908, perhaps Your Highness also recalls the reports that were then circulated in the newspapers about an engagement between the Grand Duke of Minorca and a Grand Duchess of Russia, who was said to be as beautiful as she was rich. . . and that these reports did not lack all foundation. . . For two months the negotiations were carried on by Count Fedor Obelinsky, the Russian ambassador at Madrid, on the one side, and by me on the other. . . Several official communications passed between us. . . And one day the Grand Duchess herself— during what might be called a fit of girlish romanticism— wrote a letter to Your Highness. . . a letter which was not in the same official tone... Does Your Highness remember?"

Señor Paqueno gave his master an appealing look as though begging to be excused from continuing. The Grand Duke stood absolutely still, with bowed head, and stared out of the window. The corners of his mouth were drawn far down, and it seemed as though he hardly heard.

Señor Paqueno gave another deep sigh and resumed in the same weary voice:

"That year, we were in a more desperate position than usual. The after effects of the American financial crisis were being felt most acutely... Our government bonds were quoted at 47 ½, when quoted at all, and money could not be procured at 100 per cent... And with it all, there was only the necessity of holding out for a short time until the engagement was actually arranged! But we couldn't even raise enough money for that; no one believed our promises. It was then we turned to Semjon Marcowitz... Does Your Highness now remember Semjon Marcowitz?"

Señor Paqueno's voice trembled with emotion; for the second time he looked appealingly at his master, who still stood in his former position. His cigar had gone out, and he unceasingly rolled it around and around in the corner of his mouth.

"We received two hundred thousand," continued Señor Esteban almost whisperingly, "in return for a note for three hundred thousand... and security, the nature of which was mentioned in the note... Semjon Marcowitz, who knew the disposition of the Russian court, realized that he risked nothing by lending on security of that kind. . . A letter such as the one written by the Grand Duchess Olga was worth a million as easily as three hundred in his. . ."

Señor Paqueno stopped short and involuntarily leaped back a step; the Grand Duke had sprung forward, flushed with anger, and stood towering over him, his hands in his pockets.

"Stop, Paqueno!" he cried. "You talk as though we were a couple of cold-blooded scoundrels, ready to sell our honor for a few paltry hundred thousand. Don't you know how long it took before I would have any part in the wretched business? You, Paqueno, you, who are so pious, should have stopped me!"

"Your Highness does me an injustice," answered Señor Paqueno with a look of gentle reproach. "Now that Your Highness seems to remember all the rest, perhaps Your Highness will also recollect who chanced upon the unlucky idea. It was not I. It was Your Highness, although I hasten to admit that it was first proposed in jest. That I ventured to encourage the plan no one has regretted more than I; during the last two years while Your Highness seemed to have forgotten all about it, I have conjured up in my mind a thousand wild plans by which I might make amends for my foolishness. Oh, what an old blind idiot I was—but I was tempted by the most seductive thing on earth, Your Highness, by hope! For thirty-two long years I had worked day after day to make both ends meet—almost without hope. And then it seemed as though we were saved at last.

Only to hold out a couple of months more. . ."

"And who in the devil's name could have thought that the engagement would come to naught, Paqueno? Tell me, who?"

"No one, Your Highness; but unfortunately, it was so written in the book of Fate. Grand Duke Nicholas refused his consent, and the Grand Duchess Olga in spite of everything was his dutiful daughter. . . He is dead now—I do not know whether Your Highness saw the notice in the papers a few months ago? And we, Your Highness, stand here like criminals, with the risk of being exposed at any time by Semjon Marcowitz. And yet. . . I know that what we did would be considered base in the eyes of the world, but no matter how deeply I regret it, it does not seem so reprehensible in my mind. Our intentions were of the best, and God is witness we ourselves derived no advantage from the money. Under such circumstances, many of the fathers belonging to my order would have considered our actions justifiable. But I know that worldly justice would decree otherwise; such an act would be a crime whether a person profited by it or not."

The Grand Duke stamped on the floor until the old marble slabs echoed.

"Yes, that is just what makes me so furious!" cried he. "Here we both stand, as you say, Paqueno, with the pleasant prospect of having our pictures in the press within a month's time: Further disclosures from the blemish spot of Europe—Don Ramon's latest exploits, and so on to the bitter end. And what advantage did we derive from our two hundred thousand? Unless I am mistaken, it was the moneylenders in London and Amsterdam who received the money for their interest? Or was it Mr. Altenstein?"

Without answering, Señor Paqueno gave a dejected nod, and the Grand Duke continued in the same tone but with an ever increasing roguish gleam in his eye:

"Mark my words, Paqueno, it is hell upon earth to be an absolute sovereign without money. A person in such a position is not far from turning anarchist. Don Jeronimo the Lucky was as poor as I, but his life was easier than mine, at least. He was born at the right time. If he needed money he simply issued a few letters of marque and sank a dozen merchantmen. No one thought there was anything queer in that. And he got some enjoyment out of his spoils besides— fine castles and feasts every day. I, Paqueno, commit minor transgressions, and live on rabbit week after week. I am an anachronism, a deeply deplorable anachronism. Thank goodness an absolute sovereign can do no wrong! That has always been a comfort in my hours of darkness. But now for safety's sake I shall go to a specialist in mental diseases. If I have an affidavit in my pocket stating I am unbalanced, then I can clear myself finally, and of course I can get such an affidavit. A person who would remain ruler of Minorca must be insane!"

"And how about me, Your Highness?" asked Señor Paqueno, with a slight tremble in his voice.

The Grand Duke had begun pacing the room with a

long limping stride; at Señor Paqueno's words he stopped and stretched out his hand.

"Dear old Esteban! Forgive me! I thought you understood I was joking—foolishly, of course, as usual. Naturally we will stand and fall together in this affair. But you may rest assured we will keep our heads above water. When is that wretched loan due?"

"On the thirteenth of March, Your Highness; it was signed on the thirteenth of March, 1908, almost two years ago."

"A month from today! And Marcowitz of course wants the whole of it?"

"I don't believe so. Marcowitz will be willing enough to renew it."

"H'm, I have an idea what such a renewal would mean. No, the matter must be settled once for all. I will not have it on my conscience any longer. We have a month before us in which to raise three hundred thousand for Marcowitz, and during that time, Paqueno, you can be so kind and look up some of those works on conscience written by the fathers of your order. I feel myself in need of a little consolation on that point."

Don Ramon resumed his promenade up and down the room. In spite of the tone he had assumed at the end toward old Paqueno, it was evident that his good humor had deserted him for the moment. He threw open a window and with knitted brows stared down at the harbor, where the water drowsily rippled in the sunshine, and at the small houses crowded together on the terraces rising from the shore. The palms rustled in the morning wind, from the distance came the rumbling in the streets of Port Mahon, and at intervals the odor of warm tar was wafted up from the harbor. Suddenly he turned to Paqueno, who was staring gloomily at the tips of his shoes.

"Is that German still here?"

"Who, Your Highness?"

"Binzer."

"Yes, he is here. Your Highness is well informed. How did Your Highness know his name?"

"Bah—in Minorca! But of course he is still here, since the hotel has its flag raised. What is he doing here?"

"I don't know, Your Highness. He has made a number of trips to the interior of the island. They say he has been taking photographs for a German concern."

"H'm. At least we needn't be afraid of his being a spy and photographing our fortifications, for Nature has razed them all with the exception of the old rookery here in Port Mahon. We have quietly been carrying out the peace program."

The door to the dining-room was noiselessly opened and the chef Auguste appeared on the threshold.

"Breakfast is served, Your Highness."

The Grand Duke brightened up and shook off his troubled manner as a big Newfoundland dog shakes the water from his coat.

"Share the rabbit with me, Paqueno," said he, and

pushed his old Minister of Finance before him into the dining-room. "We both need something strengthening!"

CHAPTER 2

In Which the Reader Attends a Breakfast And Makes the Acquaintance of A Gentleman from Frankfort

They sat down to breakfast by the open window in the old dining-room, the furniture of which would remind any observer how in time everything becomes food for moths. Auguste silently served the vegetal hors d'oeuvres and afterwards the delicious Mediterranean mussels which to Don Ramon's delight were boiled in wine and water.

Then came the rabbit, a generous portion of which Don Ramon served to his Minister of Finance; however he did not scorn a helping himself. Neither he nor Señor Paqueno seemed disposed to continue the conversation begun in the study. The Grand Duke ate in silence, while Señor Paqueno did but little honor to his share, toying with the bread crumbs on the tablecloth and eating only a bit now and then as though he felt it his duty. The Grand Duke filled his glass with some excellent Bordeaux—a memento from the last loan—and said:

"Well, Paqueno, don't suddenly lose your courage now; it is the excitement of seeing how things will turn out that lends the greatest pleasure to living by our wits as we do. Why, we have a whole month before us! Of course everything will turn out right. Minorca has been in need of money for the last two hundred years and has still kept going. Why should it suddenly collapse in 1910? Besides I rely on our holy patron, St. Urban of Majorca, who has never yet deserted our family. As a matter of fact he is the only inhabitant of Majorca who has not done so, with the exception of my valet Joaquin and the honorable Auguste."

Auguste returned, bringing cheese and figs which he placed on the table after the Grand Duke had declined more rabbit. Don Ramon silently occupied himself with the cheese, Bordeaux and figs. Then he ordered coffee and lit his ever-present cigar. With hands behind his head he lazily stared out at the Mediterranean, over which the gulls floated in circles as odd and fantastic as did the smoke from his cigar in the slightly moving air by the window. His large open face again expressed the most profound contentment with life. To look at him no one would have thought him what he was—absolute ruler of Minorca and a man threatened with ruin and dishonor within another month. Señor Paqueno who, after the last remarks, had in vain been attempting to imitate his master's attitude, looked at him in silent respect. Auguste appeared with the coffee-tray and a cut-glass decanter; after his Highness had helped himself from both, he again turned to Señor Paqueno.

"The stomach is the centre of the world," said he in a philosophical tone. "Look at me, Paqueno, and see how really kindly disposed I am at present! I am ready to perform the most noble and eccentric deeds—for instance to forgive those to whom I am indebted or to give my subjects a constitution. The latter I deny them only because they are much too good for it. Under my rule they have lived in peace and quiet like their forefathers, and need only think about their stomachs. If they were given a constitution they would begin to think about other things which are absolutely unnecessary. Therefore as long as possible I shall avoid giving them one. Am I not right, Paqueno?"

"Your Highness is absolutely right. Parliamentary government is entirely inconsistent with our history, and after all the care Your Highness' family has squandered on its subjects it has earned for itself the right to rule as absolute princes."

"You're talking nonsense, Paqueno, my family has in most cases acted like so many rogues toward its subjects. Think of Luis X who sold them to the West Indies. I do not desire an absolute government for my own sake but for that of my subjects. I care for them with the love which comes from long possession, a deep love, even if it does not appear on the surface. I want to see them happy. I know that they grumble about the taxes—not much, but some at least. However, I realize they are much better off paying taxes to me than being encumbered with a constitution.

For the very moment they had one industry would overwhelm them, and they would be really unhappy. I have seen enough such cases during my travels. Now, no one is in want on Minorca. They have only enough economic difficulties to give a zest to life, and I am the crowned scapegoat who, together with you, Paqueno, bears all the blame for them. But I do it gladly, for I love them, Paqueno, especially after breakfast."

The Grand Duke looked at Señor Paqueno with a slight smile. It was very evident from the old Minister of Finance's face that his thoughts were miles away from Don Ramon's fantastic ideas, and that, with his usual courtesy, he was trying to conceal the fact.

"Paqueno," said the Grand Duke, "you really show too much consideration for Semjon Marcowitz. He does not deserve your spending so much thought on him. Instead, think up someone we can fleece—that will be putting your mental powers to a much better use. What do you say if we revive some old edict and impose a head-tax on Mr. Binzer who has been living here over a month? Don Jeronimo certainly made all foreigners pay fifty per cent of what they owned, when he began his war against the infidels. Perhaps there are other precedents, too."

Señor Paqueno disconsolately shook his head, but before he could answer, the door opened and Auguste came in. There was the shadow of a discreet smile lurking in the corners of the domestic's mouth.

"There is a man outside," said he, "who requests an

audience with Your Highness."

"A man, Auguste? You mean a gentleman?"

"No, a man, Your Highness—a German." The tone of Auguste's voice was indescribable. "He has no visiting card, but he says that his name is Binzer of Frankfort."

The Grand Duke straightened up in his chair and stared at Auguste.

"Binzer of Frankfort! When you speak of the devil you. . . Listen to that, Paqueno, Binzer desires audience of me—the lamb seeks the lion!"

The face of the old Minister of Finance expressed absolute and unadulterated astonishment. Truly not every day was audience requested of the Grand Duke of Minorca—when it happened it was at the most some creditor whose patience had been tried all too sorely. This Binzer. . . who was said to be rich. . .

"What can he want, Your Highness?" he stammered.

"To take our pictures, I suppose. You said something, I believe, about his being a photographer. But he will get little satisfaction if that's what he wants. The newspapers would have too good a description of us then when we disappear a month from now!"

Señor Paqueno shuddered.

"Show the fellow in, Auguste," said the Grand Duke with a quiet laugh. "Tell him that his Highness is granting audience in the dining-room, since it is Saturday."

Auguste hastened back to the antechamber and a moment later ushered Herr Binzer of Frankfort into the

Grand Duke's dining-room and into this story.

Herr Isidor Binzer's career is to a great degree shrouded in darkness. What could be gathered together after the happenings on Minorca is not much, but we will here give a report of those facts which seem to be fairly certain.

Herr Binzer of Frankfort, it seems, was really born in Hamburg in 1876, or at least, there is record of an Adolf Isidor Binzer who was said to have been born in July of that year in the parish of Saint Felix. The Herr Binzer who played one of the principal roles in the happenings on Minorca, it is true, bore only the name of Isidor, but as it is known that at various times he changed his surname, it should not have caused him much inconvenience in abbreviating his forename to a slight degree.

The Adolf Isidor Binzer in question enjoyed the education usually given to boys of his class of life; he went through the public schools and the lower high school. Thereafter he was installed as an extra laboratory assistant in the large chemical house of Grossman and Company. For many years Herr Binzer's life flowed by behind the letter S which in a gigantic bow curled around the front of the office window at which he worked. Through the lower loop of this letter he could look out on a narrow and dusty Hamburg street, broiling under a relentless summer sun or teeming with rain turned blue from the refuse of Grossman's work rooms. Behind the window Herr Binzer busied himself making analytical tests of a simple nature, while his nose was constantly filled with the sharp stench from the chemicals, and his eyes, which longingly stared out through the letter S, gradually began to see everything from a crooked, S-shaped point of view. It was probably on this account that he left Grossman and Company in 1899 and took a position with Altenhaus and Mayer. He was employed by the heads of the firm (according to the admission they made at the police hearing) as an expert ore analyst, Altenhaus and Mayer specializing in mining property of a speculative character. In any case, Herr Binzer's work appears to have been satisfactory, for he remained in the service of the concern during the entire term of its existence, in other words, for an entire year. Then, at the very moment the police had planned to test the affairs of Altenhaus and Mayer by a thorough analysis of their business methods, Adolf Isidor Binzer forestalled them through subjecting the door of the safe to certain acid tests and silently disappearing from Hamburg. Messrs. Altenhaus and Mayer, who had not intended departing from Germany before the following Saturday, were forced through his dishonesty to leave suddenly and almost without funds. The oaths which their clients shortly afterwards hurled after them, were in turn punctiliously transferred to Herr Binzer's account by the two impoverished swindlers. The police, who quickly succeeded in capturing the heads of the firm, searched in vain for Adolf Isidor Binzer. It was not until later that they reached the conclusion he had steered his course to Mexico and Nicaragua, undoubtedly for the purpose of inspecting the remarkably productive mines which Altenhaus and Mayer had desired to popularize among the German public. However, the results of Herr Binzer's investigations, as well as his further experiences in the New World, are very little known. His persistent habit of always changing his name simultaneously with his place of residence makes it extremely difficult to follow his movements. Nevertheless, we meet with him again in October, 1909, under the name of Abraham Schildknecht, travelling as a first-class passenger on board the Franconia. Herr Schildknecht, who attracted attention principally through his parsimonious tipping and his insignificant luggage, hastily left the steamer at Cherbourg to the great disappointment of several gentlemen who expected to greet him on his arrival in Southampton. Again bearing the long since discarded name of Binzer, but no longer the full beard he had worn for many years, the crafty mine speculator hurried away from Cherbourg in search of new fields.

Such were Herr Binzer's antecedents.

Herr Binzer's appearance, as he passed by Auguste and entered the Grand Duke's dining-room, did not belie his mode of life and character. The sharp sunlight at first proved dazzling after the darkness of the anteroom; for a while he kept blinking, and every now and then the corners of his mouth twitched spasmodically, as though the muscles were not entirely under control. His head suggested a certain rough-hewn energy; it would never have been called beautiful but he had unnecessarily disfigured it by wearing his hair closely clipped in the German fashion. His eyebrows were thick, almost bushy, but so light-colored that they were hardly visible. Below his eyes were two swollen pouches, betraying a life of dissipation. He wore rimless glasses and was clad in a cutaway, rather the worse for wear, gray trousers and according to the German custom, light tan laced shoes. His figure, which was thickset, was somewhat inclined to corpulency, and his hands, adorned with various rings, were small and fat.

Auguste, who announced Herr Binzer's name in an ironical tone, retired, casting a last look at him. Herr Binzer blinkingly bowed before the Grand Duke. Don Ramon lightly waved his cigar in answer.

"You have requested an audience?" said he. "This is my friend, Señor Paqueno."

Señor Paqueno, who had risen at Herr Binzer's entrance, bowed politely and Herr Binzer acknowledged his greeting with a slight nod which made the old Minister of Finance turn red. Don Ramon smiled slightly. This species of European was new to him. What did the man want? It was evident he was trying to make as refined and confidence-inspiring an impression as possible on the Grand Duke, but if Don Ramon read his face correctly—and although an absolute monarch Don Ramon was no poor psychologist—his subservient smiles were but a very thin mask. The forehead and mouth bespoke brutality, and the curt manner in which he had acknowledged old Señor Paqueno's greeting confirmed this impression. He was too occupied with his motives for approaching the Grand Duke to have time for anything else. And what were these motives? Don Ramon hardly needed to see the lines around Herr Binzer's eyes and around the corners of his mouth to guess; as plainly as possible they said *Geschäft*! Business with the Grand Duke of Minorca! This did not happen often—but when it did it was rather certain to be a bit of bad business, through which the duke in question was predestined to lose. Smiling to himself, Don Ramon decided to make the game as difficult as possible for Herr Binzer.

With a couple of hasty glances to each side, Herr Binzer had surveyed the room; it was amusing to see the pains he took trying to conceal the feelings the moth-eaten furnishings awakened in him. Don Ramon bit his lips so as not to burst out laughing at the looks with which Señor Paqueno followed this play of features. Finally Herr Binzer opened his mouth for the first time. He seemed embarrassed as to how he should begin.

"I have requested an audience for... for the purpose of paying my respects to Your Highness... I have been here on Minorca now for some time... I thought it fitting that..."

His Spanish was absolutely correct, but he stressed his words heavily; at the same time it was evident he was trying to make the tone of his voice as subservient as the expression on his face.

"Ah," said Don Ramon politely, "that is very kind of you, Herr Binzer. It is not often that strangers come to Minorca, and it is still more seldom that they are as courteous as you."

Herr Binzer expressed his agreement through a smile,

and quickly looked around. It was evident that he was waiting for an invitation to sit down. As none came, however, he himself drew out one of the old mahogany chairs by the table and seated himself. Old Señor Paqueno turned red as a beet—throughout their greatest troubles he had preserved his old-fashioned court manners. *Santiago de Coruña!* This German to sit down without more ado even while he himself remained standing so as to remind him what politeness demanded! He was on the point of saying something when Don Ramon stopped him with a movement of his hand. There was a glimmer in the corner of his eye. Herr Binzer evidently amused him.

"Paqueno," said he, "for goodness' sake, sit down!"

Herr Binzer, who had stretched one leg over the other, again began to speak.

"I am greatly pleased with my visit to Minorca," said he. "It is a charming island. The scenery is exceptionally beautiful. I admire it greatly. And then the climate. . ."

"I am truly very glad," said Don Ramon in his heartiest tone. "People who love nature are never really bad. And as you must have noticed, Herr Binzer, the climate is almost the only thing we have here on Minorca!"

"Yes, yes, otherwise, I understand, everything is in a bad way," Herr Binzer smiled deploringly.

Señor Paqueno gave a start as though he had received a box on the ear. *Madre de Dios!* It was unparalleled, it was unbelievable! How could Don Ramon tolerate such things? Didn't he hear? Hadn't this cursed German hurled their misfortunes in their very faces? He stared at his master who again made a slight movement with his hand as though to quiet him. The expression on Don Ramon's face was more friendly than ever.

"You sympathize with us, Herr Binzer. It is really most kind of you. May I have the pleasure of offering you something to drink?" he asked, and without waiting for an answer poured out a big tumblerful of brandy. Herr Binzer lifted the tumbler and emptied it to the last dregs. Don Ramon moved his chair so that his back was to the window.

"You came here from Germany, Herr Binzer?"

Evidently Herr Binzer was beginning to feel steadier in his saddle after the brandy. He leaned back in his chair, and his smiles were no longer so numerous or subservient.

"No, from Mex. . . from America," said he. "I have been over there a long time—been around a bit, here, there and everywhere, *versteht sich*—made a bit this way and that—through houses, mines, stocks. Anything is worthwhile as long as you can make money by it, eh?" Herr Binzer laughed heartily at his own words.

"And you always succeeded in making a bit, one way and another, didn't you, Herr Binzer?" The Grand Duke hastened to hide his ironical tone through pouring out another brandy which Herr Binzer silently took. The Grand Duke's brandy was like his wine, a memento from the last loan, and as good as his financial affairs were bad. He was known to be able to withstand enormous quantities of alcohol when necessary, but Señor Paqueno, who had never before seen him drink more than a small wine-glass of brandy after luncheon, looked at his master in surprise, and with something bordering on reproach in his eye. How could the Grand Duke tolerate such a person and how could he stoop low enough to drink with him?

Herr Binzer gave a mysterious sort of smile at the Grand Duke's question.

"Oh, a bit," said he. "I have enough to get along on. Yes, things have not gone badly with me. A person must provide for his old age, *nicht*? I made my money, and got out in time. Bad times nowadays!"

His glances, which if possible were even more frank and open than the tone of his voice, again flew over the moth-eaten splendor of the room as he sipped at his brandy. The Grand Duke raised his glass to drink with him.

"Unfortunately, you are more than right, Herr Binzer. And you intend going back to Germany from here?"

Herr Binzer hastily emptied his glass.

"Well," said he, "that depends. I don't know. What is there to do at home? I have made my little pile, and I have the means to afford what I want. And here on Minorca I have found something which perhaps I would like to get hold of."

"What in the name of Heaven is it?" said the Grand Duke earnestly. "The climate is not for sale, Herr Binzer."

Herr Binzer laughed loudly.

"No, and everything else has been pawned, you mean. Ha, ha. I know that well enough. I have made a few little investigations myself, in case I might do a bit of business here; you should always know how people stand before doing business with them!"

The Grand Duke blushed slightly; this German was a bad case. For the third time he motioned back Señor Paqueno, who seemed ready on behalf of his master to murder their guest. If the latter noticed the effect of his words, which is doubtful, he at least showed no fear on that account, but continued in the same free and easy tone:

"I also know that all the land here belongs to the Government..."

"And I am the Government, Herr Binzer," the Grand Duke interrupted drily.

"Of course, so that if anyone wants to buy anything, he must come here—to the sole member of the firm, eh? And that is why I have come. I was out by Punta Hermosa a few days ago—beautiful scenery, fine situation, and I looked over the old castle there."

"Don Jeronimo the Lucky's old castle," muttered the Grand Duke between his teeth. "Well, Herr Binzer?"

"What do you want for it?"

For the fraction of a second the Grand Duke looked at Herr Binzer with such an air of reflection that the gentleman in question began to hitch uneasily in his chair; it looked as though Don Ramon were considering whether it would be better to shoot Herr Binzer on the spot or merely kick him out the door. After a moment, however, he said quietly:

"You seem to have informed yourself thoroughly about us, Herr Binzer. Haven't you discovered something rather peculiar concerning the Castle of Punta Hermosa?"

"I have never had any interest for antiquarian and historical matters," said Herr Binzer indifferently. "I like the situation, and I have the means to buy the place."

"I doubt it," said the Grand Duke drily. "If you yourself have not discovered it, I can tell you what is peculiar about the Castle of Punta Hermosa. As a matter of fact, it is a twofold peculiarity. In the first place, Punta Hermosa is free of mortgages, and secondly, it does not belong to me. It is the only bit of land on Minorca which is not hypothecated, and it is the only bit which does not belong to me—effect and cause, one might say."

"*Verflucht nochmal*," said Herr Binzer. "You are right there. The castle is not mortgaged, that is true, but if it doesn't belong to you, to whom does it belong then?"

"It did belong to me, but I presented it to a friend—have made friends through the mammon of unrighteousness, as the Scriptures say. I gave it to him so that he would remain in my service."

"I understand," said Herr Binzer, with a grin.

"No, you do not understand, Herr Binzer. My friend would not otherwise have remained in my service, because I would not have let him waste his time in such a thankless manner. The Castle of Punta Hermosa belongs to Señor Paqueno here."

Herr Binzer turned abruptly to Señor Paqueno and

looked at him with newly awakened interest.

"Really?" said he. "And what do you say to my proposition? Will you sell the place? How much do you want for it?"

All the accumulated emotion which slowly had been arising within old Señor Esteban Paqueno and which up to now he had controlled out of regard for his master suddenly broke loose. He jumped up from his chair, and as he looked at Herr Binzer of Frankfort with the keenest disgust he cried hoarsely:

"What do I say?— Will I?— What do I want?. . . Señor, how dare you come here and insult us with your offers? Sell? Never as long as I live—and to you! I would rather see Punta Hermosa lay in ashes!. . ."

He stopped short at a sudden motion from Don Ramon, who waited until he had quieted down before saying to Herr Binzer:

"Señor Paqueno is somewhat unaccustomed to affairs of this kind, Herr Binzer. He has been occupied mainly with matters of a more reprehensible character—you see, he is my Minister of Finance. In any case, you understand now that the castle is not for sale."

"I had thought of offering a hundred thousand," said Herr Binzer quietly, "but I can stretch it to a hundred and twenty-five. Well, what do you say?"

He let his glance wander from Señor Paqueno to the Grand Duke in order to watch the effect of his words. The face of the old Minister of Finance continued to be filled with suppressed disgust; the Grand Duke was still quiet and self-possessed as he said:

"I regret, Herr Binzer, that we must bring this conference to a close. It has been very kind of you to look us up and also wish to improve our deplorable condition. But you are wasting your time and, forgive me, mine, as well! You probably are a busy man, and although my position does not entail much work, still I have quite a little to do."

He rose from his chair to let Herr Binzer know that the audience was at an end, but without paying attention to this, the indefatigable man of business cried:

"A hundred and fifty thousand then, in Heaven's name! Think, a hundred and fifty thousand! A hundred and fifty— yes, let us say, a hundred and seventy-five! A hundred and seventy-five thousand! Think what that would mean to you! Do like Castro, take my hundred and seventy-five and what you can lay hold of besides, leave here and. . ."

"And begin life anew, you mean Herr Binzer?" said the Grand Duke drily. "Thank you. If the advice had come from anyone else, he would have been horsewhipped. Now, may I beg you to leave without annoying us further?"

He laid a hand of iron on the German's round shoulder and quietly but firmly pushed him towards the door, while the six figure sums, as they flowed over Herr Binzer's lips, kept growing higher and higher the nearer he and Don Ramon came to the threshold. As they reached it, Herr Binzer was up to three hundred thousand, and the Grand Duke turned around as he felt a pull at his sleeve. Old

Señor Paqueno stood there beside him, making the wildest of grimaces while his lips unceasingly kept forming the words: "Three hundred thousand—Semjon Marcowitz—Your Highness, sell!" Don Ramon gave a start. During his conversation with Herr Binzer he had forgotten the sword of Damocles hanging over his head, which Señor Paqueno now brought back to mind. Now once more his position stood clear before him, and for a moment he hesitated. Señor Paqueno was right—three hundred thousand was enough to pay Semjon Marcowitz and again become a creditable member of society; three hundred thousand—and this man Binzer offered three hundred thousand for Punta Hermosa... It would be a difficult matter to raise the money elsewhere, perhaps impossible. For half a minute he hesitated with his hand on Herr Binzer's shoulder, during which time that gentleman looked at him in tense and expectant silence; his eyes blinked behind his rimless glasses and there was a continual twitching around the corners of his mouth. Suddenly a smile came over the Grand Duke's face; he drew Herr Binzer back into the room and motioned to him to sit down. Old Señor Paqueno drew a deep sigh of relief and sank heavily into a chair.

There was deep silence in the room for several moments while the Grand Duke looked thoughtfully at Herr Binzer. Then he said:

"Herr Binzer, do you realize what Punta Hermosa means to Señor Paqueno and me? It is best that you know so that we understand each other. That castle—Don Jeronimo the Lucky's castle—and the land around it, is our place of retreat, Herr Binzer, an additional exit from their lair for two poor hard-pressed foxes. You know our position, you say, and therefore realize that at any time the state can be declared bankrupt de jure as my friend Paqueno says; it has long since been so de facto. When I took over the reins of government" (Herr Binzer involuntarily sniffed at the word government coming from the mouth of this ruined man) "the Castle of Punta Hermosa had already been mortgaged as security for a loan from Apelmann of Barcelona."

"Apelmann y Hijos of Barcelona," interposed Herr Binzer, "I know."

"No, from the old Apelmann—he did not have his hijos in the firm then," continued the Grand Duke. "The firm is our largest creditor."

"Together with Domingo Huelvas of Madrid and Viviani of Marseilles," added Herr Binzer drily.

"I see that you are well informed. Well, I—we scraped together the sixty thousand necessary to release Punta Hermosa from Apelmann; it had been mortgaged for forty thousand and the rest was interest accumulated from my father's time. Then I gave it to Señor Paqueno here, to have and to hold. Now if we are forced into national bankruptcy, abdication, and so forth, we will still have Punta Hermosa as a place of retreat, Herr Binzer. And likewise in case we get tired of keeping affairs going, which, strange to say, has not happened yet."

Herr Binzer gave a sly laugh.

"I understand the trick," said he. "Bogus transfer and breach of trust against the creditors—such actions are heavily punished by us in Germany."

"You misunderstand me. It could only be a question of bogus transfer and breach of trust against the creditors in case I did this at the last minute for the purpose of defrauding my creditors. But I did this fifteen years ago—and my creditors are of a special kind, as you have heard. And finally, taken all in all, we Grand Dukes of Minorca have had a bad reputation before this."

The Grand Duke stretched his hand across the table to Señor Paqueno, who emotionally kissed it. It was with a decidedly increased feeling of respect that Herr Binzer of Frankfort looked at him as he asked:

"Well, what are you driving at?"

"You now know, Herr Binzer, what value we place on Punta Hermosa; do you know what its real value is otherwise? I had it impartially appraised after it was redeemed from Apelmann. The highest estimated value was a hundred and twenty-five thousand pesetas. That was fifteen years ago. Let us say a hundred and fifty thousand at present on account of the change in money values. Well, Herr Binzer, and you, a smart business man from Frankfort, offer three hundred thousand . . . ."

Herr Binzer, who without asking permission, had lit a cigar, hastily put it down.

"Three hundred thousand," said he. "Yes, but I did not have time for due deliberation—you were using force, you know. I bid a hundred thousand to begin with. . ."

The Grand Duke arose from his chair. There was a shadow of a smile around the corners of his mouth.

"You withdraw your offer, Herr Binzer," said he. "I imagined as much. You are a thoughtless individual, and evidently meant a hundred thousand as little as you did three hundred thousand. Probably you did not intend buying the property at all. You wanted to have a good laugh at our expense. I regret that for the moment I thought you were in earnest. I wish you a good morning."

He took a couple of steps forward as though to conduct Herr Binzer to the door. A sudden expression of fright came over this gentleman's features.

"Your Highness," said he hastily, "you misunderstand me absolutely. If I was joking, it was just now when I spoke about undue haste and the use of force. Of course, it is possible that the property is not worth more than a hundred and fifty thousand, but *zum Teufel*, I have taken a liking to it, a charming situation, you know, and it is worth three hundred thousand to me. A few bank-notes more or less. . . I keep to my offer."

With an expression of tense expectation on his face, he looked at the Grand Duke, whose features were inscrutable as he answered:

"Forgive me, I see that you are a serious business man and that it is very possible Punta Hermosa is worth three hundred thousand to you. I am even convinced of the fact, and therefore am willing to consider your offer in the spirit it was meant" (Herr Binzer's lips began to twitch involuntarily) "but—and there is a but. For the reasons I have just mentioned, the property is worth much more than three hundred thousand to Señor Paqueno and me. If we should sell it, the lowest price, mark me, the lowest, would be, not three hundred thousand, but half a million."

A heavy sigh of despair arose from Señor Paqueno's breast. He had just seen himself freed from Semjon Marcowitz and the ruin which threatened through him; and he had been so happy about it that he hardly had heard what Don Ramon said, but only waited for him to accept this cursed German's extremely liberal offer. What would it matter afterwards if they were without a place of retreat? There was always the monastery at Barcelona—and now his Highness spoiled the whole thing by drawing his bow too taut. Half a million—the mere thought of it was ridiculous. Reproachfully he looked at his master, whose face was hard and impenetrable as an iron mask; and then he turned toward Herr Binzer to confirm his sad forebodings. . . and was struck with amazement. The German's features were a study of human passions. His small, peery eyes, as though bewitched, were glued on Don Ramon's cold face, his fat fingers were crumpling up the cloth under the table, while the corners of his mouth kept twitching unceasingly, now from disappointment and rage, now from indecision, again from momentary resolution. One minute it seemed as though he wanted to spring to his feet with a cold, scornful laugh at the Grand Duke's impudence; the next moment other ideas seemed to have entered his head and he was on the point of saying yes, when he would again appear to think it over and would stare at the Grand Duke with baffled rage. Señor Paqueno could not believe his eyes. He still hesitated, he had not yet said no!

Suddenly the Grand Duke made a little movement as though to rise, and lifted his eyebrows as much as to say: I knew of course, that the price would be too high for you! At the same moment Herr Binzer's face hardened with an expression of determination. He cleared his throat, and with an ill-assumed air of superiority said:

"Well, really, you are a hard one to deal with! Half a million, that is no trifle! Do you think you can fleece the first honest person who for a long while has wanted to do business with you? It is lucky for you that you have met someone as good-natured as I am. The price is ridiculous, absurd, my dear fellow. No one else would think of paying it for a moment, but *wahrhaftiger Gott*, I will think about it. Probably you won't believe me, but *hol' mich der Teufel*, I'll give you your half a million for the castle! What do you say to that, eh? That shows you how much I'm in love with your island, eh?"

Señor Paqueno listened no further. With a gasp he sank back in his chair: *Madre de Dios!* Miracles could still happen! Half a million—half a million, Semjon Marcowitz paid and the Grand Duchy of Minorca with two hundred thousand on hand. The next moment he jumped up from his seat. The Grand Duke had thrown himself back in his chair, shaking with laughter until the floor trembled under his heavy body. Herr Binzer of Frankfort stared at him in fright, evidently convinced that he was in the presence of a maniac—a man that had lost his senses from too much happiness. He seemed on the point of hurriedly withdrawing his too hasty promise, but before he was able to utter a word the Grand Duke stopped laughing and said in a serious tone:

"Herr Binzer of Frankfort, why did you shave off your beard and mustache?"

Herr Binzer flamed red with anger. Springing from his chair, his lips tightly drawn together in rage, he cried:

"What has that got to do with you? *Tausend Teufel*, tell me, what has that got to do with you?"

The Grand Duke looked at him earnestly.

"Now, now, Herr Binzer, don't flare up! I only ask out of interest for you. You have made a big mistake as a business man by shaving. Thanks to what I have seen from your lips, not what I have heard from them, I tell you that neither half a million nor even a whole one would suffice to purchase Punta Hermosa. Let's have everything open and above board, Herr Binzer. A big dog is buried here, as you say in Germany. It is clear as day that Punta Hermosa is of value to you for some other reason than its beautiful scenery. You don't at all resemble a lover of nature, Herr Binzer, not even a lover of nature from Frankfort. Now tell me what it is, and perhaps we can do business!"

Herr Binzer's closely clipped head was still fiery red

with rage.

"The man is raving," he cried. "*Tausend Teufel*, the man is raving. I offer a price beyond all reason and he answers by insulting me. If we were in Germany, I would force him to a duel. For the last time I ask you: will you take the price I offer or will you not?"

At each word uttered by the German, Señor Paqueno trembled in his chair as though from an electric shock. With a smile the Grand Duke continued as calmly as before:

"Perhaps I can help you along some. You are no lover of nature, Herr Binzer, and you yourself admitted you did not care about historical or antiquarian matters. But how was that? Didn't you dabble a bit in all sorts of things while in America, among others, in mines? Just think, try to remember, perhaps you may have discovered something at Punta Hermosa on one of your little outings?"

Herr Binzer quickly turned pale.

"What in the devil!" he began; then he suddenly stopped. The Grand Duke had arisen, and was looking at him in a manner which filled his soul with terror.

"Herr Binzer," said he coldly, "kindly lay aside that tone immediately; it may be suitable in Mexico, but not at all in Minorca. Let me draw your attention to the fact that people here call me 'Your Highness' and that I am absolute monarch on this island. Do you understand—absolute? The sole member of the firm, as you condescended to remark. I am a mild tyrant, but if it pleases me, within ten minutes I can put you over the border—without a boat, Herr Binzer—or throw you into prison for grossly insulting the head of the state. Our dungeons are rather the worse for age, but they could still serve for the rest of your lifetime."

"Just dare it," began Herr Binzer, but quickly changed. "Y—you m—mustn't... dare to do that, Your Highness. I—I would immediately appeal to the German consul."

The Grand Duke smiled graciously.

"You are improving, Herr Binzer, but oh—it's too bad about your beard! Why did you shave it off? I merely have to look at your chin, and then I am not at all sure whether you could appeal to any consul. No, and still less sure that your past would appeal to him."

Herr Binzer turned even paler, and the Grand Duke continued courteously:

"You see I am trying to have you look at the matter sensibly—and yet nothing would be easier for me than to send to Barcelona for a mining expert. Will we therefore act in a straightforward manner, Herr Binzer? Remember: either with me or not at all! The only member of the firm, Herr Binzer! And if we come to an agreement I will treat you fairly in spite of your behavior—I'll give you my word as to that!"

Herr Binzer's face was again worthy of a study by Forain. Hesitancy, fear and greed strove for mastery in his soul. *Tausend Teufel!* Then he gave a sigh. There was only one thing to do, to get the best terms he could.

"Well," said he heavily, "it is perhaps as you... as Your Highness says. That is to say..."

"That is to say," the Grand Duke repeated encouragingly.

"I believe I discovered a small deposit at Punta Hermosa. . ."

"When a man like you believes so," said Don Ramon politely, "it is quite sure to be a fact."

"H'm, yes, that is of course possible. You see, I am not certain yet—I thought of convincing myself later on. . ."

"After the purchase? And give me a little surprise, is that it?" the Grand Duke suggested.

"Of course—just as you. . . as Your Highness says. Now I will act in a straightforward manner, as Your Highness wishes."

"Excellent, Herr Binzer. That is by all means the best thing you can do. Only don't take too long about it."

"You see, I have made a number of short trips to Punta Hermosa lately. . ."

"I am all ears."

"The place resembles some I have seen in America—not the castle, of course, but some of the land nearest to the coast, by that mountain there—what is it called?"

"Monte Cartagen?"

"Of course, Your Highness is right. Monte Cartagen, a beautiful situation in the woods!"

"Don't waste time enthusing over nature, Herr Binzer. Come to the point!"

"I made a few investigations there and I was greatly disappointed."

"Really? And in your disappointment you decided to

buy Punta Hermosa"

"Ha ha! I had expected to find silver—silver has always been my specialty, Your Highness."

"You are to be envied. I wish I could only say the same about myself."

"However, instead of silver I found sulphur."

"Sulphur! Herr Binzer! Fire and brimstone... I can understand you were surprised. Naturally you didn't expect to find a place containing those articles for a long time to come!"

"Well, Your Highness must understand it is far from certain. But, if I am not mistaken, the deposit must have been worked before."

"You surprise me, Herr Binzer."

"Yes, there were traces of a very ancient mode of working the deposit by *calcaroni* as they call them, kilns where sulphur has been burned, a method which is even used at times nowadays. But they were practically obliterated through age. They must have been in use a very long time ago."

The Grand Duke looked at Herr Binzer thoughtfully. "You are a typical example of your race, Herr Binzer," said he. "You come here—why, the gods alone know—make a few little trips into the country, and quick as a wink, happen on something which has lain before our very noses for centuries. Sulphur! Monte Cartagen... an old volcanic territory—as in Sicily. And Monte Cartagen... Have you ever heard of Carthage, Herr Binzer?"

"Carthage, of course... Carthage..." The tone of Herr Binzer's voice showed that his knowledge of Carthage was none too extensive.

"The Carthaginians were the first to colonize this island, Herr Binzer. They founded Portus Magonis, the present Port Mahon, and carried on an extensive trade here. They also had dealings with Sicily, and one of the commodities they sought was sulphur. And their mines, which must have passed into oblivion as early as the time of the Romans, have now been rediscovered by Herr Binzer of Frankfort...."

The Grand Duke continued to gaze at Herr Binzer with the same thoughtful expression, and the latter, who had already begun to forget his late fright, made an attempt to resume his former manner.

"Yes, and I also will understand how to make the most of it. You have given me your word, and without me you can't work them, even though you were Grand Duke of Minorca ten times over. Where would you get a peseta for the purpose on reasonable terms? I am a business man, but I am willing to give you—let us say twenty per cent of the profits. But I'll attend to the managing—in a businesslike way, too, otherwise there would be nothing in it, not a thing, you understand!"

Herr Binzer's sense of security increased as he spoke, and he now looked at the Grand Duke with a challenging air, evidently well pleased with himself in spite of his disappointment a short time before. Without seeming to notice his manner, the Grand Duke asked:

"In a businesslike way—what do you mean by that?"

Herr Binzer sniffed violently at the question.

"I know well enough," he remarked roughly. "The capital must yield interest, that is the first condition. Labor is sure to be cheap here."

"Have you ever been in Sicily, Herr Binzer?"

"No. Now let's get this matter straightened out as quickly as it can be done in a half-asleep country like this."

"So you've never been in Sicily? But I have, Herr Binzer, and I had the pleasure of seeing the sulphur mines there working at full blast. Do you know what I said to Paqueno?"

"No." There was a blending of contempt and impatience in Herr Binzer's voice.

"I said to him: 'Now we need not go to Naples, Paqueno. Seeing this here is enough to give one the desire to die.'"

"Ha ha!" Herr Binzer's laugh was of the kind bestowed in reward for a boring anecdote and to avoid further ones like it.

"The working of the Sicilian mines," continued the Grand Duke, "was carried on in a way which I believe you would consider absolutely businesslike. Labor was cheap there, too—very cheap. There were workmen by the thousand—men, women and children, children, Herr Binzer; none in all these thousands were over thirty-five—they became no older, Herr Binzer—and not one of them looked like a human being. Their bodies, like their souls, were blighted and poisoned by the sulphur fumes—they have their hell with all its ingredients here on earth, Herr

Binzer, and if we can believe our religion, another one awaits them later, for they all defied authority, led lives of debauchery, and would steal whenever the opportunity arose. But the whole affair was certainly run in what you would call a businesslike manner, and the profits were all you could wish."

Herr Binzer looked at the Grand Duke with a sly smile.

"Your Highness is sentimental," said he. "I understand. Your Highness thinks twenty per cent too little to wink at the small inconveniences of having sulphur mines on the property. Well, I am not unreasonable—let us say twenty-five, but not a pfennig more, as true as my name is Binzer, not a pf—"

The recollections that Herr Binzer of Frankfort had of what followed immediately after these words were extremely confused. Without his knowing how it had happened, two hands strong as iron came booming against his closely cropped head; the next second he felt himself being lifted up from the floor and a short but gigantically strong leg inflicted an exceedingly painful kick on that part of his body where Herr Binzer's back did what Herr Binzer himself did so often—changed names. The next moment with the speed of a cannonball he flew out through a door, which in golden but very faded colors, bore the coat of arms of the Grand Duchy of Minorca: two heraldic lions, with halberds in their paws, below a five-pointed star. Then with a heavy thud he hit the stone-paved floor in the hall outside; his head buzzed as though it were filled with ten swarms of bees, and a good three minutes passed before he was able to rise on trembling limbs from his humiliating position. In the doorway, through which he had just come so unceremoniously, Don Ramon was lighting a cigar and quietly looking at him, while in the background he caught a glimpse of old Señor Paqueno's face filled with dumb despair. A servant came hurrying from a room further in the distance and looked at his master questioningly.

"Help that gentleman out, Auguste," said the Grand Duke, pointing to Herr Binzer. "If he dares to show himself in the vicinity of the castle, you have full permission to take a shot at him. You can tell the other servants that the same orders serve for them, too. See that he leaves here immediately."

But before the French servant could come near, Herr Binzer, with unbelievable quickness, had regained consciousness and rushed toward the entrance of the hall with the tails of his cutaway flapping behind him. He tore the heavy entrance door open, and flew through it almost as quickly as he had through the doorway to the dining-room a short time before. The echo from his yellow shoes was heard on the courtyard pavement; then all was silent.

The Grand Duke nodded to Auguste, and retired to the dining-room with Señor Paqueno.

"The damned scoundrel!" said he. "It was amusing to study him and see how far he would dare go with his insolence. Open up sulphur mines at Punta Hermosa, poison the atmosphere and all my poor people—and twenty-five per cent for me to wink at it! . . The damned scoundrel!"

"But Your Highness," interposed Señor Esteban with trembling voice, "isn't there some way?. . . Hygienics, you know, has made such advancements . . and think of Semjon Marcowitz, Your Highness, think of Semjon Marcowitz!"

"Ah, Paqueno," said the Grand Duke smiling again, "you are a dear old Jesuit. It is for the very reason that I am thinking about Semjon Marcowitz that I can have no dealings with any Herr Binzer. If this affair with Marcowitz is not to make me fall too low in my own estimation, I must at least protect my people against Herr Binzer. And come to think of it, how was that, didn't you write to an English firm yesterday about a loan on the olives?"

"Yes, Your Highness, an English firm by the name of Isaacs; they are said to have made a loan to Servia, so that. . . But Your Highness, Your Highness!"

"But what, Paqueno? Compose yourself. We will still find a way out. Remember, we have St. Urban behind us and a whole month before us."

CHAPTER 3

In Which St. Urban Has an Opportunity of Distinguishing Himself

Hotel Universal was situated on the Plazuela de San Cristobal in Port Mahon, and was one of the two better hotels in the town. Its patrons consisted of the few travelling salesmen who had reason to visit the island, now and then an eccentric Englishman, and at times some stray artist in search of sunlight effects. In February of the year 1910, Herr Binzer of Frankfort was stopping there. Herr Binzer, of Frankfort, was a man without refinement, and more stubborn than a mule when he had once set his mind on an object. It is unnecessary to add that his object always could be expressed in a term of figures. The fact that the object was often difficult of attainment did not, as already mentioned, frighten Herr Binzer, and attaining his ends by very dubious means caused him no qualms of conscience; but to relinquish an object through which he might earn money was something which Herr Binzer did not do until the chances against him were so great that he was in absolute danger of risking a loss.

Saturday, the 13th of February, the day on which we have seen him paying his visit to Don Ramon, had begun unpropitiously; Herr Binzer would be the first to admit it. No one could say that he was in the habit of regretting anything he had done provided he had not lost money through it; therefore no one can assert that he in any way regretted his interview with the Grand Duke; but he realized with cold, bitter resentment that for the moment he was beaten—in a most palpable manner, as diverse parts of his body bore witness. Punta Hermosa was a find, a big find, yes, an unparalleled find, unless his keen scent had led him astray. The tests he had made had shown a high percentage of sulphur, and the amount of raw material was enormous; labor in Minorca was as cheap as a person could wish, and the location excellent; no costs for railway transportation and within reach of a dozen freight lines. In a word, an affair by which one might net hundreds of thousands of marks, a tremendously big affair—which he had been on the point of getting for a paltry three hundred thousand pesetas! Time after time on arriving at this point in his reflections, Herr Binzer would call down the vilest of curses on the head of Don Ramon. The tricky scoundrel! The hypocritical devil! Managing to force his secret from him by giving his word of honor, robbing him of his own innermost secrets and then backing out of the bargain under the pretext of such idiotic nonsense as the welfare of the laborers! Yes, and in a manner which had swollen Herr Binzer's features to double their usual proportions. But *verflucht nochmal*, he'd find out it wasn't done in vain! If he tried anywhere else to raise the money for working the mines—and of course that was his little game—he might consider himself lucky if anyone was willing to give him ten per cent of the profits. Ten per cent, and Herr Binzer had offered twenty-five! And he had discovered the mines—but where could law and justice be found in this country? It should have happened in Ger—but even though this damned prince only received ten per cent if he raised the capital through others, why Herr Binzer would receive nothing! Nothing! And it was he who... several times at the mere thought Herr Binzer's wrath came near choking him as he made his way back to the Hotel Universal, but he wasn't in vain the man he was. By the time he had reached the Plazuela de San Cristobal his head was cool once more, that is, inwardly, for his ears and cheeks still burned like fire; he thrust aside until later his disappointment and thoughts of revenge, and set his brains to work on but one thing: how he could save Punta Hermosa for himself.

It must be admitted that the problem seemed incapable of solution. Minorca, and everything on it, belonged to Don Roman or his creditors; without them not a sparrow might fall to the ground. It was true, Punta Hermosa belonged to that old simpleton Paqueno, but Herr Binzer had his express word that he would rather see it burn up than sell it to him. He would have it, he must have it, no matter how, but. . . He was living in the land of an absolute prince—and even then only by sufferance! On the island of Minorca he was a man without legal rights, irrespective of the fact that such was also the case in Germany. . . And there wasn't much time to spare; naturally on the following day the Grand Duke would begin negotiations with some usurious firm about getting the business started. Damn him! As long as he ruled over Minorca Herr Binzer did not stand many chances! Damna. . . Herr Binzer gave a start, forgetting to finish his oath; of course, that was the idea he had been looking for! As long as Don Ramon continued to reign there were no chances for Herr Binzer to get Punta Hermosa; what remained for Herr Binzer to do then if, in spite of all, he still wanted to have Punta Hermosa?

See to it that Don Ramon should cease to reign.

In other words, bring about a little revolution.

Herr Binzer's career, as we have already tried to show, had not been without its stormy side; it also had not lacked a little revolution now and then. After several years spent in Central American countries such an event is looked upon as a more or less common-place occurrence, as a self-evident means when other schemes have failed. Herr Binzer had lived in the aforesaid part of the world sufficiently long to have imbibed this point of view; and although the thought that he was now in Europe perhaps intimidated him a bit, still it did not take much time for him to recall Portugal and Turkey. Had anyone interfered with the little arrangements made concerning the rulers of those countries? Unless Herr

Binzer was mistaken, no one had; and would it then be likely that anyone would have anything to say about such a tiny state as Minorca?

Answering the question with an explicit oath of denial, Herr Binzer entered the hotel, ate lunch and retired to his room. After half an hour's scheming by himself, he sent for Señor Luis Hernandez.

Señor Luis, twenty-seven years old, was the son of Porfirio Hernandez, proprietor of the Hotel Universal; but it would be difficult to imagine a greater contrast between father and son. Old man Porfirio, who had run the Hotel for the past thirty years, was a phlegmatic Minorcan, descended from an ancient family; during his sixty years he had grown accustomed to the sun rising in a cloudless sky, the wind playing through the palms and the House of Ramiros ruling the land with mild sceptre and heavy taxes. Each struck him as equally self-evident, and the thought of any change in the program most assuredly never entered his head. The life was monotonous and the earnings small, but as long as a person need not exert himself or starve, it was satisfactory as it was. Full of this philosophy of life, which he surely never had managed to formulate himself, old Porfirio contemplated his son Luis with something approaching parental anxiety. Luis' youth had been turbulent according to Minorcan standards. He was discontented with everything. Minorca was a wretched and stupid place. There was no money, nothing but heavy taxes. The hotel would never amount to anything as long as affairs were as they were and there was nothing else which a man with any desire to get ahead could take up. For, strange to say—it was enough to make Señor Porfirio at times doubt the conjugal fidelity of the late lamented Mrs. Hernandez—Luis possessed an inordinate desire of getting ahead. Nothing but old Porfirio's age kept him from going to America; afraid of losing his inheritance in case he was not on the spot, he remained on Minorca, and idled away his time, drawing up big plans for the future. He had combined with some kindred spirits; with them he was in the habit of holding secret meetings where they cursed the island of their birth and thought out fruitless schemes of how to become rich and powerful. The bacilli of discontent seemed at last to have been carried over to Minorca on the winds from the mainland.

Luis had succeeded in picking up a little English and German from the guests at the hotel, and it was his one great enjoyment to be able to pour out the bitterness of his heart to these foreign patrons. Herr Binzer of Frankfort had immediately puzzled him; he envied him his wealth, and unceasingly kept wondering why a rich foreigner should remain so long on Minorca. He made several attempts at approach, which Herr Binzer had curtly rebuffed. Therefore his eagerness was now the greater as he hurriedly responded to Herr Binzer's request that he come to his room.

He found the German slouching listlessly in the only easy chair the room possessed, a cigar hanging from the corner of his mouth. On the table by his side lay a check book and a big pile of gold coins which made Luis' eyes open wide. As the young Minorcan came in, Herr Binzer mumbled a good day, which, coming as it did from him, must be considered unusually polite. Luis noted that his face was red and swollen.

"*Guten Tag,* Herr Binzer," answered Luis with a bow, proud that he could show his linguistic abilities.

"Why, that's so," said Herr Binzer in his own language, "you speak German, don't you, Señor Hernandez?"

Now, a Minorcan is never called Señor in conjunction with his surname unless he happens to be the head of a family; Herr Binzer was well aware of the fact, and therefore in his greeting lay a hint that he considered young Luis the real leader of the Hernandez family. The bit of flattery made Luis blush slightly but he remained silent, perhaps conscious of the real extent of his German.

Herr Binzer noticed his hesitancy.

"Señor Hernandez," said he, "if it is the same to you, I prefer to speak Spanish. I have been abroad so long that I am beginning to forget my mother tongue. But it is refreshing to see a young man like you, Señor Hernandez, who even on Minorca keeps in touch with the world at large!"

Luis swelled with pride.

"I try to, Señor, but you are right, it is difficult here on Minorca."

"You are ambitious? You want to get ahead, do you not? That is the impression I have formed of you," said Herr Binzer in the same polite confidence-inspiring tone.

Luis became more animated.

"I have tried my whole life, Señor, but what can a person do here on Minorca? It is impossible to earn anything, impossible to be anything. Everything is impossible on Minorca, Señor, because it is Minorca."

"Then, Señor Hernandez," answered Herr Binzer slowly, "there is nothing left to do but change Minorca!"

Luis laughed bitterly.

"Change Minorca! You are joking, Señor. On Minorca the houses, farming, and everything else is the same now as it was five hundred years ago. Nothing changes on Minorca, and least of all, Minorca itself."

"You are mistaken," objected Herr Binzer earnestly. "Something must have changed on Minorca when young men such as you are to be found here. Who knows what you can do to improve conditions on your island?"

The expression on Luis' face became still more animated.

"Señor," he replied in a self-satisfied tone, "I am not stupid, that I know, and I will not deny that I have thought exactly as you do. But tell me, Señor, what can I do?"

"If you are the only one who thinks that way," said Herr Binzer looking at the young man intently, "there is not much you can do. But are you the only one? Have you no friends who think as you do? Friends who want to arouse Minorca from its apathy? If there are such, I cannot understand why you lack the courage, Señor Hernandez."

"Friends," cried Luis vehemently, "of course I have friends, Señor, and not so few who think the same as I. You may be sure that we have thought out many plans which would improve conditions here. We possess energy, prudence and unity. But we have the multitude against us and the people are apathetic. You see, Señor, these are two circumstances which can be overcome only by one of two means, power or money. And if money is at one's disposal it is not a difficult matter to procure power. But who has money on Minorca? No one, not even the Grand Duke, although he imposes the most exorbitant taxes upon us."

Herr Binzer cleared his throat and said slowly:

"I am becoming more and more interested in you, Señor Hernandez. You are the first congenial person I have met here. You are very clever for your age, very clever. I am very glad, Señor Hernandez, very glad indeed to hear you say you are not the only one with such ideas. Money, you say. Yes, that is true enough. But would it need so very much money to put your plans into execution?"

Luis quickly interrupted him. The word 'money', which now had been repeated several times, carried his mind back to a favorite subject of thought, and at the same time awakened his caution. What he had just said to Herr Binzer he had certainly said to many other foreigners, but this Binzer struck him as being mysterious—and although the Grand Duke ruled with a light hand, yet he did not at all like his subjects to show an interest in political matters.

"Señor," said he, in a dignified tone, "I must have expressed myself stupidly. We have no plans which we think of putting in operation. We have only discussed matters in a general way. And we have always come to the conclusion that a big amount of money would be necessary!"

He looked at Herr Binzer with a glance which plainly said: You can't fool me! You seem to be after something, but if you're a spy, you won't catch me, and if it is something else, you won't succeed by being niggardly. Herr Binzer returned his glance for a few seconds, and then replied:

"Of course, of course. In a very general way, that was also what I meant. Let us in a very general way discuss the possibility of arousing Minorca. You believe it depends on money. Well—if you get any money, what would you do then?"

As though sunk in thought, he moved his check book a little nearer and gave the pile of gold on the table a push so that it chinked. The young Minorcan turned his head to one side to conceal the struggle which was going on within him. Suddenly his eyes met Herr Binzer's; and a grin flew over his swarthy face.

"It is best to be straightforward, as my old father says. I do not believe you are playing the spy, and as far as that goes, I can always swear myself out of it. You ask what we would do if we had money; I will tell you: everything. Discontent has piled up and it is only necessary to take advantage of it. But why do you ask, Señor? Would you perhaps like to invest some money in our little enterprise?"

It was Herr Binzer's turn to lower his eyes. The young man's front attack took him by surprise. Luis continued boldly without giving him time to reflect.

"Don't be disconcerted, Señor! I am not stupid and

I understand well enough that you yourself are after something!"

Herr Binzer's hesitancy quickly came to an end. To feel his way, like a cat circling around a dish of hot porridge, did not suit him in the least; he preferred simple and brutal methods and therefore he answered curtly:

"For once, your father is right, Señor. It is best to be straightforward. I could tell you I want to help free your country of its yoke of oppression—I do, too, of course, but it is because by chance it suits my own interests. I have something in view which would put new life into you people and give you all both work and money. But as matters stand at present, I have no prospects of succeeding. Your crazy form of government prevents me. If it is this you and your friends wish to change, perhaps I can help you out with some money. But change it thoroughly, Señor! Now, do you understand? Is that what you want? And are you capable of carrying it through?"

Luis looked at him earnestly.

"Señor," said he, "if we were to succeed in bringing about such a change as you mention, what advantage would we reap from it?"

"Why, Hernandez, weren't you just speaking of the big plans you thought of putting in operation if affairs on Minorca were only different? I am perhaps disposed to give you the means to change conditions here. After that you have the field free for yourself."

Luis did not allow himself to be swayed by Herr

Binzer's eloquence.

"That is possible," said he coldly, "but I am sure that the field would be even freer for you. I am afraid that we would only be pulling the chestnuts out of the fire for you."

"Well, let us perhaps say the others might!. . ." Herr Binzer's voice was masterly in its insinuating craftiness. "All cannot earn a like amount, Hernandez. Co-operative affairs have never been to my taste. There must be a leader, you, in other words, and as such you would receive your share of the large profits."

Luis looked at him with his sharp black eyes.

"What you say is very sensible, Señor, but you have not mentioned what the little business is from which I, as leader, would share the profits with you!"

Herr Binzer's bushy white eyebrows arose threateningly and his cheeks became even redder than before. Was this booby here trying to play the same trick on him as that damned Grand Duke did in the morning? *Verflucht nochmal,* he would put a quick stop to this. To be robbed of his secret once during the day was enough.

"My dear fellow," cried he, scarcely controlling his anger, "let me tell you something once and for all; don't try to ask any questions about what I have in view unless you want a quick end to my help. That is my own private affair, understand, until you have carried out your part of the program, my own private affair, understand, and that's that! I will only say it is an undertaking which will be of benefit to the whole island—and most of all to us two, you and me."

Luis blushed, but there was a doubtful expression on his face.

"An undertaking which will be of benefit to the whole island," said he. "Only that seems so peculiar, Señor. We haven't too many undertakings here which give profit to anyone, and if you have found anything of that kind, I am sure that the Cripple up there at the palace would be beside himself with joy. It seems to me your air of secrecy is unnecessary—it makes me uneasy, Señor."

Herr Binzer looked at him quickly; then he leaned forward and buttonholed him.

"Listen to me," he whispered, "It is just because your damned Duke is in such a state, that I come to you. He would want to have all the profit himself, you can well understand that, and besides, the man is crazy! I went up to see him today, told him fairly what my plans were and offered him reasonable terms. Do you know what he answered? That he preferred to get his money as he does now and that he doesn't give a damn for the people—they are best off as they are at present, and he said so time and time again. Don't forget to tell your friends about that!" Herr Binzer's voice trembled with rage. "But I will settle accounts with the scoundrel! I will. . . and either with your help or another's. *Teufel hol' mich,* I have enough money to destroy your government ten times over, and I don't have to look for people to help me, if that is what you are thinking. But I'll keep my secret to myself, understand, and now I want an immediate and definite answer from you!"

Herr Binzer looked at Luis with flashing eyes, once more beside himself at the recollection of that confounded Grand Duke's behavior. Luis quickly thought the matter over. To follow a foreigner blindfolded did not appeal to him in the least, but on the other hand, he himself had everything to win by the move, gold, honor and position. . . yes, and if he once reached his goal then it would not be difficult to get the best of the German!. . . His mind was made up.

"Well, Señor, this is going a little too quickly for my taste, but you probably have your reasons for hurrying matters . . . I am your man. We will have a hard bit of work, Señor. The people are very thick-headed in their respect for their sovereign. But if you will give me free rein and enough money, I swear that we will succeed soon enough. But money is the most important thing, Señor!"

He cast a look full of meaning at the check book and gold by Herr Binzer's side but Herr Binzer said curtly: "The most important! For you perhaps, Luis. If things are that way, I am afraid we can have nothing to do with each other. Before you give me definite plans of what you think of doing, I will not lay out a single peseta. Or perhaps you already have your plans prepared?"

"Partly, Señor. I think I mentioned that my friends and I have made many plans which have simply stranded through the lack of ready cash. I mean to consult with them immediately, and it will not be long before I can tell you the result, Señor."

Luis spoke with great dignity; his voice had a gently reproachful tone and his eyes expressed more plainly than words: and a little in advance, Señor, would be especially suitable in arranging a revolution. But Herr Binzer's eyes were cold and did not show the least signs of comprehending this silent language.

"Very well," said he. "Talk the matter over with your friends. I will give you only one bit of advice: the sooner you are ready, the better. If you have a plan that'll do, then there is money enough here" (he nodded toward the table) "and the means of protecting it, too." (The barrel of a revolver quickly peeped out from his right hip pocket).

Luis gave a start, whether through being unpleasantly surprised or from an idea which suddenly struck him, is uncertain.

"Señor," he whispered, "there is one matter which I came near forgetting. We must have arms. You can understand that..."

"I am aware that a revolution without gunpowder would be unusual. You needn't worry; to-morrow I will telegraph to an acquaintance in Barcelona. Within a week I will place enough weapons in your hands. But in the meantime, hurry the preparations. The sooner you are ready the better, remember that, Luis."

Herr Binzer's manner, which in the beginning of the conversation had been the height of consideration and politeness, had hastily become curt and domineering. Señor Hernandez had become Hernandez and then Luis.

Now that he understood his man he evidently considered all circumlocution unnecessary. Luis did not appear to be especially flattered at this change, and seemed on the point of protesting; but after a moment's hesitation he bowed politely, murmuring: "As quickly as possible, Señor!" and disappeared. Herr Binzer turned the key to the door after him; a moment later Luis heard the click of another lock from his room. Evidently he was locking up his gold.

Halfway down the stairs, Luis stopped, struck by a thought.

"I wonder," he mumbled to himself, "I wonder why Herr Binzer's cheeks were so swollen. Did the Cripple. . ."

His reflections closed with a hearty laugh, which echoed down the old hallway of the Hotel Universal.

* * *

That was the thirteenth of February. Four days later Herr Binzer of Frankfort was just sitting down to dinner at the Hotel Universal when Luis came into the dining-room and with a bow, stood before him.

"Señor," he whispered, "everything is ready."

"You haven't taken the trouble to hurry very much," Herr Binzer answered coldly. "I had almost decided to change my plans."

Luis became noticeably nervous.

"Señor, I am sorry, but if you will come with me to our meeting place this evening, you can see for yourself what I have managed to do."

"The usual nonsense in such cases," said Herr Binzer scornfully. "Is it really necessary on Minorca? Well, where shall I meet you?"

"Outside in the market-place after you have finished your dinner, Señor. Will that be satisfactory?"

Herr Binzer nodded and Luis disappeared.

Half an hour later Herr Binzer was awaiting Luis in the Plazuela de San Cristobal. The heavens gleamed like blue-white porcelain in the moonlight. It was absolutely quiet, and the palm trees in the little square stood immovable; but in the distance could be heard the gentle murmur of the Mediterranean, seldom still, even in quiet weather. To the east the dark lines of the castle arose against the night sky.

"It's a good thing the moon is shining, Señor," said Luis, and bowed deeply to his employer. "The gas works have been shut down for a week. The taxes are heavy and no one pays his share. This way, Señor!"

He started off a couple of steps in advance and Herr Binzer, as self-confident as ever, followed him, puffing at a cigar. The way led to the oldest part of Port Mahon, which from the north side of the harbor rose up to the foot of the old fortress. The streets were hardly more than three feet broad; the houses had gaping black doorways where in the moonlight one could see the lower steps of steep flights leading to the upper floors. The windows, everywhere except in the places one expected them to be, were covered with greenish-gray barred shutters which gave the whole street the appearance of a prison corridor. Now and then at a street corner the light shone behind the windows of some pothouse, and from within could be heard the tinkling of mandolins and the murmur of voices; otherwise not a sound was to be heard. It was like a city of the dead.

"*Verflucht nochmal,* but this place here needs brightening up, Luis," said Herr Binzer to his companion.

"We will see to that, Señor," answered Luis politely. "We'll be there immediately now."

Two minutes later he opened the door to a low whitepainted house which seemed as empty and dead as the streets through which they had just come. It stood by itself in a little garden, where the moonlight glistened on a couple of lemon trees with their greenish-yellow fruit, and on some cabbages which in the dim light resembled so many severed human heads. On either side were empty plots of land where no one thought of building, while directly behind the house arose the side of the mountain, iron gray in the moonlight, on the top of which the old fortress lifted its weather-beaten walls with gaping embrasures. On reaching the entry hall, Luis turned off to the left through a stone-paved corridor on the left side of which were several small, numbered doors. Suddenly he stopped before a broader door on the right, gave five knocks and whispered: "It is I, Luis Hernandez." Thereupon the door was opened from inside, and Herr Binzer and his companion stepped in.

They entered a long narrow room with whitewashed brick walls, at one end tapering into an apse-like recess. In front of this hung a black curtain below which could be seen the feet of two big candelabra. Otherwise there were only a couple of small grated windows in the outer wall. It seemed more like a prison chapel than anything else. A large table of unplaned wood, in the centre of which stood a three-branched candle stick with smoking tapers, had evidently been brought in for the occasion. Around it were grouped six people whom Herr Binzer could but indistinctly make out in the dim light. Three of them, however, quickly drew his attention. The first was a little grinning hunchback with spindle legs and a high bare forehead above his beardless face. He looked as though he might be forty, and strikingly resembled a tailor whom Herr Binzer remembered from his Hamburg days. He smiled obsequiously as Herr Binzer entered, his egg-shaped body cringing low in a deep bow. The second was a heavy, broad-shouldered man with a black beard which covered half his face and through which his teeth now and then glimmered like foaming white-caps on a dark and murky sea. His glance was as cold and sullen as the hunchback's had been fawning and servile. He only made a slight movement with his head to show that he had noticed Herr Binzer's entrance. Herr Binzer, who apprehended a bullying nature similar to his own, immediately conceived a hearty aversion to him—a feeling which almost turned into fear as he looked from him to his neighbor, a man still young, but with a face so pale and hollow that he seemed more like a dead than living person. His eyes were deeply sunk in their sockets and glowed with a fire kindled perhaps by enthusiasm, but perhaps equally well by hate or avariciousness. He was clad in black, and when through a sudden movement he came into the candle light, Herr Binzer noticed, to his surprise, that the black garment he wore was a monk's frock, shorn off at the knees.

Luis had shut the door and now took a step in the direction of his friends. Pointing to Herr Binzer with a theatrical gesture, he said:

"Comrades, I have the honor of presenting to you the noble friend of Liberty through whom we can hope to see our plans soon realized, the tyrant overthrown and poor Minorca set free. Comrades, this is Herr Binzer of Frankfort, who in America has already fought for the cause of Freedom. If we did not need to exercise so much caution, I would ask you to cheer our unselfish patron; instead I now beg his permission to present you so that afterwards we can discuss our great plans together. Señor Binzer, you see here the six brave men who, with me, have sworn to free our fatherland from its yoke of degradation and I ask your special permission to introduce the three who with me, are to lead the undertaking."

Luis, who spoke in his most eloquent manner, paused as though listening for some protest at his words *with me are to lead the undertaking*, but no one uttered a sound. He laid his hand on the hunchback's shoulder.

"Here," said he, turning to Herr Binzer, "is our friend Amadeo, who keeps a beerhouse down by the harbor, the Commandante, a resort you probably do not know, Señor. By his side are three of his friends, Señor Quelejas, Señor

Garcia and Señor Vatello, all true friends of liberty. Amadeo, Señor, is the real leader in his part of the town, and his is the only popular place. He knows all his customers through and through, he knows what they drink, what wrongs they harbor, what they do and what they have done. Amadeo, Señor, is invaluable, for through him we can keep in touch with all the lower classes in Port Mahon and win them over to our side."

"But it will cost money, Señor," said the hunchback with a fawning grin. "I am a poor man, and I will do what I can for liberty, Señor, but I cannot ask the whole of Port Mahon to be my guest. Therefore, I tell you, Señor, it will cost money."

Herr Binzer nodded coldly, Amadeo drew back with a bow, and pointing to the man with the beard, Luis continued:

"This, Señor Binzer, is our friend Eugenio Posada, sergeant of the body-guard. Señor Posada's family has been very badly treated by the authorities and he is full of zeal for our project. . ." Luis seemed on the point of more specifically stating the wrongs done Señor Posada but stopped at a quick glance from the sergeant. "Through his position, Señor, our friend Eugenio knows the whole body-guard, two hundred men, whose duty it is to patrol Port Mahon and the rural districts. The troops have every reason for dissatisfaction. They receive their pay very irregularly, and the Grand Duke has even expressed the desire to disband the entire guard."

"Damned clever of him," murmured Herr Binzer. "What's the sense of his keeping a body-guard? Pure snobbishness!"

"Anyway, you can understand, Señor, that we cannot run the risk of having them against us, even if you supply us with weapons. Remember that the body-guard commands the whole city from the old fortress here above us!"

"That old rubbish heap!" mumbled Herr Binzer contemptuously.

"Rubbish heap—you must mean that as a joke, Señor. Eugenio tells me that several of the cannon are absolutely fit for service, and that there is a fair quantity of shot and powder on hand. But with Señor Posada's help, we have nothing to fear from that quarter. The tyrant loses his last support, Señor—but it will cost money, much money!"

"All right, Luis, all right," said Herr Binzer curtly. "And the gentleman in the cutaway?"

"The gentleman in the cuta—Señor Binzer! That is the reverend Father Ignacio. This is his house we are in. Father Ignacio had it fitted up formerly as a retreat for study, and gave instruction here to a few pupils. The room in which we are was used as both chapel and refectory. Unfortunately, the institution was closed by the Grand Duke's friend Paqueno, who himself studied at the Jesuit College in Barcelona and who maintained. . ."

"Don't bother yourself about anything Paqueno maintained, Luis," the pale man in the monk's garb interrupted in an excited voice. "I hate him, and the time will come when I can be revenged. They tell me, Señor, that you wish to further our project. You could not have come to better men than the three of us whom you see here. . ."

"And me," Luis interrupted hastily. "Than to me and you, Father Ignacio!"

"We three," continued the hollow-eyed individual, without paying attention to Luis' interruption—"we three can influence the whole populace, Amadeo, the people in the city; Eugenio, the body-guard; and I, Señor, the people in the rural districts. I was formerly a priest of the Holy Church, Señor, before Paqueno who has influence with the Archbishop, had me deposed. It does not matter, Señor, for in my heart I am yet a priest of the Church, and I refused to lay aside the cloth, as you see, although I have shortened it. The lambs among whom I continue to work on Minorca, still listen to the voice of their true shepherd, especially in the country, Señor. They have much cause for complaint. Every stick and stone belongs to the Grand Duke, the farmers are weighted down by exorbitant taxes, and the fruit-growers as well. My lambs, Señor, go where I wish them, but they are poor and if I am to start them going it will cost money, much money!"

Father Ignacio laid special emphasis on the last words of his harangue, and looked at Herr Binzer intently. It was evident that he, as well as the others, now awaited that he should declare himself. Herr Binzer spat the stub of his cigar toward the black curtains at the end of the room (Father Ignacio's eyebrows contracted threateningly), and then in his usual domineering tone began:

"Well, gentlemen, I have listened closely to what you have had to say. It is not impossible that you are the right men for the undertaking. I am willing to help you financially, but first I want to come to a clear understanding about a couple of matters. First and foremost, what goal have you set yourselves? How far do you intend to go when your chance comes?"

Herr Binzer stopped and looked hard at Luis' friends. A storm of outcries broke loose in the strange assemblage. Each and every one sought to outbid his neighbor in liberty-loving proposals. At length Luis, who during the whole time had been vociferating louder than most of the others, succeeded in absolutely outvoicing his friends and cried, turning dramatically to Herr Binzer:

"Comrades, our noble benefactor wishes to know how far we intend to go when our chance comes! I believe I can answer for all of us: our goal is to release Minorca from the frightful nightmare which oppresses it! We want to do what the Portuguese did two years ago with their wretched government—But, let us not leave as much undone as they! Let us strike the axe to the roots!"

There was an eloquent pathos in Luis' tone. He was no poor speaker; and after his listeners had seemed to hesitate for a moment before the consequences of his words, they broke loose in a wild joyful storm of agreement. Only the deposed priest and the sergeant remained indifferent. Herr Binzer, whom nothing escaped, asked:

"You do not agree, gentlemen? You do not approve of your friend's sentiments?"

The former priest gave a short nod as much as to say he did, and the sergeant followed his example, but with a quick glance at Señor Luis Hernandez which made Herr Binzer in his heart give vent to a venomous smile.

"Our friend Luis," he thought, "is an excellent orator, but I am afraid his position as president is rather shaky."

He quieted the murmur of voices with a gesture and resumed:

"I see, Señores, that you intend to make a thorough job of the matter. I am glad. That is the only thing to do. Remember Manuel is still causing trouble for the Portuguese, while Alexander of Servia has long since ceased to trouble the Servians. Luis is right: you must not leave so much undone as the Portuguese; you must strike the axe to the root. Besides, that is the only condition under which I will finance the project."

Herr Binzer stopped a moment so as to let his words sink in.

"But there is one more matter. I am a businessman, and perhaps you therefore understand that I do not put money into such an affair as yours and simply let it go at that. I am willing to advance what I consider necessary, but I demand security for it. The only security you have is real estate. I have looked around the island, and there is one place here which appeals to me. That is Punta Hermosa. That is what I demand as security for the money which I am to advance to you."

Herr Binzer was interrupted by a harsh laugh. It came from the hollow-eyed Father Ignacio. Herr Binzer looked at him questioningly.

"Forgive me, Señor," said the deposed priest, "but when you mentioned Punta Hermosa I happened to think of a certain passage in the Scriptures which seems especially appropriate to this case. That is why I laughed."

"What passage is it?" asked Herr Binzer coldly.

"The one in St. Mark where it speaks about driving out the devils with Beelzebub, Señor. Punta Hermosa belongs to Paqueno, and it is without doubt the only bit of land on Minorca which is not mortgaged. Now you take it as a pawn in order to drive out those who have pawned the rest."

"All right, all right," said Herr Binzer cutting him short. "I have brought a contract with me for you all to sign as leaders in this undertaking. Therein you acknowledge the object of our alliance, and give me Punta Hermosa as security for the amount I advance to you. I have not filled in the sum. Let me hear what you consider necessary."

There was silence; all the faces in that strange gathering bore one and the same expression, each and every one debated with himself what amount he would dare to suggest. Only the black-bearded sergeant seemed unaffected. He had other motives perhaps for taking part than the mere desire for gain. After a couple of moments Luis drew the priest aside and began a whispered conversation with him; gradually the others drew closer to them; Luis wrote down some figures on a paper, evidently questioning each one concerning his demands. Now and then a short but violent discussion arose between him and the others. It seemed as though he were trying to beat them down in their demands. Finally Luis motioned to Señor Posada, but the latter only sneeringly bared his teeth. Luis turned red, and seemed on the point of bridling up when Herr Binzer interrupted him and in his usual domineering tone said:

"Well, are you through now? I cannot stay waiting here the whole night. What's the amount?"

"Señor Binzer," said Luis fawningly, "we have considered what is absolutely necessary in undertaking the matter. We have come to the decision—you must remember the risk we all run, Señor—that a hundred thousand pesetas..."

"*Hol' euch der Teufel!*" interrupted Herr Binzer, "*Hol' euch der Teufel!* A hundred thousand pesetas! Why not a million? A hundred thousand to overthrow this scrap heap of a principality—do you think I am crazy? And that man there," pointing to Señor Posada, "surely is not yet down on the list. How much does he want? Another hundred thousand, eh?"

Herr Binzer looked challengingly at the black sergeant, whose eyebrows were sunk deeply over the whites of his eyes, as he slowly answered:

"Exactly that, Señor. A hundred thousand pesetas is the least I will accept for taking part in your undertaking. Wait, don't interrupt me yet! Remember that without me you can do nothing, nothing, Señor! The fortress commands the city, and some of our cannon, thank goodness, are in working order. And two hundred armed men would always have some chance against Amadeo's riffraff and Father Ignacio's friends from the country. Now tell me, if you think a hundred thousand too much!"

Herr Binzer immediately complied with the request in a Spanish which was filled with the most picturesque of oaths; the black sergeant silenced him with a threatening gesture.

"Not too many big words, Señor! Two hundred thousand would be a cheap price for Punta Hermosa—or what do you think about it, yourself? Who knows if you could have got it from the Grand Duke for half a million—my nephew is kitchen boy under Joaquin at the palace, Señor, and he thought otherwise. You know how boys stick their noses into everything, Señor!"

Señor Posada placed a bitter emphasis on his last words which hastily made Herr Binzer grow pale. The devil! Had the others understood what that sergeant there meant? Thank goodness, they did not seem to understand. Was it true that old rubbish heap up there commanded the city? Yes, *tausend Teufel,* it was not impossible. Two hundred thousand to that gang of robbers! Never! But Punta Hermosa, he must have Punta Hermosa—there were millions lying there waiting to be plucked. Just wait, Friend Sergeant, and the rest of you, Herr Binzer of Frankfort will pluck them yet—and his two hundred thousand back from your pockets, too. Just wait, you rabble!

Herr Binzer, who had taken hardly more than a minute to think it all over, quietly lit a cigar on one of the flickering candles and resumed. He declared shortly and to the point that he considered two hundred thousand a ridiculous amount for overthrowing such a Duchy as Minorca (a murmur arose among the assemblage); but rather than risk seeing them fail, he would agree to advance them two hundred thousand. Before it came as far as that, however, there was a certain document to be signed.

He drew a paper out of his pocket and said curtly:

"Here is the contract which I have drawn up in order to arrange our affairs. Read it, Luis!"

Luis took the paper which Herr Binzer held out to him, and then read:

"We, the undersigned, realizing that the unendurable situation in which our beloved Island of Minorca finds itself will not cease before the present form of government ceases, swear, one and all, to do our utmost to overthrow the government and to give ourselves no rest until a different order of affairs has been arranged. May the tyrant and his tools die and liberty live!

"To the possessor of this contract, from whom we have received the money necessary to carry out our plans (two hundred thousand pesetas), we, as leaders of the movement for liberty, promise the Castle of Punta Hermosa as security for the money advanced. Port Mahon, the 17th of February, 1910."

Luis stopped and looked at his friends.

"Well, may I kindly ask you to sign it?" said Herr Binzer impatiently. "I cannot wait the whole night."

A whining voice arose.

"Why should it be signed? What good is that contract? If it falls into the hands of anyone. . ."

It was the innkeeper Amadeo.

"My dear Señor Amadeo," said Herr Binzer coldly, "it is for just that very reason you are to sign it. It might otherwise happen that I had paid out two hundred thousand for nothing. If you should simply lie back and take life easy, you may rest assured that this contract would quickly enough come into the hands of someone. Therefore, may I kindly ask you to sign it!"

The little gathering grew silent; each stared at the other and no one seemed disposed to carry out Herr Binzer's wish. Then, emphatically spitting on the floor and scornfully looking at the others, the black sergeant took Herr Binzer's fountain pen and in a clumsy but powerful hand wrote, Eugenio Posada, Sergeant of the Body-Guard. Luis, who had become red then pale in turn (evidently he found his position as leader again in danger) seized the pen and wrote his name just above. Father Ignacio followed.

"Your turn, Señor Amadeo."

"I can't write, Señor," whined the innkeeper. "May the Madonna have mercy on me, I have never learned to write."

Herr Binzer looked at him with the contempt of a German for the illiterate.

"But you know how to reckon," he asked, "and you can

reckon out that there will be no part for those who cannot sign it?"

"Will my mark do, Señor?" hastily put in the hunchback.

"Just a moment," answered Herr Binzer, and took the pen. "For the innkeeper Amadeo, who cannot write, his mark," he wrote, as he spelled out each word in a loud tone. "Here you are!"

The innkeeper gave him a look full of hate and quickly made a flourish on the paper. The others, who had listened in silence, raised no objections but signed their names or made their mark, in the latter case each time provided with an explanatory note by Herr Binzer. After he had read aloud the contract with all the signatures, Herr Binzer drew a wallet from his pocket.

"Read out the amounts," said he to Luis. "You have a list, of course."

All accepted their money, but without much enthusiasm. The sergeant was the last of all to receive his hundred thousand, Luis omitting to mention him. Herr Binzer put the wallet back in his pocket and said:

"Well, gentlemen, everything is straightened out. Now get to work. When will you have some news for me?"

There was again silence; all stared at each other, evidently thrown off their balance by Herr Binzer's businesslike manner of arranging revolutions.

"In a month or so," the innkeeper began cautiously.

"Yes, perhaps before that," said Luis slowly, but was interrupted by the sergeant who now for the second time opened his mouth.

"Two weeks are more than enough. In case of necessity I can manage the affair alone. To-day is the seventeenth of February. Latest the first of March, Señor."

"Fine," said Herr Binzer. "See that you push your friends."

Señor Posada riveted his eyes on him.

"I have one thing to add to the contract."

"What?" Herr Binzer 's eyebrows began to bristle.

"Don't be afraid, Señor. It isn't money. I have other reasons also for taking part in this thing. There is a certain appointment I want when we have succeeded and when the guilty are to be punished."

"The guilty?"

"The Cripple and Paqueno."

"What kind of an appointment? Perhaps as judge?"

"No, Señor. Executioner."

Herr Binzer stared at the sergeant. *Gott im Himmel,* he wouldn't be a pleasant person to have as enemy. Executioner! He must hate the Grand Duke worse than he, Herr Binzer, did. Evidently Herr Binzer's eyes expressed his thoughts for the sergeant looked at him quickly and said:

"Four years ago, Señor, I had a brother who was also serving in the body-guard. He made a slight blunder and the Cripple had him hung before the troops."

He stopped as abruptly as he had begun. Herr Binzer looked at him again in amazement and then went slowly toward the door, followed by Luis.

Outside the night was cold; a last gleam of moonlight was resting on the cornice of the old castle. Behind them Herr Binzer and Luis heard the other conspirators tramping along on their way back to the city, which was sleeping as quietly as the villages and houses everywhere on Minorca; as quietly as it had been sleeping for a thousand years.

Would its slumbers be disturbed by Herr Binzer and his friends?

That remains to be seen.

CHAPTER 4

In Which A Vessel Leaves Minorca

At six o'clock in the evening of the twenty-eighth of February, while the bells of the Cathedral at Port Mahon were pealing heavily, the figures of two men in long coats might have been seen leaving the Ducal palace. With quick steps they crossed the palace court-yard; and silently turned off in the direction toward the harbor.

One was short and carried a small valise; the other was of gigantic size and limped slightly. In his hand he carried a travelling bag of pretentious proportions.

The smaller person broke the silence.

"Your Highness should have let Auguste bear the bag. Your Highness will overstrain. . ."

"Nonsense, Paqueno, with such a bag as this! When I have borne the cares of state and a guilty conscience for so many years! Besides, too many of us would arouse attention. I wish no one to know about my departure."

"But won't Your Highness let me. . ."

"Dear old Esteban, please don't worry about me. My

grand-ducal dignity will not be lowered through carrying a travelling bag. It is only a pity that it does not contain gold. In that case, I might conquer the strongest fortress, if the old saying is right."

After a moment's silence, the Grand Duke continued: "For as a matter of fact, no one can deny that I am and always have been a first-class ass."

"To think that man Isaac in London also said no," mumbled Paqueno, evidently continuing his own train of thought. "We offered him such good terms, too."

"Too fine a firm, Paqueno."

"But he made a loan to Servia, Your Highness."

"That does not necessarily mean he need make us a loan. We have had neither assassinations nor revolutions. Now we must place our hopes in my personally being able to soften the heart of Marcowitz or stir up a loan. On which side of the harbor is it that the boat lies, Paqueno?"

"On the east, Your Highness, here below. I am afraid we will have a bad crossing."

The Grand Duke looked up. In spite of the early hour, it was absolutely dark. The clouds were driving across the sky, covering it completely, and whenever a momentary rift occurred in them, the stars whirled by like electric sparks from an induction machine. Port Mahon was as though dead: the gas works, which had shut down for three weeks, left the streets in darkness, and not a person was to be seen.

"Just as well it's dark, the fewer people who see us the better," murmured the Grand Duke. "They are always quieter when they think their good ruler is watching over them. Although God knows that they are not a troublesome sort."

Señor Paqueno had put on his glasses, and with head stretched forward, peered into the dark alley along which they were going. The way led straight down to the harbor, and the swish of the water could be heard from the distance. At the end of the alley, the black silhouette of a boat's rigging could be seen painting itself against the sky; suddenly a light appeared in one of the masts and Señor Paqueno took hold of his master's arm.

"There is the vessel, Your Highness. Joaquin's cousin promised to show a light at this time."

The Grand Duke and he continued on their way and shortly reached the harbor pier. Beside it a little fishing schooner was rocking violently up and down, pulling impatiently at its moorings. A stocky man in skipper's clothes approached the Grand Duke and his companion, looked at them and then greeted them respectfully.

"Everything is ready, Your Highness," said he.

"Fine, my good Domingo. You are a cousin of my highly esteemed cook, Joaquin?"

"Yes, Your Highness. . ."

"And a Majorcan, I suppose. Ah, these Majorcans."

"Your Highness, I was born on Majorca, like my father and Joaquin, but at heart I am a good Minorcan."

"Yes? But your father does not even care to be purveyor to the court."

"Your Highness ..." The man became flustered.

The Grand Duke burst out laughing.

"There, there, deuce take it all, I was only joking. At present you'll be doing me the biggest kind of service if you take us over to Barcelona as quickly as possible."

"Immediately, Your Highness, immediately. We can put off in ten minutes."

The man made a deep bow, and then jumped on board. Evidently he was more than surprised at the passengers his unpretentious boat was to carry that night. In the forenoon, as he had cast anchor in the harbor of Port Mahon, he had received a visit from his cousin, the Grand Duke's cook, who had taken him aside and presented the proposal which in the beginning had filled him with the deepest apprehension and then with a feeling of amazement which had not yet quieted down. What on earth did the Grand Duke want to do in Barcelona? Or rather, why did he want to go there with him, Domingo, in a plain fishing smack? Joaquin had answered all questions with a categorical declaration that that was His Highness' affair and concerned nobody else—His Highness did not wish his departure to become known under any circumstances; and after some further talk, Domingo had agreed to the proposal, although Barcelona really lay outside his route of trade, which was confined to the Balearic Islands.

And consequently that evening he bid welcome to the Grand Duke, half convinced that the poor ruler had grown tired of his position and like so many Minorcans before him, was escaping from the island of his forefathers in order to seek his fortune elsewhere.

The Duke and Paqueno remained together on the quay conversing in a low tone while Domingo and the two members of his crew made final preparations for departure.

"Today is the twenty-eighth," said the Grand Duke. "How long will this fellow Domingo need to reach Barcelona?"

"We will arrive there early the day after to-morrow, Your Highness, if everything goes well."

"H'm, then we will have twelve days ahead of us. It is on the thirteenth, Paqueno, is it not, that the loan falls due?"

"Yes, Your Highness, on the thirteenth."

"Twelve days, or if we count in our trip to Paris, barely eleven. We must hope for success with Marcowitz, Paqueno, or with someone else."

"We must hope so, Your Highness. Otherwise. . ."

"Otherwise, my poor Esteban, I have finished the task which my grandfather and father began."

"What is that, Your Highness?"

"Ruining your life, my old Esteban."

"Your Highness!" Old Paqueno tremblingly grasped the Grand Duke's hand in his own. "Oh, if Your Highness had only sold Punta Hermosa to the German. . ."

"Never, Paqueno, never!" The Grand Duke clapped his old friend on the shoulder. "He may procure his fire and brimstone elsewhere."

Señor Paqueno gave a deep sigh. Suddenly Domingo's voice was heard:

"We're all ready!"

The Grand Duke helped old Señor Paqueno over the railing and threw in his travelling bag. Then he turned to Domingo.

"Now I'm coming, Domingo. Remember, 'you carry Caesar and his fortunes in your boat!'"

He hopped over the rail, the deck of the ship shaking under his gigantic body.

Domingo and the crew cast off. The little fishing smack moved slowly along the edge of the quay, drifted away from it and began to glide out through the harbor.

At just that moment a man appeared on the quay. He was fat and stubby and ran as though his life depended on it. As he came nearer, they heard him cry:

"Domingo! Domingo! I have something to deliver. Steer near to the pier, Domingo!"

The Grand Duke recognized the voice; it was his cook, Joaquin. He was greatly surprised, but did not wish to cry back, afraid that someone else might hear his voice. Domingo looked at him questioningly, awaiting orders; he nodded yes, and while the man continued to run along toward the end of the pier, the little skipper steered his boat in toward the quay in a graceful bow. When they were within a few yards of the end of the pier, where Joaquin already stood, the cook lifted his arm and threw something which fell on the deck with a dull thud. At the same moment the wind seized the boat and it flew swishing by the mole of the harbor and out to sea. Within a few seconds Joaquin was only a little spot; then he disappeared completely in the darkness.

The Duke had quickly picked up what had been thrown on board; it was Joaquin's cap, hastily tied together with a string. He loosened it and found inside the cap a stone and wrapped around this a piece of blue paper.

"Paqueno," he cried after he had raised it toward the lighted skylight of the little cabin, "a telegram for you!"

"A telegram, Your Highness!. . ."

The old Minister of Finance came carefully across the sloping deck and tried to open the telegram. But the smack careened too much and it was too dark; holding him firmly under the arm, the Grand Duke opened the door to the companionway, and helped him down the cabin stairs. Then he himself followed.

In the middle of the floor under the smoking lamp he found his old friend standing with wide open mouth and eyes as though fixed in death. His staring glance sought the Grand Duke's face, and his lips tried to move, but brought forth no sound. There was a twitching of the wrinkles around his eyes. He held the opened telegram in his hand, which trembled so that the piece of blue paper rattled.

Full of fear the Grand Duke rushed forward; at the same moment the lips of the old Minister of Finance finally moved and with shaking hand he gave the telegram to his master.

"Fr-from our agent, P-Perez in Barcelona," he stammered in a voice almost unintelligible. "His private code words stand at the beginning. Read... Your Highness... read...."

The Grand Duke seized the piece of blue paper and this is what he found written there:

> *Barcelona, February 28, 16.10 o'clock.*
>
> *Paqueno, Minister of Finance, Port Mahon, Minorca.*
>
> *Zp 99: Between 10 and 10:30 this morning through a coup on Paris, Madrid, Barcelona exchanges eighty per cent of Duchy of Minorca's entire national indebtedness purchased for unknown account; last quotation 42 ½.*
>
> *Great excitement prevails in financial circles most closely affected; received telegrams from Viviani, Altenstein, Apelmann; greatly excited, wish explanation. Telegraph you further to-morrow.*
>
> *Request information whether you backing affair or can give explanation; await instructions regarding Viviani, Altenstein, Apelmann.*
>
> *Perez, Agent.*

The Grand Duke read through the telegram twice and then again, at last letting his hand sink down as he stared at Señor Paqueno.

"A coup in our bonds, Paqueno!" said he. "A coup in our bonds! Eighty per cent purchased for unknown account—and Altenstein and the others begin swearing by wire... By Saint Urban!..."

The boat keeled far over from a violent puff of wind which threw the Duke against the bench, where old Paqueno had sunk together with puzzled eyes and lips tightly pressed together. Don Ramon looked at him mechanically as he caught hold of the cabin table to steady himself.

"By our holy patron, St. Urban of Majorca!" he murmured. "The market cornered in the Duchy of Minorca's obligations—now it won't be long before we have a revolution!"

BOOK TWO

Kings in Exile

CHAPTER 1

In Which the Reader Either Meets with Two Former Acquaintances or Is Introduced to A Great Financier

"What is it, Crofton?"

"A gentleman wishes to see you, sir."

"A gentleman? Who is he? Didn't he give you his calling card? You ought to know how busy I am, Crofton."

"An elderly gentleman, sir. He told me to say 26 Southport Avenue, sir."

"What did he tell you to say!"

"26 Southport Avenue, sir. He said, 'Say that, that is enough. In case it is not, then say five thousand preferred shares of the Digamma Company.'"

Honest Mr. Crofton, whose face as he delivered this greeting expressed the greatest bewilderment, became still more astonished at the effect the words had on his employer. Mr. Ernest Isaacs, London banker, of 27 Lombard Street, the City, was not known for his especially good humor and least of all when the Stock Exchange showed a downward tendency, but on hearing the message which had made Mr. Crofton scratch his head in perplexity, he threw himself back in his chair and let out a ringing shout of laughter. Mr. Crofton, who was fifty-six years old, a Low churchman and of a strictly serious turn of mind, raised his light eyebrows in disapproval. His character being such as mentioned above, he did not look with favor on a person laughing at anything he had said. Although he admitted that the message he delivered was strange, nevertheless he considered it highly unsuitable for Mr. Isaacs to receive it in the fashion he did.

"Oh, the professor, the professor!" cried Mr. Isaacs between two bursts of laughter. "That is just like him! Always the same, rain or shine, brazen-faced as Beelzebub himself!"

"Shall I have him thrown out, sir?" Mr. Crofton's bearing became milder at the thought of thus gaining his revenge on the unknown person.

"Have him thrown out! No, not by a long shot! Show him in immediately, Crofton. We have something to talk over. He has simply been amusing himself a little at our expense."

Mr. Crofton's manner became twice as disapproving as he saw his hopes of revenge come to nought. He disappeared, and a few seconds later threw open the double doors for a white-bearded gentleman with gold-rimmed glasses, clad in a rather soiled jacket and trousers with braiding down the sides. He walked with a gait as stooping as though his shoulders bore all the cares of the universe, and he gazed from behind his spectacles with a look as weary and distressed as though his eyes beheld all the iniquities of the five continents. As Mr. Crofton closed the doors, he saw him sink heavily into a leather armchair while Mr. Isaacs, who greeted his entrance with a new burst of laughter, arose to shake his hand.

"Oh, you are too good, Professor. The devil himself would not know you again in that dress. You look even more venerable than old man Booth."

"You are really very kind, Mr. Isaacs. Well, between ourselves, I have a certain amount of talent along this line. My get-up today is one of my simplest; it is the same I wore when I arrested Kenyon the detective with a warrant for my own arrest. Do you remember?"

"Do I remember? That was two years ago when you rented out the whole street where he lived to summer visitors in London. It was devilishly funny. But you have played worse tricks than that, Professor!"

"Why, Mr. Isaacs, haven't you forgotten that little affair yet!"

"If you have a fellow kidnapped through the help of a movie operator who has been duly licensed by the police, it is not likely that he will forget it so very quickly. Especially not when you send Crofton in to him with the address of the street where it happened!"

"Well, well, Mr, Isaacs, let's forgive and forget! As a matter of fact, you are as little angry with me for that affair as I am with you for palming off on me those shares of the Digamma Company which I also told Crofton to remind you about."

"H'm, why should you be angry with me about that? Shares which you made me buy back at an outrageous price—you earned quite a few pounds yourself by that affair!"

"And also risked quite a few pounds myself which I would have lost if I had not shown the ready ingenuity I did."

"H'm, a ready ingenuity which cost me eighty thousand, Professor."

"And which some fine day will make you a peer of England."

"You are a good prophet! That was three years ago, and I haven't noticed any trace of the peerage yet—nor even of plain knighthood."

"But you got into Parliament, just as I told you."

"Yes, and a devilish lot of pleasure I get from that! A lot of expense greasing the palms of the voters—just between ourselves, Professor, just between ourselves—and the privilege of being bullied once a day by the conservative press."

"Good Lord, Mr. Isaacs, you must remember that you are a thorn in their flesh, a brand pulled out of their own fire. You began as one of their candidates—if I may be allowed to remind you of the fact."

"Why not? You quite calmly remind me of matters which are far less pleasant to remember." The tone of Mr. Isaacs' voice was not without bitterness. "But enough of that.

I am getting along tolerably well, and I am glad to let other people get along too, when it is not at my expense. I do not begrudge you your little triumph in 1907—although it rather hurt at the time. I have forgiven you much on account of the pleasure I experienced afterwards through your sublime audacity. How about a smoke?"

"Thanks." Mr. Isaacs' white-haired visitor bit off the end of the cigar offered him, and held a light to it with hands which did not seem at all unsteady through age. He luxuriously exhaled a cloud of smoke and bowed:

"Your cigars, Mr. Isaacs, are as much to my taste as certain parts of your business are the reverse. But I interrupted you. You were speaking of my audacity, and were kind enough to call it sublime. I judge, therefore, that you had some special reason for trying to find me through an advertisement in the papers?"

"You are not only a great man on account of your audacity, but also through your acuteness, Professor. I need your valuable help. That is why I advertised. I didn't know your address. My own I did not wish to insert, as the police probably are keeping an eye open after you. Therefore I only signed my initials, E.I. I am glad I did not misjudge your abilities."

Mr. Isaacs stopped for a minute, and then resumed:

"I have a little job to propose to you. I will not say that I could not get somebody else to attend to the matter, but I come to you for the same reason that I go to my tailor in Sackville Street—because I want to be certain that everything will be carried out in an irreproachable manner."

Mr. Isaacs' guest bowed in acknowledgment.

"I need you to deal with a man who arouses a deadly hatred in me."

"What on earth are you driving at? I hope you don't think I am running some sort of assassination agency!"

"No, perhaps not—why, no, of course not. Besides I want to avoid all extreme measures. I am a good-natured, peace-loving man."

"As well as a member of Parliament. You did not intend, then, to have him assassinated. May I ask his name?"

"Adolphus Hornstein."

"German?"

"No, Polish, which is twice as bad. Do you remember Mrs. Daisy Bell, Professor?"

"Do I remember your delightful friend Mrs. Bell! *Mais naturellement*. What has become of her? Has this man stolen her heart away?"

"Not quite that. He has obtained possession of something which is worth far more to me, namely, my letters to her. How it happened, nobody knows; whether he got them from her or from her maid. Anyway there is only one person who matters now, and that is Adolf Hornstein. Have you heard of him before, Professor?"

"Hornstein, Hornstein... I don't know. Wasn't it a Hornstein who was mixed up in the Birchell divorce case?"

"Yes, precisely. It was he who turned over to Lady Alice the compromising letters from his lordship. And it is the same amiable gentleman who is now threatening to separate me from my constituency. You know there is to be a general election on the twenty-second of February, that is, in a week, on account of Lloyd George's budget. You also know what a strictly moral constituency I represent; you pointed that fact out to me three years ago. Oh, Professor, that movie affair! It was a clever scheme, but. . ."

"Why, Mr. Isaacs, I thought we were going to forget all about that. Your letters, then, would not lend themselves as suitable reading matter for your constituents?"

"Not as election literature, Professor, that I am willing to swear. They are a little too. . . h'm. . . liberal in style, even for a liberal candidate. If they are published, it is simply the end of me in Parliament. And in any case Hornstein can make my life a hell—as long as he has them."

"As long as he has them, yes. That is why you sent for me, Mr. Isaacs?"

"Yes, Professor, that is just why. Relieve me of Hornstein, and. . ."

"You mean relieve Hornstein of your letters. And what then?"

"You will earn my eternal gratitude. Isn't that enough?"

"That depends on the manner in which you express it. I am a poor man and earn my bread through the sweat of my brow. Last autumn proved a bad time for my little speculations. A firm by the name of Walkley & Smithers. . ."

"I have the pleasure of knowing them. Well, so you were in that, Professor? It is some consolation that such a shrewd man as you were duped by them. I myself. . ."

"Don't exaggerate, Mr. Isaacs. The pupil does not stand above his master. In business I am a little child compared to you."

A smile played around Mr. Isaacs' black, Mephistophelean beard. It was evident that the praise touched him in a tender spot.

"Oh," said he, "business! You can't imagine the sort of things people propose! Look at this letter here. It came this morning."

He tossed over to the gray-haired professor a letter bearing a foreign postmark. Opening it, he looked at the signature with a tired glance.

"For His Highness, the Grand Duke of Minorca, Esteban Paqueno, Minister of Finance," he read aloud. "For Heaven's sake, are you doing business with the Duchy of Minorca, Mr. Isaacs? I thought such things were below you."

"I am not doing any business with them, Professor. The Grand Duchy of Minorca proposes that I should. Read the letter, and you will see."

> *Mr. Ernest Isaacs, Banker,*
> *27 Lombard Street,*
> *London, England.*
>
> *Dear Sir:*
> *Although unacquainted with your esteemed firm. . . as it has come to my knowledge that through a loan you have assisted the Servian government. . . I turn to you*

privately in an affair, which should be of interest to you as a man of finance... The present depressed state of the stock market cannot have escaped your notice, and in your country even less favorable conditions may be expected on account of Mr. Lloyd George's budget... it becomes more and more apparent that instead of industrial paper, exposed to each day's unaccountable fluctuations, greater advantages are to be obtained from an investment in an enterprise both safe and profitable... government bonds however in general hardly being desirable investments... the highest interest they pay seldom exceeding five per cent... in consideration of these facts, both in your interest and our own, I venture to bring to your notice an undertaking which combines the solidity of government bonds with the larger profit of a private undertaking.

"By Jove, Mr. Isaacs, doesn't it make your mouth water! Whoever this Señor Paqueno is, he knows how to present his subject in a seductive manner."

"Yes, if one hadn't heard the likes before! But continue, Professor."

... can be seen from the accompanying tables our olive crops show an increasing yield year by year. The figures for 1909 show an increase of thirty-five per cent since 1900... naturally these figures, coming from the Grand Ducal Bureau of Statistics are absolutely trustworthy.

"Hm..."

As you will perceive the yearly returns at present are estimated at 125,000 pesetas... on behalf of the Grand Ducal Ministry of Finance make you the following proposition... to grant us a loan of 600,000 pesetas, either to be made directly by your banking firm or to be underwritten by you...

"To underwrite an issue of Minorcan Government bonds, Professor! A fine idea, eh?"

... to run for a period of thirty years with interest at eight and one-half per cent, plus, as administration fee to you, a third of the tax receipts each year from the said olive industry, which tax will be delivered in toto as security for forming a sinking-fund and paying the interest. According to the grand-ducal decree of 1885 a tax of thirty per cent is imposed on the gross receipts from the entire olive industry on Minorca and the dependent islands, an income, which, as we have already shown by the annexed figures, is steadily and safely increasing...

"But, Mr. Isaacs, why, these are unbelievable conditions! Eight and a half per cent, and a third of this thirty per cent tax—which gives you besides a yearly bonus of 12,500 pesetas! And in thirty years—with an ever increasing yield from the olives! Of course you intend to accept?"

"Accept, Professor! You are crazy. How on earth could I accept? There isn't a reputable banking house in Europe willing to do business with Minorca. My Lord, nobody wants to keep company with the worst usurers and money-sharks in the world!"

"And therefore you let the usurers pocket the 8 per cent and a third of the taxes!. . ."

"What else can a person do? You have to keep up your reputation."

"But you raised money for Servia, a murd. . ."

"Sh, sh, Professor. That deal only paid seven per cent., and a Servian decoration looks as well as any other, eh? I am a strictly moral man."

"As well as a member of Parliament, that is true. May I take this letter and the figures? My sense of morals is not as strict as yours, you know."

"Certainly. But let us return to the matter in hand. Will you take care of this Hornstein affair?"

"For your sake, yes, Mr. Isaacs. Just to make up for the little trick I played you in 1907. How long a respite has Hornstein given you? I imagine it isn't long."

"Until the twenty-second—Six days."

"How much does he want?"

"An outrageous sum. . . twenty thousand pounds."

"How many letters are there?"

"Six, I think."

"And what value do you place on them yourself—that is, between friends?"

"Between friends? Ah, I understand. Let us say six thousand pounds."

"You are a prince among autograph collectors. You shall have the letters within five days. What is Hornstein's address?"

"12 Furlong Lane, E. C. Have you already thought out a plan?"

"Three. We'll see which one suits best. As soon as I can I will bring you some news. Until then, goodbye, Mr. Isaacs. It is better never to sleep on a matter like this."

Mr. Isaacs' white-haired guest rose heavily from his chair and shook hands. The great financier watched him as with bended back he disappeared through the baize-covered swinging doors, and then sitting down again at his desk, he murmured:

"A shrewd fellow, Professor Pelotard! Mighty shrewd. I wonder who he really is!"

CHAPTER 2

In Which The Reader Will Realize By What Thin Threads The Fate Of A Nation May Hang

The question which Mr. Isaacs asked himself at the end of the last chapter, has been answered for the benefit of our readers in a series of stories entitled "The London Adventures of Mr. Collin." These stories, which should have a place on every bookshelf, depict the life and adventures of Philip Collin, student of law, during the period from 1875 to 1910.

Mr. Collin was one of those Swedes, unfortunately not so few in number, who from various causes, are obliged to take up their residence abroad. His career at home—he had practised law in the city of Kristinehamn—came to an end when in September, 1904, he departed thence after collecting the funds for his travelling expenses from various banks. He was twenty-nine years old at the time. Three years of unfortunate speculation on the stock exchange had been enough to ruin a promising future and bring Mr. Collin into hopeless conflict with five paragraphs of the penal code. The next two years of his life he devoted to revenge; he spent them in Copenhagen settling affairs with the Danish brokers who had "dragged him to perdition" (as he himself expressed it in the papers he left behind him). When this task was settled, in a manner which cost these shady firms some seventy thousand Danish crowns, Mr. Collin hastily departed from Copenhagen in the month of January, 1906. He steered his course to England, landing there full of plans for the future growth of his already rather bulging pocketbook of crocodile leather. The irony of Fate, as well as poetic justice, saw to it that on the train he happened to fall in with an English pickpocket, who, at Liverpool Street Station, kindly relieved him of his pocketbook containing the fruit of several years' dishonest toil. How he wreaked vengeance on this gentleman is more fully described in the above-mentioned series of stories which should have a place on every bookshelf. There also is depicted his first meeting with Mr. Ernest Isaacs, referred to by that financier in the last chapter. This meeting closed with a decided defeat for Mr. Isaacs, who at first succeeded in selling a large block of worthless stock in the British Digamma Company to Mr. Collin. We do not need to add that the name under which Mr. Isaacs knew him was pronounced Pelotard instead of Collin. Under the name of Professor Pelotard, Mr. Collin, after his revenge on the pickpocket, had started on a professional life which is more fully described in the "Story of the Absent-Minded Gentleman.[1]" Mr. Isaacs, who was a shrewd man with a sense of humor when it concerned other persons' affairs, gradually learned to appreciate Mr. Collin for the clever manner in which he operated and avoided the consequences of his operations. His anger at his own defeat had slowly faded away and at a chance meeting in Paris he and Mr. Collin had decided to bury the hatchet. In the uncomfortable position which he had been placed by Mr. Adolphus Hornstein, the well-known member of the Stock Exchange had hastened to seek the help of his former enemy as we have seen in the foregoing chapter.

Five days had passed since then without Mr. Collin giving any signs of life, and Mr. Isaacs, who had spent his time roaming between London and his constituency, was already beginning to be anxious at his silence when Mr. Crofton that morning came in with the same strongly disapproving manner he had shown at Professor Pelotard's last visit.

"The old gentleman from Southport Avenue wishes to see you, sir."

Mr. Isaacs gave a start of joy.

"Excellent, excellent. Send him in at once, Crofton, and don't let me be disturbed for the present, you understand?"

Mr. Crofton, who on the contrary did not understand the matter at all, showed that fact plainly enough in every feature of his sanctimonious face. However, he went out slowly and shortly afterwards ushered in the aged Professor

---

1. Available for free download from Kabaty Press at https://shop.kabatypress.com/b/1BuYH

Pelotard. Mr. Isaacs jumped up from his chair with a tense expression on his face.

"Well, how did you get along? Tell me immediately. Have you got them?"

"How did I get along! Why, Mr. Isaacs, you are not very courteous. If you have your check book handy, a draft for six thousand pounds would suit me extremely well."

Mr. Isaacs gave a nervous laugh of relief.

"Oh, Professor, you are a wonderful man. Sit down and tell me all about it. How did you manage it? Have you really got them?"

Philip Collin nonchalantly drew a package of letters from his pocket and tossed them over to Mr. Isaacs.

"I hope they are all there," said he. "Anyway, you have nothing more to fear from Mr. Hornstein. I followed him myself to the night express from Charing Cross last evening and made sure that he left for Paris."

"Left? What do you mean? For Paris?"

"Yes, never to return to England. That is to say, unless he wishes to have Dartmoor as his residence."

"You more than astonish me, Professor. You relieve Hornstein of my letters—how I do not know, but I imagine you did not pay him the twenty thousand pounds he wanted for them. Afterwards you send him out of the country and promise to throw him into Dartmoor Prison if he returns. You're really a marvel!"

Philip gave a grateful smile.

"When I left you, Mr. Isaacs, I had three plans for recovering your letters from Hornstein. The first was through burglary—there is precedent for that since Sherlock Holmes himself did not hesitate to use such methods in a similar case. What the second plan was doesn't matter. It was the third that I followed.

"I went directly home and made a slight change in my appearance. I had decided to beard the jackal in his den. Consequently I dressed up like a better-class servant off duty. 12 Furlong Lane, where Hornstein lived, I found to be a rather dilapidated house on a side street leading off Lloyds Avenue; Hornstein had rooms on the ground floor. I rang, and the door was opened by a large rough fellow with a pock-marked face, who evidently was stationed there as Cerberus. He looked, too, as though he could play the role, if any of his master's victims should lose control of themselves while visiting him. Cerberus announced me to Hornstein without raising any objections.

"A more loathsome animal than that man Hornstein it has never been my lot to see. Mr. Hornstein combined insolence and an ability to look grimy from the tips of his fingers to his very soul. Every feature of his face bespoke an unscrupulous graspingness, and every detail of his manner showed he was ready to satisfy it.

"Well, I introduced myself to him as Charles Ferguson, employed by a very well-known conservative statesman; I hinted (as the whole world knows through the newspapers) that my Lord and his lady were not on the best of terms with each other, and that she had every reason for a divorce. Hornstein immediately pricked up his ears, but was extremely careful and asked what I was driving at. I answered that I had heard about him through Arthur Sanders, who was in the service of Lady Birchell—his name stood in the papers you know, and as he is in prison now, I risked nothing. Then I came straight to the point and asked what he would give for complete proof against Lord— yes, against the Lord in question. He became still more interested, more eager and importunate—*enfin,* I caught him on the hook, but entrenched myself behind the price. He bid a hundred pounds, I laughed and demanded two thousand. He burst out with the most frightful oaths and I proposed fifteen hundred—enough so that he would not say yes. Then I started to go, at which he became extremely persistent, almost threatening. I promised to think the matter over and left.

"You may ask, perhaps, what my idea was with all this. Nothing else than to make a close study of Mr. Hornstein's features and get a general idea of the place. I had no thoughts of selling him any kind of bogus letters, although it might have been a good trick. After our interview I let four days pass by, which I devoted to other matters (Mr. Isaacs looked at his guest reproachfully). Then, yesterday, I sent Hornstein a note, asking him to meet me at the Cafe Monico. I asked him to wait there from four to five, as I was uncertain when I could get away from his lordship. I hadn't the least doubt about his coming, since I hinted I was bringing my goods with me.

"At half past three, about the time I thought Mr. Hornstein would be getting ready for our rendezvous, I myself began my preparations at home, and at ten minutes past four I arrived at 12 Furlong Lane with Lavertisse. Have I ever told you about my old friend Lavertisse? A wonderful man in his way—I have never met his equal, where antiques are concerned and when it comes to a question of an acute sense of hearing. I knocked at the door. I forgot to mention that I had made myself into a rather true copy of Mr. Hornstein. It was dusk by that time, and I was quite certain of success.

"Well, Cerberus opened the door. I pointed to Lavertisse and said in a fair imitation of Hornstein's thick voice: 'I must have left my key on the desk. I've changed my plans. This gentleman and I have some matters to talk over. You may do what you like for the next hour.'

"Cerberus disappeared without even a thank you, and Lavertisse and I hurried into Hornstein's study. Within a minute Lavertisse was at work on the safe, while I kept watch at the door. Have I told you that I never met a person with such an acute sense of hearing as Lavertisse possesses? Then, perhaps, I forgot to add that this applies especially to combination-locks. M. Lepine, who is chief of police in Paris—but that doesn't matter. Within twenty-five minutes Lavertisse had coaxed out the secret of Hornstein's fire- and burglar-proof safe (for cases where a combination-lock is not used, Lavertisse has also learned the elementary working principles of the jemmy), and I began my investigations.

I must say they were not a little surprising. The first thing I discovered was that Hornstein's name isn't Hornstein at all."

"What on earth is it, then, Professor? Of course I suspected right along that he might have other names, too. What is his name, then, instead of Hornstein?"

"Semjon Marcowitz, and under that name he evidently has a branch of his nice little business in Paris. That was the first thing I discovered. The next was your letters, bound around with a pale pink and a baby blue silk ribbon—I hope it is Hornstein and not Mrs. Bell who has such poor taste. Then I came across an overwhelming number of documents, confirming my first discovery—that Hornstein's name is Semjon Marcowitz and that he transacts his affairs on a large scale, both here and in Paris. If you could only guess what sort of a document I found deposited from his branch in Paris! Really, Mr. Isaacs, Hornstein, or Marcowitz, is no plain, every-day bungler in his profession; what would you say, if I told you he counted reigning princes among his clients?"

With wide-opened eyes Mr. Isaacs looked at Philip Collin, who seemed on the point of continuing, but then burst out laughing and shrugged his shoulders.

"No, I'll keep that as my own secret for the present. But what I discovered last of all I will not keep from you. I seemed to notice that the dimensions of the safe inside and out didn't coincide. In order to be sure I let Lavertisse fumble around a bit on the inside; and true enough, it was not long before I had my suspicions confirmed. There was a secret compartment, and Lavertisse—who is a jewel in his line, and will receive a thousand pounds from me for this as sure as he gets one—had it open in less than ten minutes. And do you know what I discovered in that secret compartment—beyond any question of a doubt? Why, that Hornstein or Marcowitz on top of everything else is a German spy!"

"The devil, you say! The devil, you say!" Mr. Isaacs' eyes were glued on Philip Collin like those of a child on a person telling a fairytale.

"Yes, no doubt about it! Some of the documents were in cipher, some just in German, a language which gives me no trouble. I made certain that Hornstein has been a German spy ever since 1905, the fleet being his special care, and then I emptied the safe of its entire contents. I dumped everything into the grate and set fire to it all, with the exception of your letters, the document from Paris and a few other things which could serve as proof of his being a spy. Then I quickly wrote a letter, in which I pointed out what fate awaited German spies in this country, and advised Mr. Hornstein to leave England without too much ceremony, at the latest by the night express from Charing Cross that same evening. I signed the letter Charles Ferguson and left it on the desk. Then Lavertisse and I took our departure. That was a little after five o'clock.

"We waited at the corner of Lloyd's Avenue until six; at the very moment the clock struck, we saw Hornstein come running along in company with Cerberus, who seemed ready to murder the first best person they met. They disappeared in 12 Furlong Lane and it took about twenty minutes before they came out, the one paler than the other. We had the pleasure of seeing Mr. Hornstein-Marcowitz question a police-constable, who pulled out a pocket railway-guide and gave him some information which, I have every reason to believe, had to do with the departure of the trains for the continent. Thereupon Cerberus and his master stepped into a cab and disappeared. Certainly I had no doubts as to the effects of my letter, but to make sure I showed up at Charing Cross in my present costume at a quarter to twelve. Mr. Hornstein-Marcowitz had been waiting there for the past half hour, whiling away the time by asking all the station employees whether the night express would be late. I enjoyed this pretty sight until the train left and then went home and to bed. The only thing I regret is that I could not see Marcowitz' expression as he opened the safe.—That is the way it all happened, Mr. Isaacs. You have your letters, and I have the pleasure of looking forward to my check. Made out to bearer, if you please!"

Mr. Isaacs, who had been listening to Philip's simple little story with wide-open mouth, silently drew a check book from his inside pocket and wrote out a draft, which he handed over without a word. Mr. Collin read it through and bowed.

"Ten thousand pounds! Mr. Isaacs, you pay me the greatest compliment I have received for a long time. *Apres tout,* it was one-third luck—and Lavertisse and I."

"You are a great man, Professor," said Mr. Isaacs. "I am liberal-minded and will say nothing, but you could be a big man in other ways. . ."

Philip interrupted him with a movement of his hand.

"*Tous les genres sont bons,*" said he, "*hors le genre ennuyeux.* All ways are good except those that are tiresome . . . I have something else I would like to talk over with you, Mr. Isaacs."

Mr. Isaacs answered through silently pulling his chair nearer. He did not even look at the clock; it was as great a compliment as the check, coming from a man who was more occupied than most of his class in London and whose word on the Exchange controlled the fortunes and misfortunes of thousands.

"Have you answered that letter you showed me when I was last here, Mr. Isaacs? The letter from Minorca?"

"Minorca? Ah, about the olives. Why yes, certainly I have answered it."

"That you are not interested?"

"Of course."

"H'm. And it was simply the fear of bad company spoiling your good reputation that kept you out of the enterprise?"

"Principally. People here in England are so refined in their feelings. One should hardly lend money to China, to say nothing about Portugal. A man in a position such as mine must think of public opinion as much as of per cent.

Business with Minorca would ruin his reputation if not his financial standing."

Philip Collin looked at Mr. Isaacs with a long glance from his intelligent black eyes.

"If," said he softly and with emphasis on each word, "if he himself appeared in the transaction! You surely have not thought about that, Mr. Isaacs!"

Mr. Isaacs stared at his guest.

"By Jove!" cried the financier. "Do I understand you correctly? You mean I should lend the money to Minorca through you?"

"No," replied Philip Collin quietly, "I mean that through me you should buy up the entire government indebtedness of the Grand Duchy of Minorca!"

If Mr. Collin, in order to astound his host, had proposed to him that he should stand on his head atop of St. Paul's Cathedral, it is most certain he could not have called forth more genuine amazement. Mr. Isaacs, who looked at him intently, sank back in his chair; his well-groomed beard dropped way down on his cravat, and he stared at Mr. Collin as though the latter had lost his senses. Philip looked at him with a quiet smile. At last the banker found his tongue:

"Buy. . . Professor, are you crazy or are you making fun of me? What was it you said I should do?"

"Mr. Isaacs, I am neither crazy nor impudent enough to make sport of you; and what I said was: you should buy up the entire government indebtedness of the Grand Duchy of

Minorca!"

Mr. Isaacs vehemently stroked his Mephistophelean beard.

"You are otherwise a clever fellow. There must be some sort of method in your madness. Anyway, I will listen to you. Explain!"

Philip Collin nodded.

"There is method in my madness. I will show you immediately. Have you heard the story about Columbus and the egg?[2]"

Mr. Isaacs gave an impatient flourish of his hand.

"All right. I will jump over Columbus and the egg. Otherwise, I had intended to say that the plan I had thought out for our mutual benefit is just like that story. Nobody had thought of placing the egg just as Columbus did, and nobody before me has thought of cornering the market in Minorcan bonds. Many of the smaller money-lenders have reaped their harvest of varying percentage during years and years. Some have earned much, some little; some have probably lost, but all have stood in each other's way, and none have thought of transacting the affair on a big scale. And still this is the age of trusts and the time for carrying matters on in a small way has passed. May I take another of your excellent cigars?"

Mr. Isaacs nodded. Philip lit the cigar and continued:

"I have made use of the last few days to procure all the

---

2. Apocryphal story regarding Christopher Columbus, who challenged guests at a dinner party to make an egg stand on one end. After they had one by one failed in the attempt, he took the egg, crushed one end of it on the table and it immediately stood upright – Ed.

information I could about the Grand Duchy's affairs. Of course, I have not obtained all the details, but I have the most important.

"The Grand Duchy of Minorca's indebtedness exists in the form of bonds issued at 100, 500 and 1,000 pesetas, guaranteed by the state. If they have procured a loan of 600,000 pesetas they have then issued at least 600 bonds with a face value of 1,000 pesetas, usually a larger number of bonds and smaller denominations. The banks which have loaned the money demand some collateral—either real estate, a monopoly, or a tax on some industry. So far this is the normal procedure; now comes the outrageous part of the affair (apart from the rate of interest being at least 7 ½ per cent). In case that for even one year there should be a default in paying either the interest or instalment on the loan, the banks have expressly reserved the right to take over the management of the security; at the same time they have stipulated especial 'costs of administration' for running and keeping the collateral in good condition, and last but not least, these stipulations are to remain in force until all back interest, instalments and the interest on these have been paid! You can understand the outrageousness of it, Mr. Isaacs. They knew that all honorable bankers had the same viewpoint as yourself, Mr. Isaacs, and they knew better than anyone else, what position the Duchy was in. Burdened with debts, which go back even to the Eighteenth Century, there was every prospect that the interest and instalments could not be paid at the appointed time. Consequently the banks thought out this disguised way of increasing the interest: as soon as there was a default in payment of interest and the instalments were not forthcoming they hurried to put their rights in force. They took over the management of whatever was pledged, and you may rest assured that the expenses, which they charged for this, did not fall below 20 per cent of the whole returns. Those poor Grand Dukes could really swear to the truth of the proverb: give an inch, and he'll take a mile. From the fact that once upon a time, one of them turned to the usurers, it became a duty with his descendants unto the fourth and fifth generation. Well, at times, the usurers cheated themselves. I do not believe that the one who loaned money on the mineral springs in the northern part of Minorca has any reason to be satisfied with his bargain. Rest assured his cries will rise to Heaven!

"Well, Mr. Isaacs, all that is not so very unusual. There are similar cases with Turkey and China—perhaps they are not practised with quite such brutal openness, since both Turkey and China are larger and have larger debts than Minorca. But now I am coming to the ridiculous part of the affair.

"Do you know what those money sharks have done besides? If you didn't know it to be true, you could hardly believe your ears. Listen to this, Mr. Isaacs! They loan money to Minorca, never under 7 ½ per cent, and issue the bonds at a figure never higher than 90. After a couple of years, when by chance there is some trouble in the payments, they take over the 'management' of the collateral, which, remember, is not considered as payment of any instalment or interest. But that does not satisfy them.

"A payment, they say to themselves, of 7 ½ per cent every eighth year or so, when the Grand Duke has raised money elsewhere, means nothing for us, others are very welcome to it—people who invest their money in government securities! Let us put the Minorcan paper on the market, then we will get back the money we loaned; the people who buy up the paper get the interest which comes in every eighth year, and we continue to manage the collateral and get our 20 to 30 per cent. In that way all parties are satisfied!

"That is their little idea, which they immediately hurry to put in practise. The bonds are listed on one or several exchanges. The prospect of seven and a half per cent sounds fine, and of course government securities are so safe! The public takes up the bonds willingly and everything goes according to the usurers' plans.

"I will admit one thing: this has been the case up to the last few years. Ever since the Parisian papers began to poke about in the Minorcan affairs the banks have hardly been so successful in disposing of the bonds, and therefore some of the Grand Duchy's obligations are still in the hands of the original lenders.

"But, Mr. Isaacs, now you understand what I am driving at, why I have found another instance like Columbus and the egg; how incredibly stupid avariciousness can make people! You understand: through greed the money-lenders have dug their own graves. For decades these graves have been open and waiting for them, yet probably would never have received their ashes if I had not happened to see that letter from Minorca a week ago! My modesty forbids my laying emphasis on the personal pronoun. Just think how matters stand, and be happy! By what right do the banks 'manage' the pledges given as security and grow fat on the exorbitant rates of interest they receive? Solely as owners of the Grand Ducal debentures, but who possesses the debentures? The people, the common people, who paid over 90 per cent of the nominal value for them, and who are willing any day to sell them on the Exchange at 45 ½—the latest quotation!

"The banks have delivered over their only weapon—to those who are strong enough to take it. Tell me the truth, Mr. Isaacs, is this another case of Columbus and the egg, or not?"

Philip Collin had talked himself into a heat and looked at Mr. Isaacs with glowing eyes. The great financier said seriously:

"Professor, you are a great man, and I believe you are right about Columbus and the egg!"

"But a golden egg, Mr. Isaacs, a golden egg!" cried Mr. Collin. "And the poetic justice of it! Cheating the usurers! Relieving the common people of their burdensome investments and enriching ourselves! Can you think of a better combination? Ah—the Grand Duchy of Minorca has long been little among the thousands of Judah, but through

Professor Pelotard it shall become a gold-mine!"

"But the details," interrupted Mr. Isaacs, "the details, Professor!"

"The details? Here are all the figures I have gathered together during the last four days; through them you can see in what position the Grand Duchy is, what the different loans are and with what bankers they are doing business. The details as to what I thought of doing are as simple as possible. The bonds are at present listed on the Paris, Marseilles, Barcelona and Madrid Exchanges. We prepare for our coup through the help of your newspapers—pessimistic articles that will make people ready to sell at any price; and then some fine day, when the Exchanges open, we will buy up the whole lot of the Minorcan government bonds... You take over the management of the pledges and become lord and master of the Duchy from one end to the other, and rich as Rothschild—together with me! If you are at all eccentric, you will lower the costs of management five per cent and let the Grand Duke, as a token of gratitude, dub you Baron of Jericho. He himself is Count of Bethlehem."

"Baron of... too near home," remarked Mr. Isaacs drily. "But you smile so queerly, Professor; are you holding something in reserve?"

Philip nodded with a little grin.

"Public gambling," he answered slowly, "is tolerated at present practically only in France and Monaco. In Monaco M. Blanc has the monopoly. In France it lies in the hands of very powerful financial interests, who even rule the parliament. In all other countries, the gambling situation is threatened, if it is allowed at all. At the present moment there is only one prince in Europe excepting the Czar, who offhand can grant a license for a new, really first-class gambling hell, and that prince, Mr. Isaacs, is the Grand Duke of Minorca! Minorca has all the requisites—nature and position. A steamship line to Barcelona could be established at a moment's notice. The Casino at Monte Carlo earned forty-three million francs last year and the Casino at Enghien over thirty."

Philip stopped. Mr. Isaacs arose, looking at his guest with thumbs in the armholes of his waistcoat.

"A corner in government bonds," said he, "and a new Monte Carlo held in reserve! By Jove, I have heard of less pretentious plans!"

He looked intently at his guest for a few moments.

"That is the biggest thing I have heard, the biggest scheme I've been in on—and I wasn't born yesterday. It is worthy of you, Professor—but I am afraid of one thing. It will be too big for me. Too big an order, sir!"

Philip Collin waved the objection aside with his hand.

"I doubt whether I could give an order too big for you, Mr. Isaacs. It is the novelty of it which frightens you, and makes you underestimate your own abilities. Do you know what the total amount of Minorca's state indebtedness is?"

Mr. Isaacs shook his head.

"When I give you the figures, you will realize how

unjustly a person can acquire a bad reputation in financial matters. If my information is correct, the sum total of the Duchy's indebtedness is not over 89 million pesetas—three and a half million pounds, if we reckon the peseta as equal in value to the franc, which is clearly too high. What does 45 ½ per cent of that amount come to, Mr. Isaacs? Hardly a million and three-quarters pounds, if you want to make a clean sweep of it. But that isn't necessary unless you wish. Assuming that you only buy up 75 per cent of the entire indebtedness, you will be absolute master of the Minorcan government; for one and a third million pounds. Have you never wished to experience the fascination of possessing unlimited power? And to be paid for it in a manner which would make a miser green with envy? Besides you would not even need risk £1,350,000; although I am only a poor, hard-up professor, I will contribute what I can."

"How much?" asked Mr. Isaacs smilingly.

Philip Collin caressingly fondled his newly acquired check.

"Ten thousand, at least," said he with a serious air. "But now look at my figures!"

Mr. Isaacs began to go over them, at times stopping to give a long look at his guest, then, for several minutes in succession adding up figures on a piece of paper. Professor Pelotard, who had sunk back in his leather chair with a tired air, smoked his cigar to an end and lit another. Outside could be heard the dull morning rumble of London. Suddenly Mr. Isaacs arose.

"I'll be damned, Professor," said he slowly, "but I do believe you have found the golden egg as you said! Perhaps I'll regret what I'm doing, but I rely on your shrewdness once more. Anyway, I am going into the biggest affair of my life."

"Until now," remarked Mr. Collin. "Until now, Mr. Isaacs! Gradually we'll do bigger things yet!"

"Unless this here breaks us," said Mr. Isaacs dryly. "We'll go into the details after the voting in my constituency. The election takes place to-morrow, as you know. Until then you have my promise that I will place one million three hundred and fifty thousand pounds at your disposal on the day you have everything ready."

"One million three hundred and forty thousand," Philip Collin corrected. "You forgot my contribution."

The great financier laughed, and with heavy step and bowed head his white-haired guest disappeared through the baize doors.

CHAPTER 3

In Which The Reader Finds Himself In Paris And Gets A Glimpse Of A Mysterious Young Lady

It was the first of March, 1910, half-past six in the evening, and a veil-like fog spread itself over Paris. The overflowing of the Seine, which had stopped but a short time before, had been followed by delightful sunshiny weather which during the day drenched the metropolis in a haze of white light; on the other hand the evenings were cold and not infrequently foggy.

On the boulevards that March evening the traffic rolled along in a steady stream. The lights from the automobiles crossed one another like threads in some complicated Oriental pattern, woven one second to be unravelled the next. The motor-buses rattled on their way, bulky and overgrown, while now and then a horse-drawn cab passed by, proceeding at a tired, funereal pace. The coachmen's faces were red and swollen under their white waxed-cloth hats and the horses' heads were sunk wearily toward the ground. The hoarse cry of the newspaper-vendors cut its way even through the harsh rumbling of the motor-buses: *La Presse, un sou, la Presse!* The electric signs flashed up, flickered, disappeared in an eternal series of green, red and white rays. Outside the cafes, in spite of the chilly weather, sat devoted crowds of boulevard habitues indulging in their favorite absinthe or vermouth.

At one of the tables in front of the Café de la Paix sat a good-looking young man of around 34 or 35 with an absinthe before him. His face was friendly and open with short clipped black mustache and intelligent black eyes. Whether he was a Frenchman or not was difficult to determine; the waiter with whom he exchanged a few words would have sworn he was; on the other hand the young man's clothes and a couple of English papers which lay beside him, financial papers, seemed to point toward his being an Englishman.

He sat leaning back a little in his chair. His table stood on the outer row and was the only one occupied there; at times some passerby jolted against it, but he hardly seemed to notice when such incidents occurred. His face wore a steady smile, expressing a certain amount of self-satisfaction; now and then he threw a quick glance at his papers and the smile deepened. It seemed as though he were day-dreaming and as though his dreams were especially pleasant.

It was decreed that these dreams should come to a hasty end.

A bright red motor car with blinding white lights suddenly swung around the corner from the Rue Auber. It was going at such a pace that it leaned dangerously over to the left side. With a quick turn it drew in toward the curb at the Café de la Paix. Long before it could come to a standstill the door flew open and somebody in a long automobile coat jumped out. The door slammed to; and the red car, which had not even stopped, only lessened its speed a trifle, made another quick turn toward the Boulevard des Capucines; then, by a hair's-breadth avoiding a collision with a horse-drawn cab, it disappeared at its original violent pace across the Place de l'Opera, followed by abusive oaths from the cabby.

The whole occurrence had hardly taken thirty seconds. The young man at the cafe table who had slightly lifted his right eyelid to watch the scene, suddenly sat up straight in his chair. What had happened a moment before was but an ordinary boulevard episode; what followed had the immediate effect of arousing him from his reveries.

Before the red motor car had reached the Place de l'Opera the person who had sprung from it made a couple of hasty steps—jumps, one might say—across the sidewalk to where the black-mustached man sat and without a second's hesitancy, sat down at his table. The next moment a little gloved hand lay on the sleeve of his coat and he felt a warm breath at his right ear. Then, as his senses seemed to return, he heard in a quick, hurried whisper:

"Save me, Monsieur, if you are a gentleman. They were

following my car—perhaps I have succeeded in putting them off the track. Act as though nothing... look as if I were with you... talk to me as though I were your... sweetheart.... Oh, God, there they are!"

All this had taken hardly half a minute more; now the voice stopped, the grasp of the little gloved hand on his arm became tauter, and he became conscious of the hot, quick breath of his unknown companion fanning his cheek. As he followed the direction her glances took through her automobile veil, he saw a black, noiseless motor car suddenly spring into view at the corner but a few steps from them. For a few moments, which suddenly seemed endless to him, it looked as though the car intended to stop; the white headlights, half turned toward the Boulevard des Capucines, gleamed coldly and defiantly; then it darted forward again in the tracks of the red car which was giving vent to shrill signalling honks from across the Place de l'Opera. It was evident that the second motor had only stopped on account of some hindrance in the traffic and that his unknown companion's plan had succeeded. Involuntarily he drew a deep breath of relief and turned hastily toward her to offer his congratulations.

He did so just in time to see her eyelids close behind the veil and feel the grip on his arm suddenly loosen. At the very moment the black motor car had disappeared the unknown had fainted!

The young man, quick as a flash, and without any apparent unwillingness threw his right arm around her shoulder and with his left hand quickly and skilfully lifted her veil. On the table stood a water carafe; he moistened a silk handkerchief and passed it quickly over the pale face beside him, while his eyes devoured the beauty which suddenly had been laid bare to him. The face under the veil was young and beautiful but deadly pale; the hair under the motoring hat heavy and black. The eyebrows were straight and almost grown together in a little dent at the top of the nose as though accustomed to knit together commandingly. The lips were firm. It was impossible to tell the color of her eyes for the lids still lay peacefully drooping over them.

"*Garçon*," cried the young man, "*une fine*—a glass of cognac, and quick as lightning! Madame has fainted!"

As he continued to bathe her forehead with the water, thoughts kept chasing one another through his head. Truly, it was just like his luck to have adventures thrown at him! Who was she? Of what nationality was she? The voice which had whispered so warmly and persuasively in his ear had spoken an irreproachable French but he thought he had noticed an accent. What had she meant by saying 'talk to me as though I were your sweetheart'? And who could the enemies be who were pursuing this charming young woman in the very heart of the boulevards of Paris? He suddenly remembered the manoeuvre through which she had outwitted them, and a thrill of admiration came over him at her daring. Truly, not many young ladies would be willing to equal her performance! What should he do? Perhaps she was simply an adventuress. . . but she was so young and

beautiful... and his train was to leave at half-past eight!...
Allons, he must....

"The cognac, monsieur!" The waiter, at a half run, had returned, bringing the order. "Isn't madame better yet? Shall I call a doctor, monsieur, or somebody from the pharmacist's?"

Without answering the young man took the glass of cognac and tried to press its contents between the half-opened lips. Hardly had the strong fluid reached the mouth of his unknown companion before she hastily sat up in the chair and opened her eyes. To his delight the young man saw they were a deep blue.

"Where am I?" murmured she. "Ah, I remember... I feel better now... thank you, you have been very kind to me..."

The waiter still remained near the table.

"Shall I send for a doctor, monsieur?"

She shook her head violently and answered the question herself.

"Certainly not," said she shortly. "I feel perfectly well now. I should like to pay and go."

She instinctively made a movement toward her left arm as though to grasp her bag, but the next moment her eyes opened wide and her face turned a deep red. There was nothing on her left arm. If there was a bag... it was evidently in the motor car!

The young man quickly motioned to the waiter to go.

"Everything's all right," said he. "I'll call when

I want you."

He turned to his unknown companion and smiled in an amused but at the same time respectful manner.

"Madame," said he, "your sortie from the motor car did not give you time to think about any baggage. With your permission, I will consider you as my guest. Nothing would give me more pleasure, excepting the knowledge that this should not be the last time. And now let me know what else I can do for you."

She sat there pale with lowered eyes.

"You are much too kind," said she shortly. "Perhaps you take some words of mine too literally." (He recalled again her strange words 'as your sweetheart'). "Will you. . . will you accept a ring as security for what you pay out for me?"

She stopped at a look from him.

"Madame," said he coldly, "a short time ago when you kindly sat down at my table, you took me for a gentleman; in any case, I am not a pawn-broker. Once more, may I ask you to let me know how I can help you—but only on condition you retain your first impression of me."

She did not answer.

There was the suggestion of a tear in the corner of her eye. He suddenly forgot his bit of irritation.

"Forgive me," said he quickly. "I'm a brutal lout. Once more, I beg you to let me be of service to you, no matter what idea you have of me!"

Two eyelids slowly lifted over two moist deep-blue eyes.

"You have no reason to beg forgiveness," she said quietly and stretched her hand across the table. "It was I who was stupid. You have been very good to me; you have not doubted me for a moment—what prevented my being a criminal escaping from the police!"

He laughed gaily in answer and then became serious again.

"Madame," whispered he, "forgive me for drawing attention to an unpleasant matter. You are sitting unveiled on one of the busiest boulevards of Paris. Are you sure the black motor car will not return?"

She gave a start and hastily let her veil fall, but could not resist replying:

"You prefer seeing me then with my veil down?"

"When it is for your good—in spite of the fact that I am a great egoist!—And now, what may I do for you?"

The voice behind the veil was very hesitant.

"I—I don't know. It isn't right for me to take up your time. Why, you do not know me. . ."

He leaned forward and looked earnestly at the veiled face.

"*Voyons,*" said he. "I thought we had come to an agreement on that point. I do not know who you are, and unless you wish it, I will never know. But I know you are in distress and furthermore without money. Please do not hesitate any longer. My time stands absolutely at your disposal."

As he said this he involuntarily cast a look at the watch on his wrist. It was now after seven and therefore he had less than an hour and a half longer in Paris, if he did not wish to miss the night express on which he had reserved his sleeping compartment. Miss the night express! He gave a start of surprise at such a thought. What on earth had he to do with this young lady who had crossed his path by chance?

She was young, helpless, and had bewitching blue eyes. . . But if an hour before anyone had told him that now at seven o'clock he would do anything else but have supper at Voisin's, he would have laughed. But *allons*. . . no matter about supper at Voisin's for this once, and her little affairs probably would not hinder him from catching his train.

He had not betrayed his thoughts through the slightest change of expression and his unknown companion, who had been studying his face carefully through her veil, seemed to arrive at a sudden decision.

"If—but you surely have time to spare?"

He nodded quietly.

"And you are willing to help me? Without asking questions?"

"I am not a detective," said he curtly. She plainly regretted her last remark and begged forgiveness with an appealing glance through her veil. "Would. . . would you then be willing to take me to Hôtel d'Écosse?"

"Is that all!" He burst out laughing at the contrast between this simple request and the hesitant manner in which she made it, called the waiter and paid. He stuffed his newspapers into his pocket and they got up from the table. As they reached the curb and he was just on the point of calling a taxi, she said hastily:

"Not an auto . . . . Take a cab."

"For goodness' sake, why?" He stared at her. Was she afraid of motor cars after her adventures that day?

"I have heard that they are ch-cheaper. . ."

He laughed and motioned to the first taxi which came along.

"Madame," said he, "you show me entirely too much consideration; it is an attitude which your sex otherwise has not showed me in such a pronounced degree. But in order to relieve your feelings, I may mention that an auto and a cab both charge the same."

They had not gone more than a few hundred yards before he felt her hand on his sleeve. He turned toward her and looked at her questioningly.

"Forgive me," said she, "but. . . I have happened to think of something."

He bowed his head to show he was listening.

"You see, per-perhaps the people in the black motor car have arrived ahead of me and are waiting at the hotel. . . what shall I do—oh, I don't know what to do!"

He stared at her, for the first time giving the matter really serious thought. Who were the people in the black car? Was he rushing headlong into some unpleasant affair— some affair with the police? Various recent exploits by the Paris bandits loomed up in his mind for a moment, quickly to be driven out by another recollection—two moist blue eyes and a confiding, smiling mouth. Bah, what a lot of nonsense! Apaches and girl-bandits—she was so young, hardly twenty. . . but the apaches, both men and women, he had heard about were not so terribly old either. . . and so beautiful. . .

"Madame," said he, "I will get out at the hotel and reconnoiter. I give you my word, I will ask no questions about you. But as to the people in the black car—will you give me some sort of description of them" (she clearly hesitated) "or shall I use my own judgment in finding out what I can?"

She nodded thankfully and settled back in the corner. Five minutes later they arrived at the hotel. The young man jumped out and rushed into the foyer.

In a couple of minutes he returned with a troubled look on his face. She stared at him anxiously from the darkness of the car.

"Well?" said she in a trembling voice.

"Well, madame, fortune seems against you. The red motor car—your car—showed up twenty minutes ago, the black one following in its tracks a few seconds later. The chauffeur of the red car hardly came to a stop before he started off again. The black motor had bad luck through a horse-drawn cab getting in the way, and the red car managed to gain half a minute's lead. Nobody left the red auto, but the black one, before it continued on its way, dropped two gentlemen, who now evidently are sitting waiting for you in the foyer."

She turned pale as death and murmured:

"Two gentlemen—what do they look like?"

"One is tall, with a face as yellow as a lemon, where it is not covered by a black beard. He wore a sack suit. The other is small, fat, of muddy complexion, with blue eyes and a blue double-breasted coat."

His tone had been rather cold as he described the two; the affair began to be too mysterious for his taste. Now he paused and looked at her. Tears glimmered under her veil and in the ensuing silence he heard the sound of a slight, suppressed sob. Again his more tender feelings got the upper hand. He made a dash into the car and laid his hand on her shoulder.

"Good God, child," he exclaimed excitedly. "There, don't cry! What is it? What do they want to do to you? What can I do for you? Tell me!"

She slowly removed his hand from her shoulder and drew herself up.

"No, no, leave me. You have already done more for me than you should. I know now I must appear to you like a criminal escaping from the police. But I swear I am not. . . let me go now!"

She made a movement to get out; he quickly drew her back on to the cushions of the car, shouted an address to the chauffeur and slammed the door. He hardly understood why he did it; but the ring of her voice had been so genuine and youthful and the remembrance of her frank smile so vivid that he now suddenly felt convinced again of her innocence. Without giving any thought as to how it should be done, he hastily decided to see the matter through with her. Of course she was innocence itself—it all had to do probably with some little escapade on her part against the authority of her parents or husband; *eh bien*, he had not, up to the present, been in the habit of fighting on the patriarchal side of the community, why should he do so now when he was drawn to the other side by two bewitching eyes and an enticing smile?

Suddenly he happened to think that he had shouted to the chauffeur the first address to come into his head, and that it would not be long before they arrived there. . . He gave a start and looked at his watch: quarter to eight. Hardly three-quarters of an hour before his train left. How about dinner? The prospects of a fourteen-hour journey with nothing else in his stomach but an absinthe was not very alluring. But if matters continued as they had begun his journey probably wouldn't amount to much, either. Well, he could at least try. He turned to his companion with a question on his lips, but she forestalled him.

"How did you manage to find out those things at the hotel?" she asked anxiously.

"Through one of the bellboys and the help of a ten-franc piece," he answered smiling. "I formerly lived in the hotel and gave rather good tips."

"Ten francs more," she mumbled with a note of despair in her voice which made him laugh.

"And they said that Jacques—that my car got away?"

"Jacques!" he thought with a sting in his heart. "The

devil take Jacques!"

"Yes," said he, with a most gloomy voice, "Jacques—your car got away."

In spite of her low spirits she burst out laughing at his melancholy tone.

"Jacques is only my chauffeur who has rendered me more service than anyone else—excepting you."

He felt gentle floods of quieting self-complacency well up in his heart. Then Jacques was only a chauffeur. But where was the man in the case? Of course there was a man. *Où est l'homme?* But that did not concern him. It was only a matter of making sure of her safety and that quickly.

"Madame," said he, and looked out to see how far they were from the address he had given, "will you give me straightforward answers to three questions? I will make them as impersonal as I can. Afterwards I will do my best to serve you as proficiently as M. Jacques."

She nodded a yes, and there was a flicker of a smile behind her veil.

"In the first place, have you any friends in Paris to whom you might wish me to take you? Some place where you will be out of reach of your yellowish lemon friend and his florid red companion?"

She gloomily shook her head.

"No," she murmured in a low voice, "I am unknown . . . I am alone in Paris."

He became more and more mystified but continued in the same quiet tones:

"Secondly, is there any place outside of Paris where you would like me to take you?"

She hesitated a moment; then came her answer and it proved more dumbfounding to him than all else up to now.

"Ye-yes, there is. I was thinking of going to Marseilles by the half-past eight train to-night. . ."

"Then you have friends there?"

"N-no, not exactly. . . no."

He stared at her in dumb amazement. The eight-thirty train to Marseilles! His train! Truly, the workings of fate are strange! Why on earth did this young girl, whom people had been chasing by automobile around the boulevards of Paris, want to go to Marseilles, unless she had friends there? Was it to prevent her going there that they had followed her in the motor car? He mastered his surprise as well as he could and continued:

"Thirdly, where do you think M. Jacques will go if he makes good his escape, and can you manage to meet him then?"

"Where will he go? That I don't know, but he knew that I was going to Marseilles to-night. I had ordered my ticket although I did not have chance to get it, because I was followed. Of course, he will look for me in Marseilles, as soon as he can."

She stopped and nervously twisted the tips of her fingers together. Evidently the thought of the forgotten bag and her helpless position had again struck her. He had made up his mind. He turned to her and filled with astonishment at himself for giving way to the impulse which was driving him on, said:

"Madame, it is more than strange, but actually true, that I myself, who am sitting here beside you, have ordered a sleeping compartment on the same express you intended to take... You have no friends here in Paris or the vicinity to whom I can take you, and you have reason to believe that M. Jacques will seek you out in Marseilles. Therefore it is plainly my duty to take you to Marseilles and save you from the people in the black car.... Will you entrust yourself to my protection?"

She had drawn back her veil, and looked at him for a few seconds so intently that he began to blush. Then she asked:

"Do you show such ready courtesy toward all ladies whom chance in this manner brings in your way?"

"In this manner?" said he lightly. "Of course I should do so if, as at present, I could arrange it without sacrificing my own comfort."

"Of course," answered she, "because you have not sacrificed your own comfort to-night! Of course it fitted in with your own comfortable plans to have me on your hands in the cafe and to drive me around Paris? And afterwards to accompany me to Marseilles? I doubt whether you ever thought of going to Marseilles!"

"*Parbleu,* madame, you do me an injustice! I swear that I thought of going there... as far as that goes, I don't need to swear. I can give you proof."

He hastily brought out a pocketbook from inside his coat and drew out a first-class Cook's ticket for Marseilles as well as one for the sleeping car (entire compartment). She looked at them inquisitively and spelled out the name.

"Professor Pelotard, London," said she. "Oh, you are English; I might have thought that, although you speak French like a native. . ."

"I live in London," answered he, suppressing the question which burned on his tongue about her nationality. "Well, you have seen that I am speaking the truth. Will you accept my offer?"

She gazed into his eyes with a clear and quiet look.

"Yes," said she simply, "if you really care to show such wondrous chivalry to an unknown. . ."

He interrupted her:

"Thank you for your faith in me. But then I must ask you one more question. Do you think your enemies are aware of your intentions?"

"Th-that is possible," she stammered. "I did not say anything about it at the hotel, but. . . Do you think. . ."

"I think it more than probable that they have people watching at the principal stations—that is, if they have the means and courage to do so?"

He looked at her questioningly. She nodded in a somewhat haughty manner.

"Then there is only one thing left to do. You must assume a disguise, and quickly, too."

"Disguise! How? Where? And how much time have we

before the train leaves?"

"A little over a quarter of an hour. Where? Here in the taxi. Wait, and you'll see."

Mr. Philip Collin, whom by now the reader should have recognized, again stuck his head out of the window and whistled to the chauffeur. The car stopped.

"How long does it take from here to the Gare de Lyon?"

"A quarter of an hour."

"Won't do. You can have ten minutes."

"Impossible."

"You must."

The little chauffeur hesitated.

"It will be at a good deal over the usual speed," he mumbled.

"It will also be at a good deal over the usual price. Let us say four times the usual price, and I'll pay the fines if there are any."

The chauffeur brightened up.

"*Mais alors, naturellement,* monsieur!"

He wanted to start his motor going, but Philip Collin stopped him with a gesture.

"Wait until I call! I need five minutes here myself; you'll still have your ten minutes to get there."

While the chauffeur in amazement stopped the car again, Philip Collin quickly brought out a little travelling case from his inner pocket. The next moment, with a muttered, "You must forgive me, madame," he had loosened the blue veil from his companion's head and taken off her hat. Then his long, slender fingers began to dance between the little travelling case and her face. Silently and hastily, cream, rouge, powder and cosmetics were applied here and there. The light from an arc-lamp fell in through the window of the automobile and by aid of a pocket-mirror the young lady followed, with wide-open blue eyes, the change that took place in her appearance. What time would have needed at least twenty years to accomplish took not more than four minutes under Mr. Collin's fingers; her face became flabby, the eyelids wearily drooped toward the corners, a wrinkle showed at each side of her nose and there were two or three across her forehead. The chin took on an expression of indolence and high living; next came her hair. Several careful touches with a little comb and to her amazement she saw small gray strands appear at the temples and neck. Without giving her time to admire his work, Philip quickly took her hat, and murmuring: "Barbaric, but unavoidable," removed the two long feathers with which it was decorated, stuck them in his pocket and put the hat back on her head. He draw the veil over it and tied it behind in the indescribable way which elderly English ladies affect when travelling.

"Can you take off your automobile coat without catching cold? It would be far too easily recognized."

She nodded, smiled in a bewildered way and took it off. Under it she wore a blue walking-suit. He quickly rolled up the coat and pushed it under the cushions.

"Fairly well done," he murmured, and looked at her

critically. "Remember to walk as heavily as you can and lean on my arm. Do you speak English? Fine. Then I'll look out for the rest.—All right; five minutes exactly."

He shouted to the chauffeur; the whirring motor suddenly let forth a shrill rasping screak and the car shot forward with the speed of a cannonball. Evidently the chauffeur, with a quadruple fare looming up in his mind, considered it entirely too dangerous making his way through the principal streets, for at the first corner he made a sudden turn which sent the young lady sprawling in Philip's arms; then they started off at a mad speed through long, narrow streets where the gas lamps scarcely threw more light than would a penny tallow candle. At every street crossing, which the chauffeur with utter disregard for public safety and all traffic regulations took at express train speed, they were hurled halfway to the roof. Once or twice they caught an indistinct glimpse of figures running out from the side streets and then suddenly by the greatest of wonders escaped running into an unlighted barrier, which showed that the street was closed. The brakes were applied so quickly and hard that for a moment it seemed as though the car would fall to pieces; but in another second the chauffeur had turned into a cross-street and continued at the same frantic speed through a network of alleys, none more than two hundred metres long. To both passengers the auto seemed to have changed into some growling sort of cat which with lightning rapidity made a gigantic spring at the beginning of each alley only to check itself as quickly when it reached the end. Philip Collin, although he had long known the ways of Parisian chauffeurs, involuntarily held his breath and pledged a wax taper to the Madonna if everything went well. Suddenly the chauffeur slowed down, and turning into an open square stopped before the entrance to the Gare de Lyon. Philip looked at his watch.

"Nine minutes," he murmured. "By Elijah and the chariot of fire, that was worth five times the regular price!"

He jumped out and handed a hundred-franc note to the chauffeur, who, filled with Gallic self-satisfaction, stood by his throbbing motor. Then he motioned to his companion:

"Ethel, dear," he cried, "hurry please or we'll be too late for the train!"

The chauffeur, a pale black-eyed Parisian gamin with all the shrewdness of his race, stared full of surprise at the person who appeared in answer to this request.

"*Nom d'un nom!*" mumbled he as his fingers grasped the bank-note. "A young lady in an automobile coat gets into my taxi on the Boulevard des Capucines and when she gets out at the Gare de Lyon she's an Englishwoman of forty, who looks as though she can hardly manage to move! *Nom d'un chien*, I'd better hurry and change this bit of paper as quick as I can!"

While he quickly started off to put this resolution into effect, Philip Collin and his faded bride hastily passed through the railway station. Philip filled the place with his nasal protestations that they must hurry and she seconded him with a histrionic ability which he would never have thought she possessed. After a few seconds' quick walk along a platform, they arrived at car number five of the eight-thirty express; she climbed in heavily, assisted by Philip. As they entered, he bent toward her and whispered:

"Did you see anyone?"

"Yes, but I don't think he recognized me. Where do we go?"

"Here," said he, after looking at his ticket, and showed her into a coupe. "Look out again carefully; don't let the light fall directly on your face, and tell me what you see."

She bent forward and looked out. At the same moment, the last doors were closed. There was a jerk and the train slowly started to move. With her glance fixed on a point near the entrance to the platform she whispered:

"Thank goodness the danger is over. The one who was on the lookout for me has just left with a very disappointed air."

Without her noticing it, Philip had followed the direction of her glance and saw a tall, lanky man disappear at the end of the platform. Philip gave a violent start. Where had he seen that face before? He could swear by everything in the world that he had seen it somewhere, that he knew the person by sight and perhaps even personally. But where, where? He decided to think it all over later when he was alone, and turned to his companion who had sunk down in the corner of the compartment.

"Well, madame," said he "so far everything has gone well. Let us hope our luck will continue. Now there is only one thing which I forgot to mention."

"What is that?" she asked, giving him a thankful smile.

"Your name. I haven't the honor of knowing what your name really is, but I do know the one you are to bear for the next twelve hours."

"And that is?"

"Madame Pelotard."

She jumped up, her eyes filled with surprise and indignation. He shrugged his shoulders and smiled sarcastically in return.

"Since you are travelling on my ticket, yes," said he. "Thank goodness, I always reserve two compartments. And you may rest assured, madame, there are walls between and the door can be locked!"

CHAPTER 4

IN WHICH IT IS SEEN THERE ARE TIMES WHEN THE VOICE OF THE NEWSBOY, EVEN AS THE VOICE OF THE PEOPLE, IS THE VOICE OF GOD

The air which streamed in through the doors to the hotel vestibule was cool and clear; the light green bamboo trees in the hall rustled slightly in the draft and the roses in the crystal bowls sent forth waves of perfume. The sunshine flooded in through the draperies of the large windows, and outside the heavens formed an arch of light blue over the large and noisy city.

It was the Hôtel d'Angleterre in Marseilles on a warm spring morning in the third month of the year. The clock was just striking eight as the hotel omnibus drove up from the station. It brought four passengers—two elderly Englishmen and a black-moustached gentleman of thirty-five, who was accompanied by a lady evidently about ten years older. The two Englishmen hurried to procure rooms, while the other pair motioned to the porter that they would wait and sat down in the lounge out of hearing distance. The young man was apparently in brilliant humor, while his companion seemed depressed and constantly looked woefully at herself in the mirrors of the lounge. It was he who began the conversation.

"Well, madame, we are safe and sound in Marseilles. If there is anything you may especially wish, please mention it."

"No-no, only that Jacques comes."

"All right; however there will be a delay of at least a day, if he succeeds in escaping your enemies. During that time, you should let him know you are here. M. Jacques is an intelligent sort of person, I suppose?"

"Yes, very. If it were not for him and you. . ."

"Then you would not be in Marseilles. My first call, then, will be to a newspaper office."

"To a newspaper office?"

"In order to insert a notice for M. Jacques. Were you in the habit of calling him Jacques?"

"Why, yes." The voice sounded almost embarrassed. "He was only my chauffeur, you know."

"Of course. I will address it to Jacques, then. But I must sign it in some way so that he will understand who has inserted it. What shall it be?"

"O, that is sufficient."

"O?"

"Yes, that is my initial?"

"Your initial? Was M. Jacques in the habit of calling you

by your first name, too?"

"How dare you? What do you mean? Call me by my first name! A chauffeur!"

"Forgive me—that was stupid of me. Was he aware you had no money with you?"

"I don't know. It is possible."

"I hope he didn't. For then he would hardly expect to find you in Marseilles. But perhaps he has seen in the newspapers that you have managed to get away."

"How can you think—do you really think it would come out in the papers?"

"Why, of course. . . The papers in Paris stick their noses in everything which they hear talked about and then talk even more about it."

"You needn't worry about that! Nothing will ever appear in the papers about me."

"You surprise me more and more. I had never believed that a young lady could puzzle me so, but you have certainly succeeded. Now, there is something else which is equally important."

"What is that?"

"Under what name you are to live here."

"Under what name. . ." There was again a note of deep embarrassment in her voice. "I think. . . I think. . ."

"Yes?"

"If you do not object, I think it is best to let it remain as it is."

"Madame Pelotard?"

"Yes. . . Madame Pelotard."

"All right, that is decidedly the best. No one will look for you under that name. But if you are to bear my name, madame, I must impose a certain condition."

"A condition?"

"Yes, that I am to assist you at your toilette."

"How. . . What! At my toilette?" She flew up from her chair with flashing eyes. "How can you! I thought you said you were a gentleman! You seem. . ."

She stopped. Philip Collin had suddenly burst out in a ringing laugh.

"But madame, I must. It will not do for you to grow younger too quickly. When you are ready with the rest, you can let me come in and see to it that you retain your mature respectability."

"Need I. . . need I go around with this frightful make-up any longer?" Her voice became half tearful. "Why, I look like a. . . like a scarecrow."

"Of course you don't, I assure you. You look as though you were forty and wanted to be thirty-five. But the main point is that you look genuine. Until M. Jacques comes, it will be better to have everything remain as it is. You may be sure that no one wishes him to come more than I!"

"So that you can be free of me!" She arose, again flushing with anger. "I will not trouble. . ."

"No, *chère madame*, so that I can see your real face again."

Mr. Collin bowed and his mysterious companion

laughed as heartily as though she never had been given a greater compliment. Her spirits seemed to be rising a little under the influence of his good temper. Mr. Collin looked at his watch and said:

"Do you know what we have earned for ourselves most of all? According to my ideas, a substantial breakfast, and as quickly as possible. It is eighteen hours since I had anything but an absinthe. I am hungry as a wolf, and I imagine you can say the same for yourself. We can attend to your toilette later."

He offered her his arm and led her into the dining-room, gave orders for a generous breakfast and then begged permission to leave her for a couple of minutes.

"I am going out to immediately arrange for our message to Jacques," said he. "If you want something to read during that time, here are yesterday's papers which I have had with me since we were at the Café de la Paix. They won't have later news here."

He handed her the papers and disappeared.

Hardly prepared for the surprises awaiting him from her side, he returned to the dining-room five minutes later, carrying a large bunch of violets in his hand.

"Everything is all right, madame," said he. "I have ordered rooms for us on the first floor, and I telegraphed a notice to be inserted in the Parisian papers. In passing, I arranged to have some toilet articles put in your room. May I offer you these violets as a sign that we have come to the land of springtime?"

She took the bouquet with a preoccupied smile; she was absorbed in reading one of the papers. *Excelsior* or *Matin*, he thought; then he saw what paper it was which had so captivated her. The *Sentinel of Finance*, by Jove! An English financial paper! Did the new-fledged Madame Pelotard dabble in stocks? Before he had time to ask himself further questions the subject of his thoughts herself interrupted his meditations. Knitting her eyebrows lightly, she asked:

"Tell me, have you read this paper?"

"Yes, Madame."

The paper was Mr. Ernest Isaacs' special medium, and Philip read it regularly, the leading articles amusing him more than *Punch*; this number had special reasons for interesting him.

"Will you explain one of the articles to me?"

"Gladly. Which one?"

He bent over, feeling sure he would find her absorbed in one of the optimistic articles with which Mr. Isaacs' secretary, Mr. Bass, was accustomed to greet the birth of a new Isaacian company. He was so amazed when he saw where her little finger pointed that he came near gasping.

"This article here," said she, "the one about the Minorcan bonds."

By Jove! By Jove!

For fifteen long seconds Philip stared at the dark-haired head beside him. Minorca! By all the stars in heaven, how could an article about Minorca and its bonds interest this young lady? The very same article which had made him smile so complacently when seated at the table in front of the Café de la Paix. Minorca! As he saw the name before his eyes again he was on the point of bursting into laughter. It was the day before yesterday that the biggest venture of his life had been launched, the same venture which a couple of weeks before he had proposed to Mr. Isaacs at his office and for which the latter had advanced the money, the most daring scheme which up to now had been hatched by his inventive brain and which had made even Mr. Isaacs tremble: to buy up the entire national indebtedness of an absolute monarchy and make himself complete master of its destiny (a small realm to be sure, but, by the Lord, with so much the larger national indebtedness!) A week had gone by preparing for the coup. Mr. Isaacs' *Sentinel* together with various friendly and subsidized organs in England and on the continent had without intermission published pessimistic articles about the condition of affairs in the Duchy of Minorca, and the desired results were attained. The wish to sell had become general, almost approaching a panic; the bonds had been dumped on the market, and the quotations had been forced down from 45 ½ to 43 ½. Meanwhile Philip and two trusty assistants held themselves in readiness with the million three hundred thousand Mr. Isaacs had advanced and the fifty thousand Philip himself had decided to invest in the undertaking, and two days before, on the twenty-eighth of February, they struck home. The exchanges in Paris, Madrid and Barcelona opened with an official quotation of 42 ½. They had hardly been open twenty minutes when eight-tenths of the national indebtedness of the Grand Duchy of Minorca had passed into new hands; half an hour later the wires spread the news over the whole of Europe, and immediately afterwards people throughout the world were asking the same question: What in heaven's name did it all mean? Cornering the market in Minorcan government bonds! People had been confined in asylums for less—if any confirmation of this opinion were necessary it was given by the evening papers in short but especially ironical editorials. The article which had amused Philip most, as he looked over the comments of the press next day, was the one which Mr. Isaacs, with good-humored courtesy, had hastened to send him by special post. Naturally it stood in the *Sentinel of Finance*, and needless to say it was "inspired." It bore the title "A Fool's Action—or What?" And it was this article which now, to his indescribable amazement, excited the interest of his pretended wife.

Controlling his astonishment, he said:

"What do you wish me to explain? The article goes straight to the point—the title as well as the rest of it."

"That is just it," she answered impatiently. "Why should anyone be a fool to buy Minorcan government bonds? Aren't they good?"

"Aren't they good!" Philip suppressed his desire to laugh. "Excuse me, but what do you know about government bonds? And what do you know about Minorca?"

She seemed to hesitate.

"When a country borrows money, the obligation is represented by government bonds, is it not? At home in. . ." she stopped. "And why should Minorcan bonds be worse than ou. . . than others? As to Minorca, I only know it lies in the Mediterranean and has a duke. . . Roland or something."

"Ramon XX, madame, who moreover is said to be a very pleasant person. So far you are perfectly right. Minorca lies in the Mediterranean and when a country borrows money the obligation is represented by government bonds. But unfortunately Minorca's affairs are not as attractive as its surroundings—not as ready flowing, one might say. You see, it has lacked money, not only on occasions, like your country. . ."

"My country," she flared up. "What do you know about my country?"

"Nothing. Only that a country with such daughters cannot long be in hard straits." She laughed, evidently pleased.

"Well, to continue, Minorca has been without money for the last couple of hundred years, and has been borrowing the whole time. Thereby it has fallen into the clutches of usurers, people who get twenty or thirty per cent for their money. Do you know what per cent is? *Mon Dieu,* what a highly distinguished political economist! Well, after once falling into the clutches of such gentlemen. . ."

She interrupted him.

"But the Grand Duke, do you know anything about him?"

"Nothing special. He was born in 1875, the same year as I, is well educated, tall and stately, but unfortunately he limps."

"Limps! He limps? You can't mean that?"

"Yes, madame, I know for a certainty. The burden of Minorca's unfortunate affairs has weighed him down until. . ."

"Oh, how I pity him! Is he lame? But handsome and stately, you said. He looks so in his pictures. And thirty-five years old?"

"Yes, madame, thirty-five years old. Just the right age for a man to get married. You seem to be very much interested in Don Ramon."

At first she seemed not to have heard him; then she impatiently shook her head.

"Not at all," said she. "Let's have breakfast, if you please. I am absolutely famished. Why, you keep on talking so much that the food will get cold."

Philip cast an appealing glance to heaven.

"I forgot to ask what you would like to drink," said he.

Without paying attention to his remark she absent-mindedly toyed with the food before her; then she resumed:

"This newspaper here claimed that it must be someone out of his senses who bought up the Minorcan bonds. Mentally unbalanced or an anarchist, it said. Do you believe it? You know all about such matters, do you not? Of course you do."

Philip assumed an expression of deep earnestness.

"Know all about such matters? Why, no one knows anything about this coup, you can see that even from the papers."

"Well, but what do you think? Do you think he is mentally unbalanced?"

Philip looked at her carefully before he answered. What on earth did this intense interest for everything connected with the Duchy of Minorca mean?

"H'm," said he. "If you want to hear what I personally think about the person who made the coup on the exchange, then I do not believe he is unbalanced. No, I do not!"

She listened intently and seemed, strangely enough, somewhat relieved at his statement.

"You do not," she repeated. "How nice, how nice! I am delighted, you know."

"My Lord, yes, I am, too! But why should you be so delighted about it?"

"I was only thinking about the poor Grand Duke, Raoul. . ."

"Ramon XX."

"Of course, Ramon. . . I mean, if it had been a madman who had bought up the bonds, then he could absolutely ruin the Grand Duke."

"H'm, yes, that is very true. Through this coup he is of course absolute master of the Duchy."

"Absolute! Really?"

"Yes, one might say that. So, if he were a madman, he

could even force the Grand Duke into bankruptcy, perhaps make him abdicate. . ."

"But you do not think he is one? You said you didn't?"

"No, I don't think so. On the other hand, if he were a good-natured fool, an eccentric and friendly fool—there are such, you know—he might have done it to remit the entire national indebtedness."

"And then Ronald would be free?"

"Ramon; yes, then Don Ramon would be free. But, between you and me, such fools are very few and far between. Especially on the Exchange. No, the one who carried out this coup" (Mr. Collin's voice involuntarily trembled with self-satisfaction), "is a mighty smart businessman, nothing else. That is my idea. A mighty smart businessman, who, like Columbus in the story about the egg, made a very simple discovery which nobody else even dreamed about. You may be sure that he has done it in order to make money by the transaction, and that he will succeed, too!"

She stared thoughtfully into her tea-cup.

"And nobody has any idea who it is?"

"No, nobody has an idea. It is generally admitted that he went about it with unusual shrewdness."

"You haven't any idea, either?" She looked at him in a manner which said plainly enough that she thought she was asking the highest authority.

"No, madame, not even I."

She became thoughtful again and seemed to be deliberating about something.

"Would you, perhaps, like me to try and find out for you?"

She hesitated a moment. Then an expression of determination quickly came over her face.

"Yes, thanks, if you will. . . I would be very grateful. . ."

She stopped short and drained her tea-cup, which was already empty.

Philip looked at her silently, with, if possible, increased amazement. Truly, she was the most mysterious person of the other sex he had ever met! Truly!. . . Then he shrugged his shoulders and promised himself that he would soon solve this little problem. It shouldn't be very difficult for a wily old fox like himself to outwit such an inexperienced young lady as this one here. Although, by Jove, he had to admit that she knew how to keep her own secrets.

Not once had she made a slip of the tongue; not once had she let fall a single word which could give a solution to the problem. And the man at the Gare de Lyon in Paris remained as much of a mystery as ever; no matter how much he thought about it, Philip had not succeeded in remembering the name he was searching after. Well, the reason for her interest in the Duchy should be easier to ferret out—if he only had time! For on the next day but one the boat he intended to take would leave for the island which, for varying reasons, interested her, him and Mr. Isaacs so deeply—the island of Minorca!

He looked at his watch. It was approaching half-past ten. Suddenly an idea struck him.

"Madame," said he, "I have just happened to think of something. You are absolutely without baggage, and it may be some time before your Jacques arrives. We must go out and buy what you need for the present."

She brightened up, then hesitated.

"Do you really mean it?" said she. "I. . . but Jacques will surely be here to-morrow. And you are right, I need some clothes. . ." she threw an embarrassed look at herself in a glass opposite, "especially at my present age."

"All right then, let's start."

They went out into the spring sunshine.

It was on their way back from the shops on La Cannebière that Mr. Philip Collin received the big shock. He and his companion had been into the branch-establishment of one of the large Parisian houses and had bought various things which he found she needed: a spring hat, a veil, perfume, gloves and a pair of light walking shoes. He had in vain tried to persuade her to include a light walking suit, and had then left her while she provided herself with certain details of dress during the purchase of which his presence was declared to be unnecessary. With hat pulled over his nose, he waited outside on the sidewalk for her to finish, in the meantime letting himself be saturated with the hot March sun. Finally she came out and they were on the point of getting into a cab when she stopped him by laying her hand on his arm. With head stretched forward she stared at a newspaper kiosk opposite.

"What is that there?" asked she. "Can you see?

Minorca—I think. . ."

"Always Minorca," laughed Philip. "Will you tell me what could happen on Minorca!"

And, as though in answer to his laugh and his words, suddenly, through the noise of the street, there burst the hoarse cry of a Marseilles newsboy.

"Mi-i-inorca!" he bawled. "Mi-i-inorca! Full details about the revolution on Minorca! Buy *Le Petit Marseillais*! Murder in the Bois du Boulogne and Mino-o-orca!. . ."

Had this newsboy been called on to give evidence about what followed next, his testimony would have run somewhat as follows:

He suddenly saw a black-mustached gentleman of thirty-five come running directly across the street, at the risk each moment of being knocked down and run over by the passing traffic. Without a word the gentleman rushed up to him, pointed dumbly at the pack of newspapers he held in his hand, and threw him a five franc piece. He—the newsboy—cursed in good Marseillais for he did not care to give up all his change so as to sell a paper for five centimes. However, he drew out from his pocket an unusually dirty hand filled with silver and copper coins and prepared to make change.

It was then that the wonderful part began.

The middle-aged, black-mustached man did not see the dirty hand, nor did he see the silver and copper. He had eyes only for the copy of the paper which he had bought.

He held it so tightly that the tips of his fingers grew

white; his eyes flew up and down the columns, his black mustache sticking out the while like the whiskers of a cat. For a couple of minutes he kept on reading, then he let the paper sink and stared at the crowded street. The newsboy, who with a sly grin, had stuffed his money back into his pocket, and had drawn several steps back, took good care not to disturb him by word or gesture; 4.95 could not be earned as easily as that every day.

Suddenly the stranger's lips opened and there gushed forth a torrent of words which he—the newsboy—easily recognized to be oaths although they were hurled out in a language strange to him; the next moment, to his joy, he saw this eccentric monsieur start forward and throw himself into the whirl of the traffic. Full of hopes that he would see him run over and thereby unable to demand his money, he followed him closely with his eyes. To his bitter disappointment, he saw him reach the other side, safe and sound. A lady who seemed rather advanced in years met him with a stream of words. As answer this eccentric monsieur handed her the copy of the paper. The newsboy watched them excitedly to see what effect it should have on her.

It exceeded all his expectations.

The elderly lady seized the paper, but was hardly able to read more than four lines before she let it drop, tottered and fell prostrate in the arms of her companion.

That number of the Petit Marseillais which had filled the strange monsieur with such interest that he paid four francs and ninety-five centimes too much for it had made the elderly lady faint on the spot!

The strange gentleman carried her into an apothecary's shop. A moment later he came running out to get something. What?

Nothing else but the copy of La Petit Marseillais which he had bought just before, and which his companion had let fall in the street. This newspaper he stuffed into his pocket and disappeared into the apothecary's. Ten minutes passed; then a cab was called to the door of the apothecary's and the elderly lady came out, leaning heavily on her companion's arm. They stepped into the cab and started off uptown.

At the same time a thoroughly amazed newsboy, forgetful of all his business, for the third time in succession began to read through his paper instead of selling it, determined not only to discover what it was which had called forth this drama, but also in the future to deeply despise the moving pictures.

And shortly afterwards the former member of the bar, Philip Collin of Sweden, alias Professor Pelotard of London, sat, with a strong early morning whiskey beside him, in the lounge of the Hôtel d'Angleterre. His companion, silently, with staring eyes, and without paying attention to any of his amazed questions, had gone to her room; and he with the help of the whiskey, went over in his thoughts for the hundred and fiftieth time all the questions he had for the past seventeen hours been asking himself about her, while his eyes for the hundred and twentieth time read through the article in *Le Petit Marseillais*, which suddenly had thrown him from the brightest heaven of self-satisfaction into the blackest depths of despair.

The article read thus:

> REVOLUTION ON MINORCA!
> A CENTURIES OLD KINGDOM FALLS
> WHERE IS DON RAMON XX?
> NO CERTAINTY ABOUT HIS FATE THE WORST IS FEARED.
> MINORCA–REPUBLIC! ITS DEBTS–REPUDIATED!

These were the headlines; the text was not less startling:

> *Late this morning a telegram of such unusual purport was received from Barcelona that we immediately took pains to verify the report before we were willing to give it out to our ever-increasing public. We have now had its genuineness confirmed beyond any doubt; and with its usual speed Le Petit Marseillais hastens to place the more than astonishing telegram before the public. It reads as follows:*
>
> *Barcelona, 1 March, 1910, 22.50 o'clock. The captain of the English freighter Lone Star, Blue Star Line, arriving here from Port Mahon (Minorca) reports under oath to the representative of the line as follows:*
>
> *"Arrived at Minorca yesterday, eleven o'clock in the morning, to load cargo (olive oil) for shipment to London. Found the city in revolt; great excitement raging in the streets; people streaming this way and that,*

the cannons from the fortress thundering continuously. Almost hit by a shot. Went on land, inquired about the reason. On account of the general excitement difficult to obtain definite information. Certain that the populace on the whole island has arisen, that the grand-ducal castle has been stormed, windows smashed and the castle flag torn down. The fate of the Grand Duke unknown or kept hidden from the people. As leader of the movement a certain Hernandez (Luis) is mentioned, as well as a Catholic priest. No signs of massacre, only general excitement. Was visited during the afternoon by said Hernandez; reported in broken English that Minorca had arisen and 'thrown off its burden of centuries'; refused to give information about the fate of the Grand Duke; declared that the island would follow the example of Portugal, become a republic with him as president, and above all repudiate the debts 'under which the island had groaned for hundreds of years.'

"Could not take on cargo on account of the general excitement."

Captain Simmons, very well known here, departed an hour later for Lisbon in answer to orders which were awaiting him from the main office; possibly he will stop at Gibraltar. Unfortunately, the Lone Star is not equipped with wireless and in trying to obtain connection with Minorca from here, it was found that the cable had been cut or put out of service.

However, no doubt exists as to the captain's story. Great excitement reigns in Barcelona. Such was the telegram, full confirmation of which we received not only from our correspondent in Barcelona but also from the office of the Blue Star Line.

The Grand Duchy of Minorca, founded in the Thirteenth Century, has thus come to an end.

Its present ruler, Don Ramon XX, was a young man of thirty-five, of whom one can only speak in the highest terms. As appears from the telegram his fate is unknown. It is only to be hoped that the populace on Minorca will show more mildness toward its deposed ruler than the populace in Portugal did against King Carlos!

This is to be hoped, but if the contrary proves to be the case, it would not be so very strange.

For the last hundred years, ever since Minorca was occupied by Napoleon, it has been in a very unfortunate position. The taxes have been heavy, the industry has amounted to nothing, and the enlightenment of the people has been poor. The populace has remained on practically the same footing as in the Eighteenth Century here in France, and everything which could be gathered up by the rulers through taxes and assessments has been squandered on their private pleasures. Leading the existence of idlers they have forgotten the first duties of a prince—to take care of the people.

The near future should show what the results of the revolution on the island will be, whether this Hernandez, *whom Captain Simmons mentions, will take over the leadership of its destiny after Don Ramon, and with better luck. The telegram in this respect speaks promisingly; it is intended first and foremost to repudiate the burden of debt under which Minorca has staggered. With regard to the historical conditions we cannot do otherwise than approve.*

As our readers probably remember, it was only three days ago that a coup took place on the Exchanges in Paris, Madrid and Barcelona through which practically all the government indebtedness of Minorca changed hands. The author of this movement is still unknown, but it is considered fairly certain that it is a foreign syndicate. Undoubtedly its members will read the telegram from Barcelona with mixed feelings!

Probably no French capital worth mentioning is still interested in the island...

No French capital worth mentioning!... We cannot but approve their repudiation of the debts... It was the epitaph over your big coup, Philip Collin, over your pride and your triumph!

Still, Mr. Isaacs should have a word to add to it! One million three hundred thousand pounds—a good bit of money, Philip Collin. What is fifty thousand from your own pocket in comparison? Nothing.

No, my dear Philip, never again have anything to do with government bonds! Remember the history of Sweden in 1809, and how the chronicler so beautifully says: "After the Revolution it was the first task for the new men to arrange the desperate economic position. Upon mature consideration they cancelled half of the government indebtedness ..." That was the way they did in Sweden; in Minorca they are more thorough. There they cancel it all.

A fine bit of business, Mr. Collin! A mighty fine and prosperous bit of business!

CHAPTER 5

A Spring Evening In Marseilles

At five o'clock on the following afternoon a middle-aged man with a black mustache and wearing a well-fitting gray suit and grayish-green ulster could have been seen passing through the Rue des Olives in the harbor section of Marseilles. The evening had become cool after a beautiful day; the man with the black mustache had turned his coat collar up to his chin and his hat was drawn so far over his brow that one could hardly see more than his mustache and a gleam of the whites of his eyes. He went along with rapid steps, now and then casting a scrutinizing glance at the numbers on the houses. As he reached Number 19 he stopped and looked at the place for a moment.

Number 19 stood somewhat apart from the other houses, and offered certain peculiarities in its exterior. It was surrounded by a garden. Above the doorway hung a miniature reproduction of a ship and over the roof a French marine flag flapped in the evening breeze. To judge by all appearances it was the home of a sailor.

The gray-clad man opened the garden gate and after

taking a few steps reached the front door. He rapped with the knocker; a maid opened the door.

"Is Captain Dupont at home?"

"Who will I say wishes to see him?"

"A gentleman who wants to hire his yacht."

"Please step in, and I'll tell him."

The stranger was shown into a little reception room, where he sat down in an American rocking-chair.

After a moment the door opened, and in came a thick-set, somewhat corpulent man with the rolling gait peculiar to sailors. He was almost completely bald, with a ruddy face surrounded by a gray-sprinkled beard.

"Are you Captain Dupont?"

"I am."

"I've been told you own a yacht."

"You've been told no lie."

"And that it is for rent."

"At times."

"Also for long trips?"

"Only for long trips. Do you think I'm a coast-hugger?"

"So much the better. How do you reckon your price?"

"That depends. By the week, unless it is some unusual matter."

"Good, and your price per week?"

"Three hundred francs, not counting provisions and coal."

"That sounds reasonable. You go along yourself?"

"Always. Do you think a man forgets his trade simply

because he's reached fifty?"

"Of course not, Captain. Are you disengaged at present?"

"H'm; yes."

"Do you know the Balearic Islands?"

"Somewhat. Have been there three times."

"Minorca?"

"Yes, but you do not mean?. . ."

"Minorca? Yes, I mean Minorca."

"But a revolution has broken out there."

"You have heard about it? Yes, they say there is a revolution. They say, Captain. I'm a journalist, and I'm interested in finding out whether they have lied."

"H'm. I'm not a journalist, and it doesn't interest me whether it's true or not."

"You aren't interested in such unusual matters?"

"That depends. Not under five hundred per week."

"That also depends. When can you start?"

"Day after to-morrow."

"Won't do. To-night at the latest."

"Not very much time. I might say an unusually short time."

"Let us say six hundred then, without provisions, and you are to be ready at ten-thirty."

"Excellent. But it looks as though we were to have a blowy night."

"Are you afraid of a little windy weather, Captain?"

"I! I was thinking of you. Don't know how a journalist stands windy weather."

"You'll find out to-night. I've been told your yacht is lying at the east pier."

"You've been told the truth again. Who sent you here?"

"I tried to get passage with the Algier Company's boat to-morrow, but I was told the Company's boats no longer touch at Minorca."

"I can well believe it. And they sent you to me?"

"At last. I went to some other places first."

"But no one wanted the job; I can well believe that. Can you find your way down to my yacht or will I call for you?"

"Oh, I will find the way well enough. Keep an eye out for me around ten o'clock. Here is for a week in advance, and a like amount for provisions. I forgot to ask one question: what's the name of the yacht?"

"The *Stork*!"

"Doesn't matter, as we are to have no women passengers. Good evening, Captain Dupont."

"But don't you want a contract?"

"I've been told it was unnecessary with you."

"I am glad to hear it, Monsieur; I am glad to hear it! You may rely upon it, we'll sail at half-past ten. Excuse me, but what is your name?"

"Professor Pelotard. I am stopping at the Angleterre. Good evening, Captain."

The captain's guest took his leave, evidently satisfied with the result of his visit. The captain accompanied him to the door. He had hardly closed it before there was another knock. He opened, thinking the stranger had forgotten something. Instead of his late guest he found, however, two other gentlemen.

One was small, his hair sprinkled with gray and he wore gold-rimmed glasses. His companion was of gigantic size, about thirty-five years old, with dark mustache turned up at the corners, and dark eyes, with a half-languid, half-jovial expression. As he took a step forward to greet the Captain, the latter noticed that he limped.

"Am I speaking to Captain Dupont?"

"Yes. What can I do for you, gentlemen?"

"May we have the privilege of a moment's conversation with you?"

The captain, somewhat surprised at two calls in such quick succession, led the way into his little reception room.

"You must pardon me, gentlemen, but I cannot give you much time. In five minutes at the latest I must start down to the harbor."

"Good, I hope we can arrange matters in even shorter time. You have a yacht for rent, have you not?"

It was the taller of the two gentlemen who conducted the conversation.

"As a rule, yes."

"We have been told so. And it is fitted out for long trips?"

"Yes, Messieurs, but. . ."

"Whereby you yourself serve as captain. We have been told that you are an excellent one. What price do you charge in renting your yacht?"

"Usually three hundred a week, Messieurs, without

provisions and coal. But. . ."

"Do you know the Balearic Islands?"

The captain burst out laughing.

"I do, gentlemen. Also Minorca. You probably wish to go to Minorca?"

The two strangers looked at each other with a surprise which they could not conceal. Thereupon the one who up to now had conducted the conversation scowled and said:

"If this is a joke, Captain Dupont, it is a very poor one. What reason have you for thinking we intend to go to Minorca?"

The captain stopped laughing as he noticed his guest's change of manner.

"No other reason than that a few moments ago a gentleman called on me who asked just the same questions as you have, and who hired the yacht for a trip to Minorca."

"Hired the yacht? You mean that your yacht has been rented?"

"Yes, ten minutes ago."

"You must cancel the agreement."

"Under no conditions."

"We will pay you four hundred francs a week for the yacht. You said you usually ask three hundred, did you not?"

"It has been rented for six hundred."

"We'll pay seven hundred."

The captain reddened slightly.

"Messieurs, it seems that you have not received as reliable information about me as the gentleman who hired the yacht. I never break my word."

The strangers looked at him; it was unmistakably evident that he spoke the truth. Again they looked at each other in dismay. Then the one who had been leading the conversation continued:

"But we must get over to Minorca, captain. Must, you understand."

"Well, hire another yacht."

"There is no other yacht in Marseilles which will go to Minorca. And we must go there, you understand."

The captain shrugged his shoulders.

"Well," said he, "then I know only one way out."

"And that is?"

"That you look up the gentleman who has hired my yacht and talk with him. The yacht is small, but there is room for four."

"By Saint Urban, Captain Dupont, you are right! And what is the gentleman's name who has hired the boat?"

"Professor Pelotard, and he is stopping at the Hôtel d'Angleterre. Messieurs, you must pardon me, but I must be off. I have already given up too much time. We sail to-night."

"To-night? Excellent. The professor seems to be in as much of a hurry as we are. At what time?"

"At half-past ten. Messieurs, I bid you good evening. Talk with the professor and let me know immediately on account of the provisions."

The captain, who had put on his cap, led his visitors

through the hall. Outside it had grown dusk and the gaslights were already lighted. The heavens were clouded over and threatened rain. Captain Dupont pointed silently to the sky in order to draw his guests' attention to its appearance. Then he smiled courteously and hurried along the Rue des Olives.

Reaching the next street light, he stopped with a laugh and called out to his guests who stood talking with each other outside his gateway.

"Messieurs!"

"Captain?"

"May I ask you a question. Are you journalists?"

"Journalists?"

"Yes. Because in that case the professor will probably not let you go along, as he is one himself."

"Is he a journalist? No, we are not."

"*Au revoir*, then."

Captain Dupont disappeared, half running down the street, and his two visitors made their way to the corner where they signalled a cab.

"Hôtel d'Angleterre, and as quickly as you can."

They started off. After a quarter of an hour they were at the hotel.

"Is M. Pelotard in?"

"Monsieur is at present writing letters in the writing room. Who shall I say wishes to see him, when he is free?"

"Tell him the Count of Punta Hermosa, and please inform the professor that it is important and very urgent."

"*Parfaitement.* Please take a seat."

The Count of Punta Hermosa sat down in the lounge with his friend.

"What can there be of interest in Minorca for this man Pelotard, Paqueno?"

"Why, Your Highness heard. He's a journalist, the captain said. News about the revolution on our unfortunate island has spread over the whole of Europe. Oh, if Your Highness had only expelled the German! He is back of it all, Your Highness, take my word for it."

"But that anyone can be interested in a revolution on Minorca!"

"Why, Your Highness, when it comes to murder and slaughter, then people are always interested."

"You are right, Paqueno. A revolution is interesting even in Montenegro. The principal point for us is not to awaken this man Pelotard's professional jealousy. The interests which draw us to Minorca must appear innocent in his eyes. What do you say to our being soldiers of fortune starting out to offer the new president our services? The army needs to be built up in order to fight the tyrant."

"H'm."

"You don't seem to think my plan a good one then, Paqueno?"

"I thought of proposing that we simply have private interests on Minorca, that our property is in danger. That would be just as good, I think, and true besides."

"You are right, Paqueno, and I know you respect the

truth although you have been our Minister of Finance for thirty-four years. But hush! If I am not mistaken, here is the professor. By Saint Urban, no one would say that he looks like much of a bookworm."

They both stared at Mr. Philip Collin, who after exchanging a couple of words with the porter now came toward them.

"Messieurs, you wished to speak to me! My name is Professor Pelotard."

Philip smiled expectantly. The gentleman who called himself Count of Punta Hermosa bowed.

"I am glad to make your acquaintance. I am the Count of Punta Hermosa and this is an old friend, Señor Esteban. We have taken the liberty of seeking you out in a matter which is of the greatest importance to us."

"I am at your service!"

"Thanks. We will not need much time to explain the purpose of our visit. Very likely you will show us the door as soon as you have heard it."

"Oh!"

"To come straight to the point: you are sailing for Minorca to-night?"

Philip looked at the supposed Count in surprise.

"What reason have you for thinking that?"

"You will understand when I tell you that we come from Captain Dupont!"

"Ah, you come from Captain Dupont?"

"Yes, and the cause for our visiting him is the same

which brought you to him."

"Namely, that you wish to go to Minorca!"

"Precisely. And in the whole of Marseilles there seems to be but one person who dares sail to that den of murderers."

"That is just the experience I had myself."

"And that person is Captain Dupont. We looked him up and wanted to hire his yacht. He said no. The yacht had been hired by you and the price agreed upon. We overbid you."

"Ah; you overbid me!"

"You see, I am straightforward with you. Captain Dupont refused. The honest captain even became angry."

"Captain Dupont is a gentleman; I noticed that immediately."

"You are right, Professor. After refusing to accept our proposal the captain made a suggestion."

"And that was?"

"That we should look you up. My friend and I have reasons which oblige us at any price to reach the island. Captain Dupont's yacht has room for four. If you have no objections, may we beg as a favor that you allow us to go with you? Of course we will pay our share."

Philip Collin looked thoughtfully at his visitors. The straightforward manner in which they told about their call on Captain Dupont pleased him, as well as their appearance in general. Economy was a virtue when a person had lost fifty thousand pounds; and it should cause no discomfort having the two gentlemen accompany him. Instead, it might even be of advantage, as they seemed to know Minorca.

He nodded.

"I have thought it over, gentlemen, and I accept your proposal with pleasure. I make only one condition."

"And that is?" There was an anxious tone in the Count of Punta Hermosa's voice.

"That you will be my guests at dinner."

The Count and his old friend laughed.

"That is really too good of you. We will return the compliment at Minorca, although it may be difficult under present conditions. The hotel proprietor there is the father of the president to be. But we have our luggage. . ."

"Gentlemen, we cannot take much luggage with us. The yacht is small and as little as possible will be best. Are you stopping far from here?"

"At the Hôtel des Princes, a couple of steps from here."

"So much the better, for then you will have sufficient time to arrange everything before dinner. If you will have the things brought here, we can start together after dining."

The two visitors bowed. At the same moment a servant came up to Philip.

"Madame wishes to speak to you, Monsieur."

"Tell her I will come immediately. Good evening, gentlemen. We will meet here in three-quarters of an hour."

Philip took leave of them with a slight bow.

"Paqueno," whispered the supposed Count of Punta Hermosa. "He is married!"

"So I understand, Your Highness."

"Doesn't that seem strange to you?"

"Why, Your Highness?"

"I have never heard that journalists are in the habit of taking their wives along with them on their expeditions."

"Perhaps she is a journalist, too. You hear such strange things about women, nowadays."

"Then she would be going to Minorca with him, but he said nothing about it. Do you know, there was one thing that frightened me for a moment."

"What was that, Your Highness?"

"When this Professor spoke about our going on one condition. By the Lord, I thought he meant payment in advance. Then we would have cut a pretty figure, Paqueno!"

"Unfortunately, that's true. We must hope that we can pay later."

"No, this won't do! The Professor is a gentleman. Do you know what I think I shall do?"

"Give up the trip? Yes, that would be the very best. The populace is excited; and without weapons. . ."

"Paqueno! Before I'll give anyone else the pleasure of suppressing this revolution I'll abdicate or swear fealty to President Hernandez! And then that man Binzer!. . . No, but I will not dine with a gentleman, and then perhaps later on cheat him out of his money. Before we sit down to table I intend to tell him how matters stand."

"Your Highness, Your Highness!"

"Yes, Paqueno, that is the only thing to do!"

The old Minister of Finance assumed an especially woebegone air, but he knew his master's stubbornness of old and giving a sigh refrained from trying to influence him further. In silence the two gentlemen passed through the door to the hotel.

In the meantime Philip hurried to the room where the supposed Madame Pelotard awaited him. He had not yet informed her of his departure and it was ⏑ ven clear in his mind what he should do with her. ⏑ d been heard from Monsieur Jacques, a⏑ d Philip, ⏑ ⏑ ⏑ssed the day wondering over many thin⏑ had also ⏑ ⏑d what had become of the faithful chauffeur. He had ⏑ ⏑ined the papers carefully without finding any notice about the adventure in which he had taken part in Paris. It might mean that the chauffeur had escaped, but it could also mean that the mysterious Madame Pelotard was right in her strange assertion: Nothing will ever appear in the papers about me!

Philip found her walking up and down the room. As he came in she ran toward him and cried: "Where have you been so long? I have had word from Jacques!"

Philip congratulated her.

"He has escaped, but cannot leave the place where he is hiding. He saw your notice, and sent a message by a friend. I am leaving to-morrow."

"And I at half-past ten to-night."

She interrupted him.

"Now I want to straighten matters out with you, please.

Will you tell me how much I owe you?"

There had been plenty of opportunity by this time for Philip to learn his companion's character. Two days before he would probably have tried to wave the matter aside. Knowing what he did, he took a piece of paper from the table.

"Let me reckon it up," said he. "One ticket to Marseilles."

"Wait, wait; you are in too much of a hurry. First at the Café de la Paix, there was a cognac."

"Of course," said Philip seriously. "One cognac, one franc."

"After that a taxi to the Hôtel d'Écosse and the station and ten francs to the boy in the hotel."

"But I should pay half of the taxi," Philip interposed in as serious a tone as before.

"No, that isn't fair," she objected; and so they became engrossed in their calculations. Finally she was satisfied and took out a small pocketbook.

"Four hundred and fifty-six francs, forty centimes," said she. "I have no change; here is five hundred francs."

"I will give you the change immediately," answered Philip, in his most businesslike way and began to feel in his vest pocket. She took the money with the same calm seriousness and put it in her bag, from which she then drew a little case.

"Monsieur Pelotard," said she, "you have proved yourself a gentleman toward me in every way. Not for a single second have I regretted confiding myself to your care as blindly as I did. If you will accept a remembrance from your travelling companion, then you will give her much happiness. . . much pleasure. . ."

She stopped, and with a slightly embarrassed manner handed over the case which at the same moment sprang open from the pressure of her finger. Philip stared in astonishment at its contents. It was a scarf pin of gold, set with ten small diamonds encircling a large dully shining pearl. Confidentially, it was worth a thousand francs if it was worth one. His first impulse was to refuse but before he was able to say anything he was forestalled by his mysterious travelling companion.

"If you try to refuse," said she, "I will never forgive you."

She smiled as she said it but at the same time she wrinkled her straight black eyebrows in such a manner that Philip started: so might Anne of Austria have looked as she gave the famous diamond ring to d'Artagnan. His study of her character during these eventful days made him again give way to her wishes. He bowed deeply and murmured some expressions of thanks but she interrupted him with a motion of her hand, almost as worthy of a queen as her manner a while before.

"It is I who am your debtor," said she. "I can never repay you for what you have done."

She was silent for a moment, then continued:

"You are leaving. May I ask where you intend to go?"

Philip smiled.

"You will admit that I am more communicative than you,

if I answer? I am going to a place in which you have shown a very lively interest during the time I have known you. . ."

"To Minorca?" she added breathlessly and with wide-open eyes.

"To Minorca."

She stared at him for fully half a minute. Then she said slowly:

"This is more than strange. We meet in Paris; you are on your way to Marseilles, I too; although without your help I should never have reached here. We are together in Marseilles for two days, and when we are to leave, it turns out that you are going to Minorca. . . to Minorca, just where I am going to-morrow!"

It was Philip's turn to open his eyes wide. She going to Minorca too! She too! She too! Truly, by Jove, she was right, it was more than strange! Was the whole world then going to that little island? Then he quickly gained control over himself again.

"Madame," said he, "you are right. It is really a combination of circumstances more than strange. There is really only one detail lacking to make this combination still more strange, and I believe I can supply it."

"What detail is that?" she asked frowning slightly.

"You said that in Paris you were on your way to Marseilles but would never have reached here without my help, and you may believe me or not, the case is exactly the same if you wish to go from Marseilles to Minorca!"

She sank down on the sofa and looked at him with

mistrust.

"Y-you can't mean that," said she. "The boat goes at three o'clock to-morrow."

"The boat, madame, should leave here for Minorca at three o'clock to-morrow, if it were not for a certain event: that the Minorcans are indulging in their little revolution. I am sorry on your account, but all communications with Minorca have ceased since yesterday!"

She stared at him, still mistrustful.

"And you then—how can you go there?"

"Because," said Philip politely, "I have formed a trust in the vessels which are still willing to go to Minorca."

"A trust!"

"Which I must admit was unusually easy to do; namely, there was only one captain in the whole of Marseilles who was willing to risk making a trip to the island."

"And you have engaged him?"

"I have engaged him."

She looked at him intently for a good half a minute before she spoke again.

"You must have very important reasons for going to Minorca?"

"Just as you, madame."

It became quiet in the room; she sat looking before her without saying a word, and Philip's brain, which already had more than enough to think about, was whirring with thoughts. How should he act in this new and more than strange phase of his adventure? Could there be any justification in taking a woman with him to a country where a revolution was in full blast? And what, *what,* what were her reasons for going to that country? In other words, who was she? He looked at her intently, so intently, that she finally noticed it and blushed. Philip became embarrassed and turned his head toward the window. As he found nothing of interest there he turned his glance to the desk which stood before the window, and the next second he let out a half-choked cry of surprise. On the table stood an unframed photograph of a man.

Following a sudden impulse he pointed to the portrait and asked:

"Madame, is that Jacques?"

She gave him a slight look of annoyance.

"Jacques? Do you think I would have my chauffeur's portrait on my desk? That is my brother, Peter."

Now Philip, as well as she, knew the photograph was not a likeness of Monsieur Jacques, for at the very moment he saw it he had recognized who it was and his question had only been a little ruse—an attempt to see if this mysterious young lady might not betray herself at last. And wonderful to relate, she had fallen into the trap! She had finally given him some information about herself!

The portrait on the desk was a picture of her brother.

But as truly as Philip stood in that room, it was a likeness of nobody else but the man at the Gare de Lyon, the man who had spied on their departure without recognizing them and whose name Philip's brain had been hunting after for two days! This man, then, was her brother.

And his name was Peter...

But where had Philip met this Peter? For as truly as Philip now recognized the portrait on her desk, just as truly did he know that he recognized the person himself at the Gare de Lyon from some earlier occasion.

Peter... Where?...

Suddenly, and to his hostess's inexpressible surprise, Professor Pelotard gave a jump worthy of an Indian but hardly of a sedentary scientist. Eureka! He had found it! He knew who this Peter was, where he had met him, when!

Hamburg!... A night in January, 1909... The night cafe Le Papillon de Nuit!...[3]

But if that Peter, whose portrait stood on her desk, was identical with that crazy sort of man Philip met in Hamburg in 1909 and with whom he had miraculous adventures which resulted in a fabulous reward for himself—if that Peter was her brother, who then was she?

The sudden conclusion he drew made Philip Collin's Indian jump end as quickly as it had begun; his lips, which had opened to let out an involuntary cry, closed again, and, silent and overcome by his discovery, he sank onto a chair from whence he looked respectfully at his travelling companion.

She had awakened from her thoughts with a start at sight of his strange antics, and now stared at him filled with

---

[3]. Described in the short story 'Becoming a Landlord', available for free at https://shop.kabatypress.com/b/7g8N9

alarm. Philip pulled himself together and said hastily:

"Forgive me, madame. A violent pain in the small of my back. . ."

"Do you have such pains often?"

"No—very seldom. But when it rushed on me I was just thinking of asking you an obvious question."

"What is it?"

"If you will continue to entrust yourself to the protection of Professor Pelotard? Do I need to say that the yacht and everything I have is at your disposal, if you still wish to go to Minorca?"

Her face brightened up like a summer sky and she looked at Mr. Collin with a radiant smile.

"You are really too kind, really too kind," cried she. "I did not know whether I dared. . . I was afraid that you would feel it as an unpleasant encumbrance. . ."

He interrupted her with a bow.

"Madame, you pay me too many compliments. I should have made my offer immediately if I had not thought of three things and had that pain in my back."

"And what were the three things?"

"For the first, there is a revolution on Minorca, and a woman. . ."

"Revolution! I have seen bigger revolutions. . ." She stopped and Philip, who could well believe what she said after the discovery he had made a few minutes before, hurriedly continued:

"Secondly, it will be bad weather to-night."

"That doesn't matter. I am accustomed to the water."

"So much the better. Thirdly, we shall not be alone on board."

For the first time she seemed to be disturbed.

"Not alone? I thought you had formed a trust, as you expressed it."

"Exactly, but an hour ago two gentlemen sought me out who had as pressing reasons as I myself for going to the island, and they begged permission to accompany me. Since I am not so pitiless as other trust magnates, I said yes."

"What are their names, if I may ask?"

"The Count of Punta Hermosa and a friend of his, Señor Esteban. They have interests to protect on the island. But you will soon have opportunity of convincing yourself as to the sort of gentlemen they are."

"How is that?"

"I have invited them to dinner, and if you have no objection. . ."

She laughed.

"You are the most delightful trust magnate I can imagine. I do not object! But did I understand correctly? You are leaving to-night?"

"To-night at half-past ten."

"And you did not tell me before. Why, I must pack!"

She waved to him gaily.

"Go now," said she. "I must pack, and I must dress for dinner!"

It might have struck another as strange: she was all at

once in radiant humor, now that she was certain she could go to Minorca! But to Mr. Philip Collin who went to his room, whistling like a canary, it did not seem so strange.

For, thanks to chance, he knew not only who his mysterious travelling companion was, but also why she was going to Minorca.

When, ten minutes later, Philip entered the hall of the hotel, he found the Count of Punta Hermosa and Señor Esteban awaiting him. The Count of Punta Hermosa arose and came toward him. For the first time and somewhat to his surprise, Philip noticed that he limped.

"May I have a little talk with you, Professor?"

"With the greatest pleasure."

They stepped over to a corner of the room, while Señor Esteban remained seated in his armchair.

"When I have told you what lies on my heart, Professor, you will either think I am crazy or that my audacity exceeds all bounds."

Philip raised his eyebrows.

"You see, it is this way. Captain Dupont did a good bit of business to-night when he refused our offer and kept to yours. Honesty is its own reward, one might say."

"How is that?"

"We could not have paid him."

Philip stared at the Count to see whether he was joking. But no, he was apparently in earnest.

"You do not seem to understand me," the Count repeated quietly. "We could not have paid Captain Dupont, or perhaps I should say, we could not have paid him now, but possibly at Minorca."

"Possibly at Minorca?" repeated Philip mechanically.

"Depending on what the rebels leave of my landed property. . ."

The Count of Punta Hermosa broke off in the middle of the sentence and hastily looked at Philip as though to see what effect these words had on him. As Philip, with his head still full of the discovery he had made about his travelling companion, hardly had room for other thoughts, his face showed no signs that he had found anything unusual in the Count's remarks; and with a shrug of the shoulders the latter continued:

"Well, you can understand what held good in the case of the Captain this evening holds good in your case now. I did not have the courage to admit it when I talked matters over with you an hour ago—or rather, I thought of following the example of certain passengers on the Atlantic steamers, get on board and then let you throw me overboard, if you wished. But when you invited me to dinner, you awakened my conscience. . ."

Philip burst into the heartiest laugh he had indulged in for a long time, and there came over him a sudden and irresistible feeling of sympathy for this gigantic man, who was now looking at him with eyebrows raised and with an odd expression playing around his mouth.

"Count," said he, "thank goodness I was able to give Dupont a week's pay in advance, and if necessary I can pay him for another week, too. Don't let it worry you! We will straighten matters out when you wish. But, I see Madame coming down the stairs."

"And if the rebels have destroyed everything I have, Professor?"

"Then I will have the pleasure of your company, and together we will teach them to tremble at the power of the press!"

Philip took his guest by the arm, nodded to Señor Esteban, who had watched him uneasily from his armchair, and led the two gentlemen over to his mysterious travelling companion.

It was somewhat after ten o'clock, when two cabs left a party of four at the east pier of the harbor at Marseilles. There was an elderly gentleman with gold-rimmed glasses, a very large man of middle age who limped, another middle-aged man in a grayish-green ulster and a lady in travelling costume.

Near the quay, against which the waves were dashing in white brigades, lay a small graceful steam yacht with smoking funnel. A skiff pushed off from her side as the two cabs arrived, and a few minutes later a florid-faced man with a beard sprinkled with gray climbed up the quay steps and approached the party.

"Is it you, Professor?" he called out.

"Yes, Captain Dupont."

"I thought it was the departure of the children of Israel out of the land of Egypt. Why, you are a whole crew!"

"Your proteges, Captain, whom you sent to me, and my wife. I hope you received my message and arranged for provisions accordingly."

"Ah, your wife!" The Captain stared at the gray-haired lady in the travelling costume who held herself so unusually upright in the sharp spring wind. "Yes, I received your message. But you said nothing about a lady. The Lord knows, if we can take care of a lady on board the *Stork*."

"But, Captain, Madame's needs are simple, and she is neither afraid of the water nor of the name of your boat."

The Captain laughed. Then he frowned and said:

"Has the devil broken loose today, Professor?"

"What do you mean?"

" 'Pon my soul the whole world wants to go to Minorca. First you come, then these two other gentlemen. Well, you can believe me or not, I had hardly reached the harbor before I had a call from a devil of a person who wants to go there, too!"

Judging from the Captain's language, it was evident his experiences had rather excited him.

"Another person!" Philip stared at him.

"A devil of a person!" Captain Dupont confirmed. "I told him that he could go to. . ." The Captain checked himself, spat energetically on the ground and began to arrange for the transfer of his guests to the yacht.

The supposed Madame Pelotard was the first to get in the skiff which was to take them aboard, then came Señor Esteban and the Count of Punta Hermosa. Philip was on the point of stepping in, when Captain Dupont, who was still on the quay as well, grasped him by the arm.

"By all the gods, Professor, there is the man again."

Philip turned around quickly. The Count of Punta Hermosa and Señor Esteban leaned forward to watch.

A small, thick-set man in fur coat and stiff hat had jumped out of a cab at the other end of the quay and came running toward them, waving his cane.

"Captain, Captain!" he cried hoarsely. "Wait, wait! Haven't you changed your mind? Can't I go along with you? Captain, Captain! I'll pay, I'll pay whatever you wish!. . ."

Captain's Dupont's answer was several silent but powerful strokes at the oars, which sent the boat flying from the quay. The man kept dancing up and down and tore off his hat in order to wave persuasively with it.

"Captain! Gentlemen!" he cried. "I must go, I must go!"

The light from a gas lamp fell on his face, and Philip Collin suddenly gave such a start, that the little boat rocked. That face, that face! Following an irresistible impulse, he raised his voice high above the sound of the waves and cried out with a burst of laughter:

"Go by way of London! Go by way of London, Semjon Marcowitz!"

At the same moment he felt the little skiff, which was bearing him and the others to the yacht, give a lurch that came within a hair's breadth of making it capsize. The Count of Punta Hermosa and Señor Esteban had simultaneously arisen from their seats and stood with eyes as though glued on the quay where Captain Dupont's latest prospective customer still stood in the glimmer of the gaslight. At Philip's words he had suddenly stopped gesticulating. His arms hung limply at his side, and his head was stretched forward like that of a wild beast scenting for prey. Even at that distance his eyes could be seen gleaming black and malicious at the little boat and its passengers. Just then Captain Dupont let out another oath; and as though both were answering the same impulse the Count and his elderly friend sank down on their seats.

They cast a look at the others as though to intimate that nothing had happened. But the next moment the Count of Punta Hermosa leaned over to his friend and in spite of the swish of the waves Philip heard him say eight words which made him grip the side of the boat and made him stare as though bewitched at the person who uttered them. And still these words were as simple as possible.

For what the Count said was:

"Paqueno, did you hear? It was Semjon Marcowitz!"

But Mr. Collin, in the inner pocket of whose coat lay a strange document, taken from the safe of the usurer Semjon Marcowitz, and who had the natural gift of a most excellent memory, suddenly recalled to mind the letter which two weeks before he had seen in Mr. Ernest Isaacs' office—the letter which had been the means to the greatest coup of his life, the corner in Minorcan government bonds. This letter was from the Minorcan Minister of Finance and contained a request for a loan; and it was signed: Esteban Paqueno,

Minister of Finance for His Highness the Grand Duke of Minorca.

And if the Count of Punta Hermosa now called his friend Paqueno, instead of Señor Esteban, as he introduced him—what was necessary then to make this strange coincidence of names seem still more strange?

That all the land in Minorca belonged to the Grand Duke; and that the Count in question, who was going to Minorca to protect his landed property, was lame!...

Truly, by Zeus, if Captain Dupont ought to feel great responsibility already through having charge of Mr. Collin and his welfare, great responsibility would still be his even if Mr. Collin fell into the sea.

For not every day does a little yacht with room for four passengers count among its guests a Swedish arch-swindler, a lately deposed Grand Duke with his Minister of Finance, and a Grand Duchess of Russia!

Sail carefully, Mr. Dupont! You carry a cargo of kings in exile!

BOOK THREE

Midst Rebels and Rogues

CHAPTER I

A March Day at Sea and What Took Place There

The Mediterranean dashed into spray against the sides of the little yacht; the sharp spring wind covered the sea with foam until the waves appeared blanketed in snow. The sky above was filled with white light behind large thin clouds which in turn seemed as white as though they had been chemically bleached. Slightly rolling from side to side the yacht *Stork* plowed forward between sky and sea.

It was but seven in the morning when the first of her passengers appeared on deck; the lame Count of Punta Hermosa and his old friend Señor Esteban came up the companionway and carefully picked their way along the lurching deck toward the bow.

The Count sat down on a chest which had been placed on deck and motioned to his friend to follow his example.

"Here we can chat undisturbed, Paqueno," said he. "No one can hear us except the gulls, and they probably do not understand Spanish."

"A beautiful morning, Your Highness! Only it is a pity

the boat rolls so much."

The Grand Duke laughed.

"How is your stomach behaving? Is it as sensitive as it was on our outward trip?"

"At present, I feel a little better. The air has done me good." Old Señor Paqueno tried to make his voice as hearty as possible, but his pale face showed that matters were not going any too well with him.

"Our outward trip," continued the Grand Duke, "yes, that was a journey! I hope this one will be better. Really, it is very comfortable on board. But I must say one thing."

"What is that, Your Highness?"

"That our host and his wife, although they are as amiable as one could wish, seem to me rather mysterious. Think of a journalist who has the means to charter a yacht for himself in order to see a beggarly revolution on Minorca!"

"His paper settles the bill, naturally."

"Possibly, but since when did the papers begin to show such an interest in us, Paqueno? And then his wife. Why, she is ten years older than he!"

"Perhaps he married her for her money, Your Highness."

"M—yes, that of course is possible. Well, if she were not so old, she would be rather good-looking. Anyway, it is strange that she tags along with him like this. He said nothing about it at first."

"Perhaps she herself decided the matter at the last minute. If I were to express an opinion about Professor Pelotard and his wife, I should say that I almost believe the

Professor is a bit henpecked." Old Paqueno laughed faintly, but stopped as the *Stork* gave an extra little roll.

"H'm, yes, you may be right there, Paqueno. Madame looks as though she knew what she wanted and her husband looks as though he were well aware of the fact. But, of course that can also be politeness on his part. . . But the most mysterious fact of all still remains."

"What is that, Your Highness?"

"That he knew Marcowitz! How on earth can you explain that? My Lord, I almost tumbled overboard when I heard the Professor shout out his name. And did you notice, that Marcowitz suddenly became quiet after the Professor shouted? Go by way of London! Nothing should prevent Marcowitz doing that! Decidedly mysterious! And then tell me this, what earthly reason could Marcowitz have for going to Minorca? Why, people believe I am dead or in the hands of the rebels. What reason then, can Marcowitz have for going there? It's mysterious, mighty mysterious!"

"Oh, Your Highness, everything which happens now seems mysterious in my eyes! That coup on the exchange. . . And then immediately afterwards the revolution. . ."

"You are right, one mystery after the other. So much has not happened on Minorca since the days of Don Jeronimo the Lucky. I can well imagine that speculator on the exchange letting out some pretty oaths at the present time! I would willingly have given all I have, which is not much, to have seen his expression when he read the telegram about the revolution! You may be sure he would wish me luck on my trip, if he knew that I was on my way to Minorca to punish the rebels—by the holy St. Urban, look, look!"

The Grand Duke suddenly laid a hand on Señor Paqueno's shoulder, and stared past him to the steps leading up from the cabins. Did he see correctly? Or had he been dreaming the night before, when in Professor Pelotard's wife he had seen a lady of forty, dressed in a manner somewhat too youthful for her age? Either he had been dreaming then or this was a new mystery to be added to the others; for here on the top step of the stairs, illuminated by the white light of the spring morning, stood Madame Pelotard with her hand on the banister and one foot stretched forward in the act of placing it on deck. But a Madame Pelotard who no more resembled the one he had seen the night before than spring resembles winter, than a bright March morning is like a November evening. She stood there tall and lithesome with a face which was as young and fresh as the morning light, and with blue eyes which gleamed like the Mediterranean around them. The wind that whirled through the little yacht's rigging swept her skirt tight around the contour of her body and in a moment ruffled her hair under her sport cap. Now she caught sight of the supposed Count of Punta Hermosa and his friend and came toward them with a gay smile. She moved over the deck as though she had tramped the boards of a ship since childhood.

"What a delightful morning! Have you slept well, gentlemen?"

"Excellently, madame," said the Grand Duke, who had arisen with a bow, "and you? Will you do us the pleasure of sitting down with us?"

"Thanks," said she, and took a seat on the chest. The Grand Duke could not help staring at her and with his glances devoured every movement she made. Suddenly she smiled at him a little spitefully and he stammeringly tried to gloss over his rudeness.

"Madame," said he, "I must beg your pardon—but to be quite frank I have never before known a sea trip to have such a wonderful effect."

"How is that?"

He hesitated, uncertain as to what he should say. She noticed it and began to laugh.

"Go ahead and say it. You want, perhaps, to remark that I. . . that I look a little more youthful?"

"Yes, more than a little," said he, but broke off, afraid to wound her feelings in another way.

She smiled again.

"It isn't so very strange that you notice it. I have just been going through a facial cure, you see, and the treatment ended today!"

She looked so absolutely truthful as she uttered this prodigious falsehood that the Grand Duke bowed.

"Your treatment has had a wonderful effect, madame; you are twenty years younger. May I ask how M. Pelotard is?"

"Thanks, very well, I think." Her tone was evasive, almost short.

"You decided only at the last minute to accompany him?"

"Yes... at the last minute... of course his departure came so suddenly."

"A newspaper correspondent like your husband must naturally be ready to start at a minute's notice. Would you tell me for what paper your husband writes?"

"Paper... I don't know... Why, of course, for the *Sentinel of Finance!*"

"*Sentinel of Finance*," he repeated uncomprehendingly, and with eyes astare. "For a financial paper?"

"Of course... that is to say, for others too... for a syndicate..." The supposed Madame Pelotard became more and more confused while she spoke; the name *Sentinel of Finance* had suddenly popped up in her mind from the breakfast two days before and she had clutched at it like a drowning person at a straw, without thinking that it was a financial paper and that such papers do not usually send out war correspondents. She blushed. The Grand Duke did not know what to believe, and kept quiet. The *Sentinel of Finance!* A syndicate! She hardly seemed to know for what paper her husband wrote! The little scene was interrupted by old Señor Paqueno, who hastily arose and with a mumbled apology hurried away across the deck as fast as his legs could carry him. The Grand Duke could not refrain from smiling, but Madame Pelotard looked at him disapprovingly and cast a sympathetic look at the old Minister of Finance who was now disappearing down the stairs.

"Poor Señor Esteban," murmured she. "I am sure he

wishes that we were already on Minorca."

"You are right, madame. Upheavals on firm land frighten him less than on water. At present he even longs for Minorca."

She looked at him with lively interest.

"At present, not at other times?"

"At other times it is his dream to enter a monastery in Barcelona."

"Enter a monastery? How strange! Is he a monk?"

"No, he is finan—He has held a position under the Grand Duke of Minorca for many years."

"Under the Grand Duke! You don't say so! And then he knows the Grand Duke? You, too—do you know him?"

He looked at her in surprise; her tone was so enthusiastic.

"The Grand Duke? Why, yes, madame, he is one of my best friends."

"Don Ronald, isn't it?"

"Ramon, madame. Poor Don Ramon! He isn't having a pleasant time of it now!"

"Yes, poor, poor Don Ramon. I am sorry for him, I am so sorry for him! But tell me, you don't believe. . . you don't really believe that they have harmed him in any way? That he has been murdered by those wretches?"

"Why, madame, that is hard to say. Nobody knows how far the oppressed people will go. Perhaps they have balanced out their age-old injuries with an edge of steel. . . you saw, of course, what the papers had to say? 'It is to be hoped that the populace have shown mildness, but were the contrary the case, we could not hold them absolutely wrong.'"

"The papers! The papers!" she rose, red with emotion. "What do I care about the papers? At home in my country. . . I think they speak spitefully, without any show of conscience! If they have murdered Don Roland then Europe should shoot the whole of Minorca into splinters!"

"Madame, madame, you are even more of a royalist than the king himself! Don Ramon, whom you insist on calling Roland, was on the whole an indolent idler, a parasite on his poor people, and. . ."

"Don't dare to say any more! He was a fine and noble man, and if he has bad luck the whole of his life, then we should pity him and not slander him as the horrible papers do. You who know him should say I am right instead of taking their side."

"*Mon Dieu,* madame, I gladly say you are right. As I said, he was my friend and he had many good qualities. He very frequently offered me an excellent cognac, and. . ."

"You are detestable," she cried, "detestable! Offer you cognac! And had good qualities, was your friend—why do you talk so? It is just as though you believed that he were. . . were dead."

"Madame, a dethroned prince is as good as dead."

"A dethroned prince! Then he is no longer your friend because he does not reign and cannot offer you a cognac! That's a fine trait!"

"But, madame. . ."

"Then you are nothing else than a fair-weather friend! I did not believe that of you. You don't seem to be that kind. I was already beginning to have a good opinion of Don Raoul simply on account of his friends, when in the beginning you said you were one of them."

"You are as gracious toward me, madame, as toward poor Don Ramon whom you have already called everything beginning with R except Rameses. I assure you that I really agree with you. . . no one can think more of Don Ramon than I. I hardly believe anyone has shown more patience with his weak points or more appreciation of his good ones than I."

"Now I like you; that is speaking beautifully. . . But tell me, you who knew him and know Minorca. . . what do you think they have done with him?. . . And remember they have cut the telegraph cable too! It is exactly as though they were afraid people would find out what they have done. . . as though they really had murd— "

"Oh, madame, the telegraph cable signifies nothing. If the telegraph cable stops functioning at Minorca there are so many other reasons why it could have happened! It could have been caused through the weakness of old age. Or perhaps the rebels have cut it through fear that Don Ramon might telegraph for help."

"That's so! Oh, and to think that no one in Europe has thought of helping him! It is shameful, inexcusable. If my br. . . If anyone. . . Do you think the wretches would release him for money? That he could be ransomed, if he has been captured? I have thought of that..."

"You have thought of that! You are the most kind-hearted young lady I have met! But I am afraid that you would find it difficult to ransom him, if he is held captive. No one would risk any money on him while he reigned, and probably no one would feel more inclined to do so now since he has been overthrown."

"Tell me..." She hesitated. "I have only seen his photographs. He was good-looking, wasn't he?"

"Why, I don't know exactly what to say, madame. Good-looking, one could hardly say. He limped, you know."

"Limped! What does that matter? Why, even you..." She broke off and looked at him apologetically. "I... I have heard that he was very stately and had a good figure..."

"Who said so, if I may ask?"

"Monsieur Pelotard."

"Your husband? Did your husband know the Grand Duke?"

"I... I don't know. I don't believe so. I rather think it is the first time he has gone to the island."

"You don't know? Don't you keep better track of your husband's affairs than that, madame?"

"Of course, but he could perhaps have been there before we were..."

"Before you were married, I understand. Have you been married long, if I may ask?"

To the Grand Duke's great surprise, the answer to this question was a deep blush which slowly spread over the whole of Madame Pelotard's face from her chin to the roots of her hair. Fearing that he had said something stupid, but embarrassed as to how to correct his mistake, he stammered:

"Ah, I understand, is it possible... Is this your honeymoon?"

The next moment all he saw of Madame Pelotard was her well-shaped back and the glimpse of two little patent leather shoes, which in double-quick time, bore their owner across the deck to the companionway; a second later not even so much was to be seen. Madame Pelotard, without giving him any reason for her actions, without a word in explanation and without turning around even once, had disappeared.

Truly, the yacht *Stork* was carrying more mysteries than it was entitled to according to its registered tonnage. Why on earth should a young married woman, who one day looked as though she were forty and the next, through a marvellous facial cure, as though she were a girl of twenty, blush because somebody had asked her in a highly respectful manner how long she had been married? Blush, and then flee like the chaste Diana! And this woman who is married to a journalist, writing for papers she does not know, as well as for a financial paper that sends out war-correspondents—this woman is filled with uneasiness at what may have happened to a Grand Duke whom she has never seen and whose name she keeps confusing in a shocking manner! She is filled with uneasiness on his account, does not dare think of the possibility that he may be dead, thinks that his subjects, whom she calls wretches, should all be shot, if they have harmed a hair of his head, and (without knowing it) for a half hour cross-questions the said Grand Duke about himself!

Truly, less than that is enough to make a person's head swim. Far less!

Before these thoughts, which followed one another with the speed of an electric current, had even been able to rush through his head, Don Ramon suddenly saw the husband of the lady who had so mystified him come up the stairs, down which she had disappeared, and with a quiet nod approach him.

"Good morning, Count! How are you? You are up bright and early.—Madame Pelotard just told me that you two have already been holding a long conference together here on deck."

"Yes, and a conference which was broken off by madame in such a manner, that I am afraid I have wounded her deeply. Monsieur, I beg of you to believe that I would be overwhelmed with despair if that were so! I can only say that I do not know in what. . ."

"But, Count, don't worry; it isn't as bad as all that! Between you and me, Madame found there was a bit too much sea. She told me so just now."

"Too much sea! But Madame seemed as though born on the ocean."

"Ah, you know, the ocean and women are two things which are equally unreliable!"

The Grand Duke hastened to agree heartily with the truth of this statement.

"You might say unfathomable, Professor, without exaggerating. But in your wife's case, this unreliability is even more noticeable than with other women."

"How is that?"

"It concerns not only the inner woman as with them, but her outer appearance as well. You introduced me yesterday to a Madame Pelotard of forty, and today I find one of twenty."

"Ah, Count, the difference in the light, you know! And the sea air!"

"The sea air? I thought Madame had just finished a facial cure?"

"Why. . . yes, of course! I had almost forgotten that. To be sure, a facial cure, which ended today."

"That is what she told me. On the other hand, she did not want to tell me which paper you write for. I was on the point of saying that it looked as though she hardly knew."

"Ah, *mon Dieu,* Count, you cannot expect such things to interest a woman."

"No, perhaps not. On the other hand Madame Pelotard is very evidently interested in the object of our trip. She cross-questioned me about Minorca to the best of her ability."

"Yes, she is very much interested in Minorca."

"And still more in the Grand Duke! Professor, you are fortunate that he has been deposed! Were he alive and reciprocated your wife's interest, then it might happen that you would leave Minorca without her. Remember: he is an absolute sovereign!"

"Do you think Madame Pelotard interests herself so heartily for the Grand Duke?"

"It almost strikes me that way."

"And do you think that the Grand Duke would show an equal interest?"

There was an ironic undertone in Philip Collin's voice which at first mystified the supposed Count of Punta Hermosa, and then irritated him. If the thought were not so absurd, he could almost believe that Mr. Pelotard knew something—more: that the Professor was standing there making fun of him! Without controlling himself, he cried:

"I am thoroughly convinced of it, my dear Professor!"

Philip turned his head, as though to see whether the sailor at the helm was still attending to business, then he turned to the Grand Duke.

"There came near being five of us last evening," said he. "If it had not been for Captain Dupont's instant aversion to the man, we would perhaps not have been able to avoid it."

"You knew the man on the quay?" The Grand Duke, in spite of all his pains, could not make his voice sound as disinterested as he wished.

"Knew him? A little. And you, Count, you will know him next time, probably!"

The Grand Duke made a quick movement to straighten out the end of a rope which had been lying straight enough before.

"At least, you looked at him long enough," Philip continued heartlessly.

The Grand Duke shrugged his shoulders.

"The episode, of course, was unusual," said he, but he knew that his voice was far from convincing, and he was again struck with the thought which seemed to him more absurd each time it came into his head: this Professor knows something! He knows something! He became angry at himself, then at the Professor. What else was this but groping after a lot of mysteries! He turned to the Professor and said almost brutally:

"Your paper must be very much interested in revolutions, since it is willing to stand the expense of a private yacht to get information about the revolution on Minorca."

"Yes," said Philip thoughtfully, "it really is. But you know there has been a good deal of talk about Minorca lately. It isn't more than a couple of days since that coup in Minorcan bonds took place on the exchange."

"Well, and what do you know about that?" The Grand Duke's voice was almost scornful.

"Nothing, Count. Nobody knows anything about it."

"That is just like the press. They know nothing but that doesn't stop them from writing about everything."

"You do us an injustice," said Philip as quietly as before. "With my paper, for example, it is the rule that those who write about a matter must be well informed about everything connected with the subject."

"Then you are well-stuffed with details about Minorca?"

"H'm, yes, I think I know about most things connected with Minorca... But pardon me, wasn't that the gong? It is time for us to go down to breakfast."

Almost unwillingly the Grand Duke followed his host toward the stairs which led to the little dining-saloon; with his eyes fastened on him he said slowly:

"Let's hear something of what you know!"

Philip Collin cast a quick glance at him, surprised by the tone of voice, and noticed the expression in his eyes. Philip realized that he must not say more if he did not wish to betray himself. He shrugged his shoulders:

"Ah, Count, it would take too long now before breakfast. I know at least that Minorca will be represented at our meal with something of which it has every reason to be proud."

"What is that?" cried the Grand Duke, turning on Mr. Collin the piercing glance of a detective.

"Its lobsters," said Philip politely, and motioned him to go ahead.

It was about five o'clock in the afternoon when Philip Collin came up the companionway, and after a few turns around the little yacht's deck went up to Captain Dupont who now had charge of the wheel. He took out his cigar-case and offered the trustworthy captain a cigar. Industriously smoking, the two men talked over various details of the trip; whether it would be advisable to steer direct for Port Mahon or go to some lesser harbor on the island; and how they should act in case of an encounter with the revolutionaries.

It had begun to blow again toward evening. The heaven was filled with fleeting gray clouds which, far in the distance, could be seen gushing down a whipping rain over the water; the wind which in the morning had been a fresh and pleasant spring breeze had increased to an angry, howling northwest wind. The little yacht rolled heavily and Philip inwardly felt sorry for old Señor Paqueno who would probably suffer the tortures of hell during such weather. He himself was a good sailor and where he stood by the Captain's side on the bridge, felt no discomfort either from the wind or the waves.

It grew dark quickly. The trailing smoke from a large gray ship was seen in the distance.

Suddenly, Philip to his surprise saw Madame Pelotard and the supposed Count of Punta Hermosa making their way up the stairs from the cabins. In such weather! She and the Count, however, seemed to be as hardened against the weather as he. They made several turns back and forth across the heaving and rolling deck; they were talking and evidently Madame Pelotard was asking questions of the Count which he did not answer to her full satisfaction, for she gesticulated excitedly and each time spoke at length, while he seemed to express himself shortly and evasively. A couple of times Philip saw her place her mouth to his ear while he lowered his head; she evidently had difficulty in making herself heard.

They did not seem to notice Philip on the bridge. Philip smiled discreetly.

Suddenly the wind doubled in force. The foam arose in a single white cascade along the windward side, and the little yacht began to roll so heavily that Philip had to clutch the railing of the bridge to keep from falling. As he lurched from side to side, trying to regain his balance, he saw his supposed wife and the Count hastily rush across the deck toward the companionway. The Count's lameness seemed in no way to inconvenience him for he sprang over the deck with as much self-assurance as any sailor, and Madame Pelotard in no way proved his inferior.

Suddenly, however, she let out a cry and threw her arms in the air; she had stumbled over the end of a loose rope, staggered and would certainly have fallen heavily against the railing, perhaps gone overboard, if at that moment, the gigantic Count had not sprung forward and encircled her with his outstretched arms. The next moment she lay struggling and evidently protesting in his arms, and was borne at double-quick time toward the stairs. When they reached there he respectfully set her down again; she took hold of the banister and stared at him for a couple of seconds with a queer look in her eyes, then stretched out her hand and said something.

The Count of Punta Hermosa took the outstretched little hand, pressed it—and then hastily raised it to his lips.

The next second she disappeared down the stairs and he followed slowly. . .

Mr. Collin on the bridge smiled again but was aroused from his thoughts by Captain Dupont.

"A man-of-war!" cried the latter at his left ear. "A man-of-war, Professor!"

Philip looked to where he was pointing. The big gray ship whose trailing smoke he had seen an hour before had now come nearer to them; its imposing and grotesque silhouette placarded against the light in the western sky. Without paying attention to the wind or sea, it quietly plowed its way toward Marseilles from whence Philip and his yacht had come. The foam rose around its sharp bow like two white streamers.

Ten minutes later it was so near that Philip could see its flag; white, blue and red; a Russian ship then. He took his marine-glasses and turned them on the colossus. Czar Alexander, he seemed to read. Then he let the glasses sink, nodded to Captain Dupont, and with a smile went to the companionway, down which the Count of Punta Hermosa and his wife had disappeared a while before.

Why did Mr. Collin smile?

For the reason that he began to feel himself to be a representative of Providence, whose duty it is to watch over the fate of fools and lovers.

And also because he now began to hope that he might recover his lost fifty thousand pounds!

CHAPTER 2

Which Is The Beginning of Very Adventurous Events

The wind increased during the night and the following morning; there was a heavy sea and it was not until noon that the weather calmed down again. It was one o'clock and the sun was shining down from a deep blue sky before old Señor Esteban dared come up on deck. Overhead the gulls circled gracefully like squadrons of monoplanes. The air was warm and whetted the appetite.

"Madame," said the Count of Punta Hermosa, "we are beginning to give you an idea of the best thing there is on Minorca, the climate."

At six o'clock they passed the south-eastern coast of Minorca and shortly afterwards Port Mahon came in sight. The little city, as white and quiet as ever, rose in terraces from the sea; the Angelus was ringing in the cathedral and the shadows in the west were sinking heavily over the houses and palm-trees. The crescent moon was like a fine silver rent in the opal-blue evening sky, and the gulls rested like white lily buds on the transparent water of the harbor.

The *Stork* slowly rounded the harbor breakwater and at half speed entered the harbor, which was empty with the exception of the gulls who arose shrieking at their arrival. The yacht cast anchor and for some time it looked as though nothing would happen.

Suddenly, however, a boat shot out from the inner part of the harbor and quickly approached the little yacht. A waterman sat at the oars and with him in the boat were two men in uniform, their coats richly adorned with gold lace. They wore a white band on their left sleeves.

Only Professor Pelotard, his wife and the captain appeared on the deck of the yacht. As they came in sight of Port Mahon, Philip had taken the Count of Punta Hermosa and his friend aside and said:

"Gentlemen, I have decided to put into the principal town itself. I am unknown there and think it is safe to do so. But if I am not mistaken, you have been there before? And have property there?"

"Yes."

"Then it seems wise to me, yes, the only wise thing, that you remain out of sight until I can see how the land lies. Your appearance might lead to violence on the part of the revolutionists. . . one never knows, of course!"

"You are right," answered the Count, "and we will do as you say."

Consequently only Philip and his mysterious travelling-companion stood on deck when the boat with the gold-laced gentlemen pulled alongside the little yacht. Within ten seconds these two gentlemen were on board. One of them, a young man of hardly thirty, dressed in the most brilliant of uniforms and with the larger amount of gold lace, approached them and made a military salute.

"Good evening," said he in broken English. "Whom have I the pleasure of speaking to?"

Whom have I the pleasure of speaking to! Philip looked at him, highly amused.

"My name is Professor Pelotard," he replied. "This is my wife, and this is Captain Dupont, who is in charge of our yacht. Whom have I the pleasure of speaking to?"

The young man straightened himself up.

"Luis Hernandez is my name," said he. "Perhaps it is not unknown to you?"

Philip was on the point of laughing outright: this, then, was the future or already elected president of Minorca! And he had immediately come on board to show himself to the distinguished foreign guests... Evidently that was his custom: he had also paid a visit to Captain Simmons of the Lone Star. And perhaps ten steps from him in a cabin on the *Stork* sat the man whom he intended to succeed!

"It is a pleasure to make your acquaintance, Mr. President," said Philip, bowing. "The press of the world has blazoned forth your name during the last four days, ever since the telegram from Captain Simmons was dispatched from Barcelona."

"Ah, he telegraphed! I was hoping he would, but I began to be uneasy... We had no way of telling... our telegraph cable is out of order. No one knows why. People, then, are talking about me... about us in Europe?"

"You may be sure of that, Mr. President! They talk of nothing else, and the papers are full of praise for you and your courageous countrymen. I myself come as a representative of the press... come to bring you their greeting and to place their influence at your disposal, Mr. President."

Philip spoke slowly, so as to let each word sink into the thankful soil which Señor Luis Hernandez' heart evidently represented. The presumptive president of Minorca listened with slightly parted lips and with head bent forward, while now and then his hand glided over the gold lace on his sleeve. It was Philip's wish for the moment to be on as good terms with him as possible, and it was evident that he had made a start in the right direction. Señor Hernandez cleared his throat and said in an oratorical voice:

"I am pleased to hear it, Mr. Pelotard! It shows that the press sees that its duty is to fight for truth and the triumph of justice. I am pleased to hear it... But you shouldn't call me president. I am not that yet... The election will not take place for several days."

"Ah," said Philip with his most amiable smile. "But I have heard that at times the First Consul Bonaparte was called Sire without his being displeased!"

A flush of pleasure spread all over Señor Hernandez' face, but he threw a shy glance at his companion to see whether the latter understood. Then he said:

"This is the Harbor Inspector, my friend, Emiliones. We

have come to help you in any way you may wish. . ."

He stopped and cast a long glance at the windows to the dining-saloon, as though to hint that the President of Minorca would not refuse if he were invited to supper. But Philip, who had his own plans, pretended not to notice.

"To-morrow, Señor, I will take the liberty of calling on you, and will consult you as to what we had best bring out in the papers."

"I'll be very glad to see you, Señor, very glad indeed," Luis hastened to reply. "You can meet me at whatever time you wish. Only, from ten to twelve I inspect the troops."

"And where," asked Philip, "can I find you?"

"In the castle, Señor. In the palace."

Philip again was on the point of laughing outright. Señor Hernandez, though not yet elected president, was not slow in assuming the outer insignia of power; the representative of the people had simply appropriated the dwelling of the deposed ruler!

"Ah," said Philip, "in the grand-ducal castle. . . May I ask a question?"

"Naturally, Señor, with pleasure."

"What has become of the former tenant?"

Señor Hernandez gave the representative of the European press a searching glance. . . Then he again gained control of himself.

"We will talk about that in the morning, Señor. I bid you good evening."

He jumped down into his boat with Señor Emiliones,

who during the whole time had not uttered a word, perhaps because he did not understand English, and a couple of minutes later their boat had disappeared in the darkness which was closing in. They were hardly out of sight when Philip rushed from the side of his supposed wife, who was still staring after the president of the Republic of Minorca with murderous glances, and hurried down to the cabin of the Count of Punta Hermosa.

"We have had callers, Count, important callers."

"Who, then?"

"President Hernandez. He and I are the best of friends and to-morrow I am to pay him a visit in his apartment at the grand-ducal castle."

"In the grand-ducal. . . the damned rogue. . . so, you are going to pay him a visit there? Will madame accompany you?"

"Madame? I had the greatest trouble in the world to keep her from assassinating the president during his call. You know she is a Royalist."

"I know it, and I am glad."

"There, there, Count! I really have to thank the president for one thing."

"An invitation to the grand-ducal palace?"

"No, because he has freed Minorca of the Grand Duke! If Don Ramon had still been in power, you said I would have to leave Minorca without my wife. But between you and me: I do not intend to wait until to-morrow to return the call."

"You seem to be in a hurry to see your friend the president again."

"H'm, yes, in any case, I want to see his capital and therefore I intend to land to-night."

"You won't see much. The capital's gas works are celebrated for their unreliability."

"I can get along without the gaslight. *Au revoir*, Count."

"Don't be in such a hurry, Professor. I think I'll go along too, if you have no objections."

Philip laughed inwardly.

"Ah, you think of going along too... It is very imprudent. And if I have any objections?"

"Then I'll swim ashore."

"For goodness' sake, you needn't go to such lengths. Come along if you like, but promise me that you will not telegraph your impressions to any rival paper! Do you know Port Mahon?"

"Somewhat."

The Grand Duke's tone was very short. There was a queer expression of determination on his face, and with a tingle of joy Philip said to himself that this looked as though it might develop into quite an adventure. From the very moment he had mentioned where President Hernandez was living, the face of the assumed Count of Punta Hermosa had hardened as though it were a mask; and if Philip had not mistaken the character of his guest, it meant there was a dangerous time ahead for the leader of the revolutionists—and for themselves as well! But he was in sympathy with the Grand Duke's feelings, loved adventure, and did not forget that what was happening absolutely fitted in with his own plans!

When he and the Grand Duke came on deck they found the twilight had been succeeded by night. The Grand Duke was right: not a single gaslight was burning in Port Mahon. They would have to get along with the faint light which came from the nocturnal spring sky.

Captain Dupont was having a quiet smoke by the railing. Philip called to him to have the skiff lowered. The captain gave the necessary orders, seemingly surprised.

"You are going on land, Professor?"

"Yes, captain. We will probably not be away more than two hours. But if we should be delayed, then listen carefully if you hear anything suspicious. You can't tell what may happen in a land of revolution!"

"You are right, although the Lord only knows how they can carry on their revolutions so quietly here. It isn't the same as in France."

"They are through with the revolution now, captain. You saw the new president this afternoon, you know."

Captain Dupont spat energetically as confirmation that he had.

"Ugh, yes," said he.

"*Au revoir,*" said Philip with a laugh. Captain Dupont, although citizen of a republic himself, did not seem to greatly favor republics when abroad.

The Professor and the Grand Duke jumped into the skiff. Philip took the oars and started off.

CHAPTER 3

In Which We Again Meet With An Old Acquaintance, And In Which Surprises Begin For The Grand Duke

The skiff glided noiselessly across the water of the harbor, Philip taking special pains to make as little noise as possible.

He leaned over to the Grand Duke, who had been watching the rowing in silence, and said:

"Where do you suggest we should land? I, for my part, prefer it should not be in the vicinity of my new friend Emiliones' office."

"Emiliones?"

"President Hernandez' harbor inspector."

"Aha. I agree with you. Let me row. I think I know the right place for us."

He took the oars from Philip and they glided on as silently as before.

After rowing some four minutes through the darkness

they arrived at the further end of the harbor on the western side. A few low, gray sheds with outspread nets before them showed that this part of Port Mahon's harbor was used by the fishing population. None of its representatives, however, were present to celebrate the return of their lawful ruler; the Grand Duke and Philip landed with the greatest secrecy and as quietly as possible dragged the skiff to a place among the five or six fishing boats which lay keels up in front of the sheds. The Grand Duke, motioning Philip to follow, led the way past the small gray houses, which at that side of the harbor stretched down almost to the water's edge, and entered a narrow alley. Without saying a word the two nightly adventurers walked along, the Grand Duke ahead and Philip directly behind him.

Minute after minute passed in silent order of march; in the narrow winding alleys it was difficult for Philip to judge which way his leader was directing his course, but according to his own sense of direction, it seemed toward the west; now and then as they passed some intersecting alley which led down to the harbor he saw in the west the silhouette of a building which he had already learned to recognize, and he smiled.

He realized that his friend the Count of Punta Hermosa, acting as a good guide should, intended first of all to show him Port Mahon's most noteworthy sight—the palace, where President Hernandez had succeeded his deposed master!

What surprised Philip most was the death-like stillness

in the city. Hardly a sound had been heard the whole way as they came along, and this was a city whose populace had just overthrown the yoke of centuries and who at last were imbibing the air of liberty after hundreds of years of inexpressible ignominy and oppression! Surely they seemed to take their release unusually quietly! One would expect revolutionary songs and dances, bonfires, Phrygian caps, perhaps even a guillotine erected in honor of the new republic; instead a silence like the grave reigned over all, and the liberated populace retired to rest at nine o'clock!

Suddenly where the alley they were passing through crossed a somewhat larger street, the Grand Duke stopped and stood motionless with head outstretched. From the broader street in front of them could be heard the steady tattoo of heels in the distance. Was it a watchman on patrol? It would be best to find out before they continued. Click, click, click, the steps came nearer and nearer; it sounded like the tread of a person accustomed to military life. Philip bent forward beside the Grand Duke and stared into the slightly less dark street before them. In another moment the person, whose step they were listening to, became visible; Philip heard a low sibilant sound escape his companion, and he himself gave a start of surprise.

With genuine Prussian bearing, straight as a ramrod, his square head erect, clad in a cutaway which flapped at every step, and wearing a stiff hat and yellow shoes, the latter shining faintly in the darkness, came a man tramping along the street, whom Philip's eyes with one glance registered as belonging to the species "German commercial traveller." Everything was there, the indescribable clumsiness of bearing, the unmistakable traces of military training, the dress in all its details, and so that nothing should be lacking, a smouldering cigar in his mouth, the odor of which, as the night wind wafted it in their direction, bespoke the genuineness of a five pfennig Bremen havana. Philip was on the point of bursting into laughter. Although in the throes of a revolution the people of Minorca slept, and when finally a waking member of the liberated populace came along he proved to be a German commercial traveller! The next moment, just as the man passed the alley where they were standing, his desire for laughter ceased. Without uttering a word, but with a smothered hiss, the Grand Duke had sprung from Philip's side and landed by the German. Philip saw his right hand grab the German's right wrist, while with his left he clutched at the man's throat; a quick jerk with his right hand followed, a movement such as the police make when a prisoner resists arrest, while his left closed in a murderous grip. Faintly, but with perfect clearness, Philip heard the German's heavy breathing, and then some words which the Grand Duke uttered in a whisper, but with special emphasis on each and every one:

"Attempt to cry out, Herr Binzer, and I'll strangle you on the spot!"

Although evidently half paralyzed with terror, the German made a last effort to free himself, trying to grab with his left hand first the Grand Duke's throat, then an object in his own back pocket. Philip realized he was fumbling for a revolver, and although he did not yet grasp the meaning of it all, he rushed forward. If the German succeeded in getting hold of his revolver and shooting, it would mean an end to all his plans for recovering his lost fifty thousand pounds and the future of the Republic of Minorca would be assured. . . But before he could even reach the two opponents, the Grand Duke hastily let go his hold on the German's throat, raised his left fist and let it fall like a heavy hammer against the man's right temple. The German fell to the ground as though struck by lightning or by the musketeer Porthos.

With flushed face the Grand Duke turned to Philip.

"You are probably shocked at my forceful methods, Professor, but when you know who this fellow is, then perhaps you may understand the reason."

"Who is he?"

"This," said the Grand Duke, and pointed with his foot to his unconscious adversary, "is Herr Isidor Binzer of Frankfort, and he is the person back of the revolution on Minorca!"

"In that case," said Philip quietly, "I can understand both Your Highness's feelings and mode of action!"

The Grand Duke stared at him in utter astonishment.

"You said your. . . You know who I am?"

"Yes."

"Since when?"

"Since our departure from Marseilles."

The Grand Duke, whose eyes were wide open with surprise, mumbled between his teeth:

"I suspected it; I suspected it. But then. . ."

Philip, who did not consider it an appropriate time to go into details, interrupted him.

"Your Highness has dropped a paper."

He bent toward the ground, where Herr Binzer still lay in the same deathlike stupor and took up a folded sheet of paper which lay by his side.

"Allow me!"

The Grand Duke unfolded the paper and tried to read it in the dim light. It was too dark, however, and he was on the point of putting it in his pocket when Philip came to his rescue with a pocket flashlight. The Grand Duke read it through and then gave a laugh which echoed the length of the whole street.

"Quiet!" whispered Philip, "keep quiet, by all means! Don't let us be surprised here."

"You are right," murmured the Grand Duke in a tone which almost frightened Philip, "but if you only knew what this paper is which you have just given me!"

Philip looked at him curiously, but asked no questions.

"It did not fall out of my pocket," continued the Grand Duke with another short laugh, "but out of Herr Binzer's, and it is nothing less than a contract between him and six of my subjects, who in return for two hundred thousand pesetas cash agree to bring about my downfall and assassination."

Philip's attention was aroused by a slight movement on the part of Herr Binzer.

"We must carry this man Binzer away from here. Does Your Highness know any safe place?"

The Grand Duke, who stood sunk in thought, staring at the contract, hastily came to his senses at Philip's question and looked around. Everything still seemed quiet in the street where they stood, each house presenting the same deathlike appearance; one of them, however, a one-story building a few steps away, looked even more deserted than the rest. The window-panes were broken and the door stood half open as though ready to receive the first passerby who wished to enter. Don Ramon pointed to it silently, and Philip nodded. Still silent, they lifted Herr Binzer and carried him into the dilapidated house. In spite of outward appearances it was not so completely deserted as they had thought, for in one corner of the room stood various articles, brooms, pails, a step-ladder, a lot of empty bottles, and a rope which was dangling from a hook on the wall. Following the same impulse, Philip and the Grand Duke pulled it from the hook and began to bind Herr Binzer. Just as they finished their task this citizen awakened to consciousness; his arms, which were bound behind his back, started to twitch and jerk, and his swollen blue lids began to rise, revealing two eyes, red and inflamed from his fight with the Grand Duke.

He stared in fright at his two enemies, then suddenly his tongue began to move and he whispered hoarsely: "The

Cripple! The Cripple!"

The Grand Duke gave a little laugh.

"Yes, Herr Binzer, the Cripple. The Cripple, who has come back to resume the reins of government. You can cross off your two hundred thousand pesetas as lost, Herr Binzer. The sulphur mines at Punta Hermosa will not be worked with you as director."

Herr Binzer gazed at him with a look of such intense hatred that it infected the Grand Duke.

"Do you know, Herr Binzer," said he, "what my first act of government will be? It will be a law which in your honor shall be called Lex Binzer, and it shall stipulate that no foreigner shall land on Minorca under penalty of a fine of fifty thousand pesetas. If he should be from Frankfort, it shall be under penalty of death."

He had uttered these words in Spanish. Philip, who understood the language fairly well, interposed:

"May I give Your Highness a bit of good advice?"

"What is it?"

"Let the law be retroactive."

Herr Binzer of Frankfort shuddered. The Grand Duke gave a smothered laugh.

"An excellent bit of advice, Professor. If you will lend me your handkerchief, I will insert a gag as the first step toward enforcing the law. Afterwards, we will start off again."

Philip hastened to fulfil his request. The Grand Duke quickly gagged Herr Binzer, who was still too dazed to make any resistance.

After taking the latter's revolver the Grand Duke turned to Philip and said:

"Let us go along, now."

"Where to, Your Highness?"

"To the palace," answered the Grand Duke with a grim smile, "to pay the president a visit."

Philip, who saw his smile, inwardly pitied the president.

If he and the Grand Duke had known in what house it was that they had just left Herr Binzer of Frankfort, perhaps they would not have smiled!

They started off at a quick pace through the long streets leading to Port Mahon's western terraces on whose top the massive silhouette of the palace was outlined against the night sky. The Grand Duke, who time and again looked intently at Philip, frequently seemed on the point of questioning him, but would then restrain himself; and it was in complete silence that they reached the castle terrace. Philip, who was a good pedestrian himself, had to admire the quickness with which his companion, in spite of his affliction, hurried along. He himself was sorely tormented with curiosity and there were a dozen questions trembling on the tip of his tongue about Herr Binzer, the contract and the sulphur mines at Punta Hermosa, but realizing that his best policy was to follow the Grand Duke's example, he kept quiet.

They had reached the edge of the palace square, the trees of which were faintly outlined before them, when a sound made them stop short, the same sound which had brought them to a standstill in the city; the tramping of heels. Carefully tiptoeing along in the shadow of the trees, they succeeded at last in getting near enough to see from whom the sound proceeded.

It came from a sentry marching back and forth at his post in front of the palace gate. President Hernandez did not sleep unguarded among his faithful subjects.

Philip looked questioningly at Don Ramon, and with his lips formed the words:

"Shall we attack him?"

For a moment the Grand Duke stared at the little soldier who wearily patrolled his beat before them. Then he shook his head.

"No, no. He has done nothing wrong. We can turn our strength to better account, and I believe I know of another entrance. If it can still be used."

He took Philip by the hand and carefully led the way back, turned off to the left into the palace garden and after a while stopped before a small door half concealed by ivy.

"I used to run out this way as a boy," he murmured, "when the culinary regions seemed to me the most interesting part of the palace, even though they were not especially well provisioned. We will see if it can still be used."

He put his powerful shoulder against the little door and pushed a few times; suddenly the lock creaked and snapped. The old rusty latch had broken, and the way was clear before them.

As the Grand Duke was on the point of going in he

stopped suddenly.

"One moment," said he. "Here is where I bid you good-bye."

"Good-bye! Nothing of the kind, Your Highness."

"Yes, for it may be dangerous. If I risk my life, it does not matter, since it is mine, but I have no right to risk yours. Return to the harbor and go on board. Let the *Stork* stand out to sea. If I succeed, I will send you word in the morning. If I fail, then. . . remember me to old Paqueno and Madame Pelotard."

Philip felt his heart beat quicker. By Zeus, this was a man! Alone, armed only with a revolver, he intended to seek out the enemy in his stronghold and subdue a crowd of rebels, to whom his death meant everything! No matter what his faults had been, he made ample amends for a large part through what he did to-night! Philip shook his head resolutely.

"Your Highness," said he, "the Press has its duties too. Among other things it must always be on hand when anything happens. As its representative I feel obliged to accompany Your Highness and chronicle the events of the night."

"And if I shut the door on you?"

"Then I will go in by the main entrance, and we will meet in the hall."

The Grand Duke gave a laugh and grasped Philip's hand.

"My respect for the Press has risen a hundred per cent to-night," said he. "Come along, if you wish!"

Plunging into darkness as black as night they groped their way along the passage leading from the small door to the kitchens. Step by step, with infinite care, they continued from there to the hall of the palace. A solitary lamp was smoking at the end of the room nearest to the square. Outside could be heard the regular muffled tread of the sentry on guard. Philip drew out his pocket flashlight and for a moment let the light shine on his watch. It was five minutes past ten.

Silently, with a litheness one would not have suspected possible in such a gigantic body, the Grand Duke crept forward to listen at the row of doors in the hall, A bitter smile flew over his face as he looked at them; on each and every one the old grand-ducal coat-of-arms had been daubed over with coarse paint, and suddenly on one he noticed a visiting card! He hardly needed to bend forward and read it to know what name it bore.

"Professor," he whispered with a nod to Philip. "This is where the president lives. You will find his visiting card on the door!"

Philip hastily tip-toed over, staring at the eloquent bit of white cardboard. Then both listened intently. Only the faint sound of a solitary person's step could be heard from within, and following an irresistible impulse Philip suddenly raised his hand and knocked. Steps could be heard hastily approaching from the other side, then the door opened, and there appeared on the threshold, standing clear in the lamplight, President Luis Hernandez himself.

Philip had quickly pushed the Grand Duke behind the door as it opened and now bowed serenely to Señor Hernandez.

"Good evening, Mr. President!" said he. "As you see, I have not waited until to-morrow to discuss our plans. I have taken the liberty of calling to-night."

The president's face, which at first had expressed amazement and suspicion gradually cleared as he recognized Philip.

"Ah," he replied with an air of dignity. "You are right. It is late, but you come at an opportune moment—I am just awaiting my friends—my fellow-workers. Come in, Mr. Pelotard!"

"Thanks, Mr. President," said Philip, and slowly drew nearer, "but the truth of the matter is, I did not come alone. I have brought a friend with me!"

CHAPTER 4

In Which The Existence Of The Republic Of Minorca Seems Gravely Threatened

"A friend?" repeated Señor Hernandez uncomprehendingly. "I thought you were alone on the boat. Have you friends in Minorca?"

"I have one," said Philip with an involuntary quiver in his voice, and grasped the Grand Duke's hand behind the half open door. "A person who wishes to pay you his respects, Mr. President."

Señor Hernandez stepped back in the room and looked at him with a glance which had suddenly grown suspicious again.

"How did you get by the sentry?" he cried. "Who is your friend? Tell me his name immediately!"

"His name," cried Philip, rushing into the room, "is Don Ramon XX of Minorca, whom you and your friends undertook to murder for the sum of 200,000 pesetas, and who has come back to watch you count your chickens before they're hatched!"

While he was uttering these words in an ever louder tone, Señor Hernandez turned and rushed toward a desk on whose corner lay a black shining object which Philip instantly saw was a revolver. There was a time when Philip was considered the best football player at one of the Swedish universities, that was long ago; but at sight of the article, instincts which had been slumbering long in Philip's soul awakened quick as lightning. He made three springs of which he might well have been proud twelve years before; at the very moment the presumptive President of Minorca threw out his hand to grasp the revolver, Philip's right foot arose in a stately kick; the next second the little Browning whizzed with a curve through the air and landed ten metres away at the other end of the room. However, it must be stated that Philip's foot, probably obeying certain dim laws of physics, did not stop after this fine performance, but continued its course until it suddenly came in contact with the President of Minorca's nose. Then it sank to earth, and while the Grand Duke roaring with mingled laughter and anger hurried forward, the President of the Republic of Minorca uttered a cry of pain and fell in a heap across the desk.

"Well done, Professor!" cried the Grand Duke. "Silence there, you, or I'll kill you outright without further fuss! Silence, I say."

His voice was so terrible that Señor Hernandez' cry of pain stopped as quickly as though his throat had been cut;

trembling all over, he arose from the table, looked at his ruler and then sank on his knees, while the blood gushed from his nose.

"M-mercy, Your Highness!" he panted, "Mercy! I had no part in the conspiracy. . . I swear it. . ."

The Grand Duke looked at him his eyes blazing with contempt.

"Then you swear falsely, you damned scoundrel. How does it happen that you have settled down here in my palace? Answer me! Is it because you had no part in the conspiracy?"

"Th-they thought of choosing me as p-president," mumbled Señor Hernandez with a snuffle.

"And you assumed the dignity in advance! But how does it happen" (the Grand Duke's voice again became terrifying) "that your name stands first in this contract?"

He suddenly pulled out the paper which had fallen from Herr Binzer's pocket and held it before the eyes of the presumptive president. Señor Hernandez became paler than death and for a moment it seemed as though the blood from his nose even stopped flowing. Then, without a word, he threw himself prostrate at the Grand Duke's feet and tried to grasp his knees as though begging for mercy. With a rough movement Don Ramon freed himself and said to Philip:

"Will you go to the room at the further end of the hall? I believe you will find some rope there."

"A-am I to be hung?" stammered Señor Hernandez

while big tears began to trickle down his swollen nose and mix with the still-flowing blood.

"Yes, later," said the Grand Duke, "if the courts so decree. I am no murderer, Señor Luis, like you and your friends. For the present you are to be bound. Dry your nose with this."

He threw him a handkerchief and continued:

"Now, tell me one thing, but tell me the truth! When do you expect your friends?"

Señor Hernandez' whimpering had stopped as he heard he was not to be executed on the spot. He cast a sly, wary glance at Don Ramon and began:

"I don't know... In an hour..."

The Grand Duke's brow clouded over like the heavens before a thunder-storm. It was plain as day that the fellow was lying, that he was planning some sort of trick and that his friends were coming at any moment.

"Luis Hernandez," said he, "I had thought in case the courts should sentence you to death, to make use of my power of pardoning. After the six words and two lies you have just uttered, your fate is sealed."

With the skill born of experience, he and Philip quickly transformed the President of Minorca into an easily handled package which, provided with a gag, they placed in the next room. Then the Grand Duke closed the door and said:

"Evidently we can expect Señor Luis' friends at any moment. I am afraid we will have a more difficult task with them than with the President. Have you not changed your mind yet about taking part in such a thankless job as mine?"

Philip shook his head and smiled inwardly, like another Ulysses. He knew better than his companion at arms how far from thankless this job should be for him. Fifty thousand pounds that had been lost, were looming up within reach! The Grand Duke looked at him thoughtfully.

"You are a brave man, Professor," said he. "Do you mind telling me, are you French or English?"

"My mother was French," Philip answered, "but I am neither French nor English, Your Highness. I am Swedish."

"Swedish, by St. Urban! You are the first of that nationality I have met, but I hope not the last. Lex Binzer will never apply to you!"

"Pardon me," interrupted Philip with a slight laugh, "but shouldn't we be preparing to meet our guests instead of exchanging diplomatic compliments? Since I am without a weapon and its owner can no longer make use of this, I will start by appropriating President Hernandez' revolver. Do you think we will have many visitors?"

"I have no idea. Señor Luis' inborn disposition for lying makes it useless to question him. Here on the contract are six names of which his is one. Therefore we can expect five gentlemen if only the leaders come. And one of the five is a very dangerous fellow. Posada is his name, sergeant of the body-guard."

"Does Your Highness think we should wait in here? Would it not be better out in the hall?"

"You are right! It is better in the hall. We can count our

enemies as they come in and attack when we choose."

The Grand Duke and Philip hurried into the hall and looked around for strategic points of operation. After short deliberation they decided to move the lamp, which lighted up the furthest part of the hall, to a place between the entrance door and the president's room. Then they stationed themselves at the lower end of the hall where it was now dark, and started in to await events.

For several minutes nothing happened. The Grand Duke leaned over to Philip and whispered:

"You are Swedish—is your wife Swedish, too?"

"No, Your Highness, madame is Russian."

"And are you not afraid to help me in this undertaking after what I said about myself on the boat?"

A smile, which the Duke could not see on account of the darkness, flitted over Philip's face. Then, before he could answer, came the sound for which they had been waiting.

Steps were heard outside; two or perhaps three persons conversing together were approaching the palace. Another sound immediately followed: the challenging of the sentry as they approached. A few hasty words were exchanged then a deep voice was heard saying:

"All right, you can keep watch on the lower terrace. We will look out for things here ourselves."

With a "Yes, señor!" the little soldier could be heard starting off, and the next moment the door to the hall of the palace opened.

Three persons stepped over the threshold, closed the

door, and hastily walked in the direction of the room which the Grand Duke and Philip had left a few minutes before.

Philip, who strained his eyes to see what the modern descendants of Danton, Marat and Robespierre looked like, gave a low whistle of astonishment. He had never seen greater contrasts than these three figures offered. The first was a broad, thick-set man with a big black full beard; the second was thin and hollow-eyed, and dressed in a sort of monk's robe which vividly resembled a Lutheran pastor's ceremonial costume: instead of being ankle-length as the monks' robes usually are, it only came to its wearer's knees; below it his hairy muscular legs were bare. Walking beside these two was a third figure, which in the dim lamp-light, most of all resembled some deformed insect; it was a hunchback, not taller than a twelve-year old boy, with a body the shape of an egg and long, thin spindle-legs. Philip glanced quickly at the Grand Duke as though asking what they should do.

At the same moment the latter, holding Herr Binzer's revolver in his hand, lifted his arm, and a report rang out in the little hall. The three conspirators jumped as though struck by lightning and turned around: facing them was the man they had undertaken to murder for the sum of two hundred thousand pesetas, and Mr. Philip Collin, both of whom held them covered with their revolvers. Then the Grand Duke's voice thundered out:

"Up with your hands! Quick, or we shoot to kill!"

For the fraction of a second it seemed as though the

man with the black beard and his hollow-eyed friend hesitated in spite of the revolvers which were levelled at them; the hunchback, for his part, had obeyed with a celerity which left nothing to be desired. Then, as the Grand Duke's finger slightly pressed the trigger of his revolver, their hands too flew silently in the air, while the look in their eyes fully expressed their feelings for Don Ramon. The Grand Duke turned to Philip and said:

"Professor, will you kindly search these gentlemen and see if they carry any weapons. Begin with the worthy Father Ignacio in the picturesque robe. Or would you prefer I did it?"

"Certainly not, Your Highness."

Philip hastened over to where the three stood and deftly began to empty the deposed priest's pockets. The contents were varied, and extended from the revolutionist's inevitable revolver, which Philip stuffed in his own pocket, to a bundle of bank notes and a varied collection of relics, which he returned.

"All right," cried the Grand Duke after Philip had convinced himself that Father Ignacio had been deprived of all his fangs. "Next: Sergeant Posada!"

The sergeant's pockets were found to contain nothing but two revolvers and some gold coins. Philip proceeded with him as with the priest, and then turned to the hunchback whose blood-shot eyes followed Philip's every motion as he drew out a fourth revolver and a knife of respectable size. Then Philip turned to the Grand Duke.

"I'll get some rope, Your Highness, so that we can bind these gentlemen and let the president enjoy some company in his solitude."

He rushed off for a coil of rope. Out of respect for the Church he began with Ignacio, and in another five minutes the holy man was as helpless as could be wished. Philip was on the point of proceeding to the sergeant when events hastily took a different turn.

The hunchbacked inn-keeper standing furthest to the left had very quickly noticed that it was his two companions who principally drew the attention of the Grand Duke. Softly and without attracting any notice he slunk away from where he stood by the sergeant's side. The distance between them grew larger and larger and the Grand Duke did not seem to notice. Then, at the moment Philip reverently placed Father Ignacio on the floor, Señor Amadeo found the occasion propitious to carry out his little scheme. Quickly and silently, like one of the insects he resembled, he made three or four springs toward the doorway to the square; by the time the Grand Duke noticed his manoeuvre and aimed his revolver at him, he had opened the heavy door; the next moment he was outside and the bullet from Don Ramon's revolver met no other obstacle to its flight than the panel of the old door.

The ensuing events followed even more quickly. The black-bearded sergeant who, all the time, had stood panting like a royal tiger and ready to spring forward, needed nothing more than Amadeo's flight to bring him into action. Like a great beast of prey, with bared teeth and with a hoarse roar, he threw himself against Don Ramon; before the Grand Duke could turn after his shot at the innkeeper, the sergeant's arms were around him and together they rolled over and over on the stone floor of the hall. The revolver fell from the Grand Duke's hand and it became simply a battle of muscle against muscle. But they were muscles which were worthy of each other and if the Grand Duke was somewhat heavier, this greater weight was more than offset by the black sergeant's rage. He knew he was fighting not only for life but for the success of his own plans.

And it really looked as though the sergeant would win; Philip watched the spectacle, not daring to use his revolver; the two fighters were rolling over each other so quickly that he might just as likely hit the last member of the House of Ramiros with his shot. Father Ignacio, at his feet, began a sort of exorcismal chant which sounded doubly weird in the dim light of the hall.

At last, after watching idly for perhaps a minute, Philip determined to mix in; but as he came nearer the Grand Duke hoarsely mumbled:

"Keep away, Professor. I'll attend to this myself."

At the moment he seemed to have the best of it, then their positions changed quickly and the sergeant, whose eyes were half popping out of their sockets with thirst for blood, got the upper hand. Just as Philip, in spite of the Grand Duke's command to the contrary, was about to interfere, the black sergeant partly freed himself, and with teeth bared and jaws wide open for attack his bearded face flew up toward Don Ramon's throat. Philip let out a cry and Don Ramon made a quick movement; the teeth slipped by their mark and closed on the Grand Duke's right ear, which they had half torn off before Don Ramon, with a last gigantic effort, got one hand around the sergeant's throat and thrice in succession slammed his head on the stone floor. The man's brutish muscles suddenly relaxed, his body twitched a few times and then lay still. With the blood streaming down his cheek, and his breast heaving and panting the Grand Duke arose.

"A dangerous fellow, as I said, Professor! If you will get the rope we will bind him."

"But Your Highness' ear!"

"That can wait until later."

Philip hurriedly brought the rope and in passing silenced Father Ignacio's chanting with a gesture of his revolver. They quickly bound the sergeant with a double thickness of rope. Philip proposed they should put it directly around his neck and lower him through the window to a fitting distance from the ground, but Don Ramon refused.

Thereupon Philip helped the Grand Duke wash the gaping wound caused by the sergeant's teeth and applied a temporary bandage. They were hardly through with this when Don Ramon gave a cry.

"What's the matter, Your Highness?"

"My servants, those two fine fellows!" cried the Grand

Duke. "I had forgotten all about them! If the scoundrels have murdered them, I will shoot them on the spot without bothering about trial and sentence. My big-hearted Joaquin and my honest Auguste!" He went over to Father Ignacio who now lay silent and immovable, merely mumbling to himself now and then.

"Where are Joaquin and Auguste? What have you done to them? Answer, you ornament to the church!"

"Maledictus in aeternum, maledictus, maledictus!" chanted the priest looking at Don Ramon with blazing eyes. "Maledictus in nomine Patris, et Filii et Spiritus Sancti! Nefaste princeps, perinde, perinde ac cadaver!"

The Grand Duke shrugged his shoulders and proceeded toward the room where they had put President Hernandez.

"I am afraid that Father Ignacio will have to atone for his crimes in a madhouse. We must question the president."

As he said this Philip noticed for the first time that he limped more than usual.

"Have you hurt your foot, Your Highness?"

"I must have wrenched it when the sergeant fell on me. Don't worry, Professor! It doesn't matter. It makes me more symmetrical now, limping on both legs."

They found Señor Hernandez staring up listlessly from the floor. He seemed absolutely stunned by the events of the evening and at first did not even give a sign of understanding the Grand Duke's questions.

"Hernandez," said the Grand Duke, "you have an old father who has always been the direct opposite of yourself—an honorable and industrious man. For his sake, I will once more reconsider what is to become of you, but only on condition that you immediately tell me what you have done with Auguste and Joaquin! Do you understand?"

It took more than half a minute before the former president seemed to realize what had been said. Then big tears began to run down his cheeks and he snuffled:

"In the little hunting lodge, Your Highness, in the little hunting lodge. . ."

"You damned scoundrels!" roared the Grand Duke. "In the little hunting lodge which has not been used for thirty years and which is overrun with rats! What did Joaquin and Auguste ever do to you? You damned scoundrels!"

The president did not seem to hear him and the tears continued to flow down his face in a steady stream. The Grand Duke made a wry face and went out with Philip.

"Professor," said he, "if you would like to do me a great service, then look up my poor servants and set them free. I am afraid it is impossible for me to go with you. My head is whirling around a little after all this wrestling and my foot is causing me some trouble, too. Probably you can get to them without difficulty."

"With or without, doesn't matter," Philip answered. "But where is the little hunting lodge?"

"You will easily find it if you go directly down through the palace gardens which we passed as we came in. The lodge is white and it is not too dark for you to see it. Have you a good sense of direction?"

"Excellent," said Philip. "*Au revoir,* Your Highness."

After quickly grasping his hand, Philip hurried away.

As he went out he saw the Grand Duke wearily throw himself on a chair in the hall. A few feet from him on the floor was the deposed priest, still chanting. At the lower end of the hall lay the black sergeant as immovable as before.

Philip little thought how the room would look when he should enter again.

CHAPTER 5

The Grand Duke Shall Be Hung.
Long Live The Grand Duke!

As Don Ramon sat down, he felt far worse than he let Philip imagine. The fight with the black sergeant had exhausted him; the foot which he had wrenched bothered him twice as much now that he was alone, and his lacerated ear burned like fire. It was almost as though the sergeant's teeth had been poisoned, there was such a smarting throb to the wound.

Don Ramon cast a glance at the two prisoners in the hall; they both lay in the same position they had been placed. The raving song of the priest had stopped and he now lay with his head twisted toward the Grand Duke, staring at him with a hard, burning look. The sergeant, somewhat further away, still seemed unconscious. Don Ramon went over to him and made sure that the ropes had not loosened. Then he returned to his chair which he pulled out from the wall and lit a cigar which he had found practically undamaged in one of his pockets.

Confused pictures of all that had happened in the last

few days rose up in his mind: his departure with Paqueno, the telegram about the coup on the exchange which had reached them at the last moment; and after their arrival in Barcelona the vain attempts to solve the mystery... Then, later on, Marseilles and the news about the revolution just as they were on the point of starting for Paris, to see Semjon Marcowitz... The revolution... They must have planned it to take place on the very day after his departure from Minorca; truly Chance had played a trick on them! He could well imagine their looks when they found the palace empty of all but Joaquin and Auguste! Did the people know he had escaped! Or had the news been kept secret in order to make the position of the leaders more secure? It was not impossible that even the leaders knew nothing about his departure, and that therefore his appearance to-night frightened them so much the more... His appearance to-night... thanks to that man the Professor... A Swedish Professor with a French name and a Russian wife!... Suddenly the conviction came over him again that the Professor knew more than he had said—that perhaps it was around him that the mystery circled; then he drove these thoughts away. It was true the Professor had recognized him, but there was nothing strange in that... and it was true his wife was extraordinarily interested in the Grand Duke of Minorca... Don Ramon interrupted his train of thought; it must not enter on that subject! He was not what one might call a ladies' man—he had never been; but in the few hours he had known this young woman he had noticed with surprise how quickly she had taken possession of his thoughts. She was so open, impulsive, unaffected; she had the charm of a wild bird. . . and she was so beautiful, too. . . And she was the wife of another, too—wife of the man whom he himself had to thank for his success that night. . .

Don Ramon gave a start. His cigar had gone out; he lighted it again.

. . . His success that night. Yes, it was now fairly assured. Binzer, Luis Hernandez, Posada, and Father Ignacio were the real leaders, he did not doubt that for a moment. After they had been rendered powerless the others could not cause him any difficulty. Amadeo for example! The ugly little reptile had escaped but it would not help him on the morrow! The three others on Herr Binzer's contract, Vatello and whatever their names might be, he knew absolutely nothing about, but they had surely been drawn into the affair by the gentlemen whom he had already rendered harmless. . . Poor Joaquin and Auguste—wasn't the Professor taking a long time?

Don Ramon roused himself again: he had been on the point of falling asleep in his chair! That wouldn't do. He must at least keep awake until the Professor came back. How about that? Weren't there some bottles of cognac in Joaquin's pantry some time ago? A glass of cognac was just what he needed to start the blood flowing in his veins once more and make him forget the pain in his foot and head. He arose with a stagger, threw the stump of his cigar away, and went over to that part of the hall where he and the

Professor had first entered. There Joaquin had fitted up a small closet as pantry. He opened the door and peeped in: the place was dark as the grave. He leaned forward and felt his way with his hands, for he had forgotten how it looked inside. There was a small table in the middle and a cupboard on each side. The table was bare; he began to grope around in the cup boards. On the upper shelves he found nothing. He kneeled down with his leg partly outside the closet and began to fumble around with his hands on the lower shelves.

At last he grasped a bottle which he could hear contained some liquid; he partly rose from his stooping position and smelled of the bottle. Yes, that seemed to be cognac all right.

He put the bottle to his mouth intending to take a swallow. . .

At the same moment he felt a stinging blow as some hard object hit him on the back of the head; the bottle fell from his hand; everything seemed to go around and around, and fumbling with his hands before him, he fell forward into the darkness.

* * *

When he came to his senses again he at first was conscious only of his head which kept whirring and snapping as though it were an induction-machine while a thousand red and white dots danced before his eyes like so many shooting stars. Then he became conscious of something else: he sat tightly bound to a chair; the rope cut into his throat and into his ankles, the right one feeling as though it were screwed into a vise; and round about him, indistinct as the distant roar of the sea, he heard the murmur of many voices.

Still half-stunned with pain, he wearily half opened one eye and looked around.

He was in the hall where he had shortly before kept watch over Father Ignacio and the black sergeant and on the very same chair where he had lately been sitting. Round about him, watching him, shrieking, laughing and swearing, pushing this way and that were a crowd of people, whom in his confused state his eyes at first refused to recognize; then partly through the help of his eyes which began to see more clearly, partly through the shouts and cries hailing about him, he realized who these people were! And the first one he recognized was the man who two hours before he had left tightly bound and equipped with a gag in a deserted house on one of the streets: Herr Binzer of Frankfort!

But it was not Herr Binzer's voice which gave him the explanation of what had happened; it was that of the innkeeper Amadeo. With gleaming eyes, his coarse straggling hair on end, the little hunchback was dancing up and down on the floor before the others, whom Don Ramon gradually succeeded in counting. There were six, but with the exception of Herr Binzer he only recognized three of them. These were Luis Hernandez, the sergeant and Father Ignacio.

"It is I, comrades, it is I, Señores, I, Amadeo of the 'Commandante'! If it had not been for me—what would have happened to you? What, I ask? Before to-morrow night you would all have been shot, all of you, Father Ignacio, Eugenio, the great Luis and Señor Binzer himself. Yes, Señor Binzer himself! Do you know where I found Señor Binzer? Bound up in my storehouse, in my old storehouse; bound up and absolutely helpless!"

"Yes, yes," came the German's voice, harsh and hard as usual. "But who was it that brought back your courage and made you seek our friends here?" He pointed to the three persons Don Ramon did not know. "It was I, whom you found so helpless, who did all that. And," pointing to the Grand Duke, "who was it who led the way here and struck down that fellow there?"

Don Ramon suddenly felt a little energy return to his aching body as he heard this last boast of his enemy. With an effort he found his tongue.

"If it was you, Señor Binzer," said he, "then I promise you shall hang for it before to-morrow night."

"Hang!" Herr Binzer, who now first noticed that Don Ramon had returned to consciousness, rushed over to where the Grand Duke sat bound. "Hang, did you say? There is one who shall hang, my friend, but that one is you!"

He stopped for a moment, overcome with rage and with bloodshot eyes stared at his enemy while his blond eyebrows began to bristle.

"You!" he shrieked. "You damned poorhouse Duke! You

shall hang—like any other criminal. Do you remember what you did to me a short time ago? You hit me in the face—here is your pay for it! And here! And for to-night!"

Beside himself with rage, he began to shower blows on his tightly bound opponent, on his face, on his cheeks, on his wounded ear from which Philip's bandage had been torn away. The others had grown silent. In spite of everything some feelings of respect, inherited through the centuries, remained for the princely house; only Amadeo laughed wildly. At last Luis came forward and tried to drag Herr Binzer away. His movements were almost like those of a somnambulist.

"Señor Binzer," he murmured, "Señor Binzer, later! First we must have the trial. . ."

The other stopped, still wild with rage, and Don Ramon, who in vain had made titanic efforts to free himself of his bonds, followed him with a terrible look in his eyes which were half-dimmed with blood.

"Herr Binzer," said he, "I already knew that you were cowardly, but I have received confirmation of the fact. Before to-morrow night you will atone for this through death."

His voice and looks were so fear-inspiring that the rest became silent and for a moment looked timorously at one another. Did the Grand Duke have means of help at his command about which they knew nothing? Where did he come from, anyway? Those who already had taken part in the evening's events had seen him suddenly appear like an avenging angel, and during two hours' time almost put an end to the revolution on Minorca. On the others, who only had heard tell about it all, the effect had been almost as frightening. Could what he had done be explained in any other way than that he had several accomplices about whom they knew nothing? Amadeo and one of the three persons whom Don Ramon did not know quickly exchanged a few words and then hurried over to the main door, which they locked and bolted.

During this time Luis, still wearing the same absent-minded expression, and the sergeant, whose eyes kept roaming over the Grand Duke, held a short consultation with Herr Binzer. Father Ignacio kept on chanting to himself, every now and then making wild gestures with his arms. Finally Luis came over to the Grand Duke, followed by the others, who stood around in a half-circle.

"We wish to know," said Luis, "who the other person was who took part in all this."

Don Ramon answered coldly: "You will know before to-morrow night when you all are to be hanged."

Luis, growing pale, continued:

"We know that he arrived this afternoon in a small yacht. I myself visited the yacht but neglected to find out whether there were other passengers. . ."

"You damned ass!" exclaimed Herr Binzer.

"Were you there, too?" Luis concluded.

"Are you talking to me in that fashion, Luis?" asked the Grand Duke.

"Yes, answer my question!" Luis' voice was far from steady; it could be seen that he was trying to keep up his courage before the others.

"Then call me Your Highness, Luis, if you expect an answer. Mercy you cannot expect hereafter."

Luis suddenly began to tremble all over and the next moment was pushed aside by the black sergeant.

"Were you on the yacht or not? Answer," he roared, "and no tricks!"

The Grand Duke gave him a scornful look and was on the point of answering him in the same manner as he had Luis, when a thought suddenly came into his head.

There was no sense in provoking them. All was not lost as long as the professor was free! The professor and his own two servants! If they could be given sufficient time the tables could still be turned at the last minute. At the same moment he was struck by another inspiration.

With a quiet look at those gathered about him, he said:

"I was on the yacht. But there was something else beside me which your friend Hernandez forgot to notice."

"What was that?" cried the sergeant.

"That the boat is equipped with wireless telegraphy. Have you heard about wireless telegraphy?"

There was silence for a couple of seconds. The conspirators stared at each other, half uncertain what Don Ramon meant, half frightened at the hidden threat which seemed to lie in his words. Herr Binzer was probably the only one who really understood what it all signified, and to their terror, the others noticed that he quickly seemed to lose some of his self-assurance.

"Before we went on land," continued the Grand Duke, laying stress on every word, "we got into wireless communication with an English cruiser and told them everything. You will have them down on you before morning, gentlemen, and I congratulate you then!"

Again for a few seconds it was absolutely quiet in the room. The Grand Duke seemed to have more than achieved his purpose. All were familiar with the sight of those immense British and French battleships which often stopped at the island on their cruises through the Mediterranean, and all had heard hair-raising reports about their shooting ability. If the Grand Duke was speaking the truth, it would not be long then before punishment would be upon them—and from his entire manner they had no doubt he was speaking the truth... Luis turned pale as death and the others stared with frightened glances at the Grand Duke, whose face, bloody and bruised from Herr Binzer's assault, was more awe-inspiring than ever; and then finally they stared at Herr Binzer, the father of this revolution, which now seemed on the point of ending so disastrously.

After a pause of perhaps a couple of minutes, Herr Binzer began to realize what fate might lie in wait for an unfortunate instigator of a revolution. First there was a mumbling from the innkeeper Amadeo and the three men Don Ramon did not know; then Luis' voice, half snuffling with fright, blended with the murmuring, and at last came the black sergeant's roaring bass. "Down with the German!" "He is the cause of it all!" "The devil take him—the stingy coward!" "What good would the revolution do us?" It seemed as though Don Ramon had played his cards better than he had dared hope; cries of "Mercy, Your Highness!" began to be heard here and there; then with a last effort Herr Binzer managed to make his voice heard.

"Comrades," he cried, "don't be cowardly! Are you begging mercy of him? This is the way I treat persons like him" (he lifted his hand but stopped before the new expression he saw on the faces of his fellow conspirators) "—if I want to," added Herr Binzer. "Are you going to let him frighten you with his story about wireless telegraphy? He is lying, that is all! And what of it, if he is speaking the truth? If an English cruiser does show up before morning—will we be treated any better because we have begged for mercy? Hasn't he sworn that we shall all hang before to-morrow night? If you are to prevent it, comrades—there is only one way: for you to hang him immediately! Dead men tell no tales! If you hang him and scuttle the boat he came in, I would like to see the English cruiser which can prove anything against us. Let us hang him now, and then start for the harbor!"

Herr Binzer stopped and the Grand Duke saw with a mixed feeling of rage and indifference that the German had won his point; the faces of all had brightened up at his words. Don Ramon had promised they should all hang, and if he was found alive when the cruiser came then they might be sure he would keep his word. Herr Binzer was right! Don Ramon must be hung then and there and his yacht sunk! Then the cruiser could come!

A wild murmur arose, growing louder and louder: Don Ramon was pulled out of his chair and the black sergeant threw off the coat to his uniform; there was no doubt he intended to assume the duties of executioner. He turned to Father Ignacio who was still singing and mumbling to himself in a corner, and cried:

"Here, Ignacio, your help is needed here! Come, and read the prayers for the dead over the last Grand Duke of Minorca! Confess him, Ignacio!"

"Maledictus, maledictus in externum!" the deposed priest chanted. "Nefaste inter homines, perinde ac cadaver! Maledictus, maledictus!"

Suddenly, just as the innkeeper Amadeo, assisted by two of the others, was preparing to put up a ladder and fasten the rope on a hook in the ceiling, three heavy blows were heard on the door, the sound rising above the noise and shouting of the general excitement.

For a moment silence reigned and there was a clutch of dread at the Grand Duke's heart: it was the professor returning just in time to witness the execution. What would his fate be?

Then the black sergeant sprang over to the door and cried in a loud voice:

"Who is there?"

"I, the sentry from the lower terrace," came the indistinct answer. "There is someone here asking about the way to the Grand-Ducal Palace!"

The sergeant drew back the bolt and opened the door, evidently without understanding what it was all about. Then he turned and burst into laughter.

"A little señorita," he cried, "coming to see the palace at this time of night! Thank Goodness we can show her something worth seeing!"

The door opened wide; a man in uniform could be seen outside, and a lady stepped over the threshold. The next moment as she came in line with the light from the hall, Don Ramon thought he would lose his reason.

It was Madame Pelotard.

She looked around, evidently at a loss to understand what was going on. All stared at her.

No one noticed that Luis Hernandez quietly slipped through the door and disappeared in the night.

CHAPTER 6

In Which The Republic Of Minorca's Reign Of Terror Finds Its Bonaparte

Calling out to the soldier to resume his watch, the black sergeant shut the door, and then turned with a grin to the young woman. She was still standing a couple of steps from the entrance; her eyes were wide open with astonishment as her glance wandered from one to the other of the strange gathering. It was evident that she was torn between surprise, fear and a desire to appear brave. Another grin cleaved the sergeant's black beard.

"To what do we owe this pleasure? Is it possible that you also came on the mysterious yacht, Señorita?"

She cast a frightened glance at him and turned her eyes away; the next second she caught sight of the Grand Duke. She quickly sprang forward, but checked herself almost immediately. Was she seeing right? Did that bruised and bloody face belong to the man she knew? And if she were seeing right, why was he sitting there bound in the midst of these beings who frightened her so that she almost felt like crying!

"Count!" she cried in French. "Is it you? Why are you bound? Why have they hit you? Tell me!"

Don Ramon had not yet recovered from the paralyzing feeling of pain and surprise which had come over him. It was she! And she would be looking on when he. . .

"Madame Pelotard," he answered in a half-choked voice, "it is really I. . . you are seeing correctly. . . but how did you get here? This is the most bitter hour of my life."

"I went on land with Captain Dupont," she faltered. "We were both uneasy. . . we could not understand what was delaying you. . . Somewhere in the town I became separated from the Captain, and I knew no other place where I might find anybody except at the palace. . . I found my way here, because I knew the outline of the castle. . . Then the soldier stopped me. . . But what has happened, Count, tell me? What are they doing to you? Why are you bound?"

The Grand Duke looked at her, at a loss to prepare her for the events about to happen, when he was suddenly relieved of all trouble in this respect by a third person—Herr Binzer of Frankfort.

Herr Binzer was not especially proficient in French, but he knew enough of that language to understand at least a third of what the Grand Duke and the new arrival were saying to each other. He burst out laughing.

"Aha," he shrieked. "Your Highness has been travelling incognito! Your Highness is a Count! Señorita, let me enlighten you on one subject: this gentleman whom you call Count does not bear that title!"

She looked at Herr Binzer with flashing eyes and said in broken Spanish:

"Is not a Count? Who are you?"

"You shall hear both that and more," cried Herr Binzer. "I, Señorita, am only a poor business man of Frankfort, but one who has been grossly injured by this gentleman who is not a Count. And five minutes from now, Señorita, your friend, this false Count, is to be hung!"

Herr Binzer laughed heartily at his own words. Breathing heavily, the young woman repeated: "To be hung. . . why should the Count be hung?"

Rubbing his hands with an air of satisfaction, Herr Binzer answered:

"For just the reason I told you, Señorita—because he is not a Count! Ha, ha! Yes, for just that reason!"

"Who is he, then?"

"He is—no, he *was* Grand Duke of Minorca, and his name, Señorita, if perhaps you do not know it, is Don Ramon XX!"

Herr Binzer cried this out in a voice which echoed through the hall, but if he had expected his words would have the same crushing effect as before he was greatly mistaken. The young woman drew herself up like a queen and cried to the prisoner on the chair:

"Is he telling the truth? Are you the Grand Duke of Minorca?"

Don Ramon smiled at the expression on her face, and waited a little before he answered.

"Since Herr Binzer has unmasked me, it is not worthwhile my denying it. I have been sailing under false colors, Madame! I am the Grand Duke of Minorca—and you have come just in time to see me hung by my faithful subjects!"

She almost laughed as she answered:

"Of course not! I have come just in time to save you from them! In five minutes you shall be free!"

"Ah, Madame Pelotard, you are as optimistic as ever! You do not know my faithful people if you believe you can save me so easily."

Herr Binzer broke in:

"His Highness, my dear lady, knows us better than you. For once he is right. And now enough of this. Is the hook firm, comrades? We must hurry if we are to finish everything. Are you ready?"

Amadeo and the men, who for several minutes had done nothing but stare at the mysterious visitor, gave a start and turned hastily toward the improvised gallows. They tested it by jerking the rope a couple of times.

"We are ready!"

"Good!"

Without wasting time on further questions, Herr Binzer gave a sign to the black sergeant. The cords which bound the Grand Duke to the chair were loosened, while every care was taken not to touch those around his arms and legs. He was dragged toward the improvised gallows where Amadeo and the others were waiting. Suddenly the rigidness which had seemed to bind Madame Pelotard disappeared; she rushed forward and with flashing eyes placed herself in the way of Herr Binzer and the black sergeant.

"Wretches!" she cried in her broken Spanish. "How dare you lay hands on your ruler! It isn't possible!"

"Señorita," cried the sergeant, "step aside. We will attend to you later—after the execution!"

She stared at him half petrified.

"You mean that you dare—that you dare?"

"That is precisely what we mean. Out of the way!" His brutal violence had an effect which neither he nor the others could have expected. She took a step back, lifted her hands, and cried pantingly:

"I have something to say—you must listen! You are on the point of committing a hideous crime—of murdering your ruler... How much do you demand for his life? A hundred thousand pesetas—is that enough? They are yours! Twenty thousand for each and every one of you!"

She stopped. Her words produced a stronger effect than anything else she could have said. Money was a magical word to these wild, poor souls. A hundred thousand pesetas!—Twenty thousand for each and every one of them! It grew silent in the hall, except for the mumbling of the crazy priest. All stared at one another: a hundred thousand... Don Ramon turned red, then pale, thinking furiously. Where could the professor be? Had he been unable to find the lodge? It must have been an hour since he left.

As long as he was at liberty everything was not lost... and if she could win time by offering them money, why... He looked about him: all faces in that strange circle bore the same stamp, they were torn between avariciousness and fear. What would have happened if they had been left to themselves is uncertain; but there was one among them who did not have the same reason for hesitancy as they, namely, Herr Isidor Binzer. The pause which had arisen through the young woman's words had not lasted many moments before Herr Binzer hurried to offset the effect produced.

"Idiots!" he cried. "How long would you enjoy the use of your twenty thousand pesetas apiece? Have you forgotten what your gracious ruler promised—that you should all hang before to-morrow night? That help was coming from an English warship which would be here before morning? Idiots! Much joy you would all have from her money!"

The young woman stared at the Grand Duke with a stunned expression: what was that? Had he said that? The Grand Duke nodded: his lies of a while before had come home to roost in a manner which excelled anything related in Sunday school books! Herr Binzer's speech had an immediate effect; the hesitancy on the part of his five fellow conspirators disappeared as quickly as it had come, and a storm of abuse broke loose against the Grand Duke. Sergeant Posada bared his arms and made the noose ready, while Amadeo tested the rope to see that it ran smoothly.

The young woman threw a quick glance of despair at the Grand Duke, who lowered his head, not daring to meet her eyes. Then she took a step toward the sergeant and made another attempt.

"Forty thousand pesetas for each and every one of you!" she cried. "Do you hear? Each and every one of you will be rich—and I swear that the Grand Duke will pardon you. I give you my word!"

The sergeant brutally threw her aside.

"Enough of that. If you have the money, we will get it anyway. We have wasted too much time already. Whether he will pardon us or not, doesn't matter. The Grand Duke shall be hung—long live the Grand Duke!"

She turned pale as death.

"Dare do it, you villainous wretch!" she cried with trembling voice. "Dare do it and. . ."

"Dare do it?" interrupted the sergeant with a roar, "we dare do it, never fear! You will see in a second!"

Beside herself, tense with impotent desperation, she turned to the Grand Duke with burning eyes and cried in a voice which could hardly be understood:

"Then, as true as I am Olga Nikolaievna, Grand Duchess of Russia, I will give myself no peace on earth until they have paid for this crime with their lives! I swear it, by all the hopes I had of saving you whom they think of. . . murdering. . . By. . . by my. . . by my love for you. . ."

Her voice broke, and blinded by the tears which began to stream from her eyes, she tried to force her way past the black sergeant, to throw her outstretched arms around Don Ramon—around Don Ramon, who stood there bound, wounded, powerless, his thoughts whirling around in his head as though he were delirious: she was Olga Nikolaievna, Grand Duchess of Russia! Was it all a nightmare? Or was it possible? Ah, yes, he began to understand, now, at last, when it was too late! It was she who two years before had written to him—it was her letter which he. . . he dared not complete the thought. . . And now she had risked her life. . . so as to save him. . . Overwhelmed by the thoughts which whirled through his brain, he felt the noose laid around his neck; saw how the black sergeant brutally pushed aside this woman whose beauty and passion would have conquered any other nature than his, saw him push her toward Herr Binzer, who calmly watched the whole affair. He wanted to see no more. He turned his head aside. His glance fell on the door and he gave a start which aroused him from his stupor: for the fraction of a second it seemed to him that the handle of the door turned, that someone was trying to open it. . . Could it be the professor? Or merely the sentry? The next second the handle was again still, if it had really moved, and suppressing a last cry of helpless sorrow and rage, he heard, for he did not want to look there, how Amadeo gave the signal: "All ready!" and how Herr Binzer with a chuckling laugh said:

"Well, well, my little friend, come over here to me and I will hold you up! You will get a good view here. Come on!"

Amadeo and his helpers grabbed hold of him and dragged him nearer to the gallows; the rope grew tight around his neck and he raised his eyes to take a last farewell of her who that night had dared everything for his sake—whom he had so cruelly wronged—and who had said that she loved him... Their glances met, hers hanging on his as though paralyzed; he saw that she was on the point of fainting and saw Herr Binzer open his arms to enclose her in their embrace...

Then the rope began to grow uncomfortably tight; he saw nothing more and made ready to die with this last thought running through his head: Herr Binzer would soil this glorious young being with his hands... Herr Binzer had stretched out his arms to throw them about her... about her...

Herr Binzer had done so, but it was the last movement Herr Binzer ever made!

Before his hands had been able to grasp the Grand Duchess, a shot resounded from the other end of the hall. There was a howl, a howl of deadly pain; the arms which had wanted to embrace the young Grand Duchess groped in the air and with a heavy thud the eminent businessman from Frankfort fell forward on the marble floor.

But before the echo of the first shot had died away and before Herr Binzer's death cry had ceased, six further shots cracked in such quick succession that they sounded like one; the rope which had chokingly tightened around the Grand Duke's throat suddenly loosened, he tottered and fell over; but he could breathe, he could breathe! Then from what seemed to him an endless distance he heard a voice crying out words which to him were void of meaning:

"Courage, Your Highness! Auguste, Joaquin, another volley. Death to the wretches—no quarter to any of them!"

He heard death gasps and shrieks beside him, three or four shots more, and then the next second he felt a hand press some cold object between his wrists and the rope which bound them. A slash, and they were free. Another, and the rope around his feet was gone. A couple of seconds with teeth tightly clenched, and he again could open his eyes, before which fire and rockets were raining. He seemed to make out a face which bent over him, and although hardly able to move his tongue, he succeeded in mumbling:

"In the nick of time... have you... have you by chance any cognac?"

The face above him disappeared and instead, a little further away, he became conscious of a back which was leaning over something. Suddenly the back straightened up and a figure which he in vain tried to recall disappeared with something in its arms.

Then he felt a hand under his head, something cold and smooth against his mouth, and a burning fluid rushing between his lips. It burned, it burned; then suddenly a curtain was lifted inside his head, he could see, hear, feel, understand, and he arose, leaning on an arm which he now saw belonged to Joaquin, his legs wobbling and his knees rattling like castanets. Joaquin's hand again held out the bottle with the burning fluid; he took another swallow which this time did not burn unpleasantly, and at last was master of himself.

"She?" he mumbled. "Where is she, and the Professor?"

Joaquin gently began to lead his master toward the room where President Hernandez had dwelt shortly before. Suddenly recalling the trials his trusty servant must have undergone, Don Ramon stopped and smiled compassionately at him.

"Joaquin, my poor Joaquin," said he, "you have had a hard time, haven't you?"

"Ah, that doesn't matter now I know Your Highness has been saved."

"In the white lodge, the wretches," murmured the Grand Duke, "It must have been frightful for you and Auguste. It is even better cooking for me, isn't it?"

"Ah, Your Highness... Yes, it was terrible; if the Professor had not come soon, then..."

"Was the Professor able to free you easily? Were you guarded?"

"Yes, but he overpowered the sentry and freed us in a twinkling."

The Grand Duke nodded silently.

"He managed better than I," said he, "I was easily caught off my guard. Was it you who tried to get in the main entrance a while ago, or did I merely imagine it?"

"No, Your Highness, we tried but the door was locked and we had to run around to the back way. When we came in they were on the point of hoisting Your Highness up, the whole crowd of the wretches together and the German was trying to embrace the lady. The professor simply threw out his arm, like this, and the German lay there dead. 'Shoot ahead into the crowd!' he cried to us. 'Give no quarter but simply be careful of your master!' He himself fired three shots as he said this, and it was he who killed most of them; we were afraid, Auguste and I, of hitting Your Highness. Our hands were not so very steady either after the time we spent in the lodge. . ."

The Grand Duke involuntarily cast a look behind him. The leaders of the Minorcan Republic lay there in a heap; the black-bearded sergeant with bared teeth on top of the others. Their bodies had already begun to assume the rigidity of death. At just that moment Philip Collin quietly smiling came out of the inner room.

"How is Your Highness? It was the last minute, I am afraid."

"No, Professor," said Don Ramon, and stretched out his hand, "the last second. One second more and the tyrant would have been dead and the sovereign folk masters of Minorca."

"Yes, thank the Lord I came in time," said Mr. Collin. "For you and for my poor wife."

Don Ramon's eyes suddenly burned with repressed tears. He remembered how he had seen her just before help came. . . Poor little princess! Poor child! How could she have done what she did! Her life, everything she had been willing to risk for his sake, for him who. . . With an effort he broke off these thoughts and gravely nodded to Philip.

"Yes, you came in time, Professor. For me and for her."

"But how did she get here? She is somewhat better now" (Philip motioned with his hand toward the inner room) "but I have not wanted to ask her any questions yet. Do you know anything about it?"

"She came on land to look for us, got separated from Captain Dupont, and arrived just in time to see me hung. She offered those" the Grand Duke again looked with a shudder at the stiff bodies behind them, "those friends of liberty two hundred thousand pesetas for my life. . . They answered by throwing her into Herr Binzer's arms. . . and in her fear and desperation she then betrayed who she was. . ."

Philip cast a quick glance at the Grand Duke.

"Yes," continued the Grand Duke slowly, "we have each sailed a little under false colors; I was not Count of Punta Hermosa, and she was not Madame Pelotard, but. . ."

"But Olga Nikolaievna, Grand Duchess of Russia," said Philip, completing the sentence for him. "We will talk that all over in the morning. I think it is time we should go down to the *Stork*. Good Captain Dupont will be out of his mind if he doesn't see us soon. Let's start, Your Highness. . . With all due regard for the Grand-Ducal Palace, I have no desire to sleep here to-night."

The Grand Duke looked around and shuddered again.

"By St. Urban, Professor, neither have I. But how is she. . . can she. . ."

"We will carry her," said Philip. "Auguste is just getting ready a sort of litter."

Five minutes later the palace door closed behind them

for the last time that night. Philip, Joaquin and Auguste took turns helping bear the litter, where the Grand Duchess lay in a light feverish stupor. Don Ramon, whose foot was giving him much pain, limped beside them, constantly begging that he might be allowed to help. After a fifteen minutes' march, which passed without incident, Philip started at a certain thought which flew through his head, and gripped the Grand Duke's arm.

"Your Highness, how many dead were lying in the hall?"

The Grand Duke looked at him reproachfully.

"Don't misunderstand me, I only happened to think of something; if I am not mistaken, the president was not among them!"

It was Don Ramon's turn to give a start. Yes, the Professor was right! Luis Hernandez had not been present during the final occurrences in the hall.

"I think what you say is true," he mumbled. "Luis must have escaped. Suppose we. . . Would a couple of minutes' detour do any harm?"

"Not at all, Your Highness. Just show us the way."

The Grand Duke quickly turned off down a small side street which led into a market-place where some palm-trees were softly rustling in the night air. He stopped at a two story house with a sign on the front; finally Philip was able to make out the words: Hotel Universal. The Grand Duke hammered on the door, at first without receiving an answer; then after several minutes' silence an old man's voice was heard inside:

"Who is it?"

"Open the door!" cried the Grand Duke. "Travelers who are looking for rooms."

There was a creaking of the lock, the door opened and on the threshold appeared an old man with long gray hair, a trembling hand shading his eyes so that he could the better see who was there.

"Good evening, Señor Hernandez!" said Don Ramon. "Do you recognize me? And is the president at home?"

The effect of his words was instantaneous; he had hardly stopped before the old man all of a tremble fell on his knees, and with hands uplifted to Don Ramon gasped out:

"Mercy, Your Highness, mercy! I have had no part in this shameful revolt. . . I swear it, Your Highness, I swear it."

The Grand Duke motioned him to rise.

"Very good, Señor Porfirio, I believe you, but answer my question. Is Luis here?"

"No, Your Highness, no! I swear it! He has not lived here since. . . since. . ."

"We know," interrupted Don Ramon, "we just came from his late dwelling . . . . Well, old Porfirio, I will simply give you a bit of good advice: if Luis comes here, then send him out of the country immediately. For your sake, I do not want to see him hung. Good night!"

They were about to continue on their way when Don Ramon stopped short at something which had occurred to him.

"One moment, Professor," said he. "If I am not mistaken, we are full up on the yacht?"

"Yes, Your Highness, absolutely full."

"We must then find some other place where Joaquin and Auguste can sleep. Señor Porfirio!"

"Your Highness!" The old hotel proprietor hurried forward with trembling legs.

"No need for being frightened, old friend. I only want to give you the opportunity of making some sort of amends for what your son has done. Here are my two fine servants, Joaquin and Auguste. Luis and his friends had installed them in a lodge where the rats have been the sole occupants for the last thirty years. I will quarter them on you for to-night. See that they are as well treated by you as they have been ill treated by your son!"

"Your Highness... Your Highness!" whimpered old Porfirio, and tried to grasp the Grand Duke's hand.

"Good night, Porfirio! Be prepared to receive them in half an hour."

The procession started again through the silent streets, and in another fifteen minutes they reached the harbor. A fog had arisen from the Mediterranean during the night, and the nearer they came to the water the denser it grew in the alleys through which they passed; finally when they had almost reached the water's edge the fog was so thick that the houses could only dimly be made out as indistinct shadows. To go around to the west side where the skiff from the *Stork* lay was out of the question; it would mean at least fifteen minutes' further march; and not only the Grand Duke, but his companions as well were worn out with fatigue. Don Ramon bade his friends stay where they were and left them to reconnoiter. In a couple of minutes he returned and motioned them to follow.

He led them carefully down between two low sheds similar to those he and Philip had passed when they had landed on the other side of the harbor some hours before. A flagstaff, however, rose over the roof of one and the Grand Duke leaned forward toward Philip and whispered:

"Your friend Emiliones' dwelling, if I am not mistaken! Hope he doesn't hear us!"

The next moment they had successfully passed both the small houses and were down by the waterside where the water slowly rose and fell in the darkness like the strokes of a pendulum in an old-fashioned clock. A little rowboat—evidently the same which had carried the president and his friend to the *Stork*—lay drawn up on the beach. Panting heavily, Auguste and Joaquin put the litter on the ground and the Grand Duke turning to them said in a whisper:

"Go back to the Universal, take the best rooms and provide yourself with what you wish, at least chicken and champagne, if old man Porfirio has any. Tomorrow I will come on land again and assume the reins of government. Inquire about the price of rabbits, Joaquin. We will give a banquet. Good night!"

Auguste and Joaquin silently disappeared in the fog and the Grand Duke turned to Philip.

"Now, Professor, all we have to do is to reach the *Stork*.

If you will push out the boat I will try to put our charge aboard."

He carefully put his arms around the Grand Duchess so as to lift her out of the litter; at his touch she started as though an electric current ran through her body and before he could prevent it she had thrown her arms around his neck. He felt them tighten about him, wildly, feverishly; then a whisper reached his ears:

"Ramon—Ramon—they must not kill you. They must not kill you. . . I love you. . ."

He trembled so that he almost lost his hold; then with temples throbbing he lifted her from the litter. His bruised instep burned like fire as he took the few steps with his burden; but to him it was as though he were floating along Elysian fields, not even touching the ground with his feet. Suddenly he found himself sitting on a cushion with her in his arms, trying in vain to loosen her grasp around his neck. Then he heard Philip Collin say:

"The litter, Your Highness! One moment; I'll jump ashore and hide it. Our friend Emiliones. . ."

Thereupon Philip hastily sprang back on land and the Grand Duke was alone. . . He felt nothing but the hot breath on his left cheek and saw nothing but a few wisps of dark hair which fell in disorder over a closed eyelid, but if his eyes had been able to follow Mr. Collin he would have seen a sight which would have filled him with amazement.

Philip, after picking up the litter, stood for a moment undecided what he should do with it. Was there any fit hiding place near or should he throw it in the sea? Suddenly he noticed that the door to one of the two sheds stood open and he quickly decided to hide the litter there. No one would probably find it before morning. He hurried away with it, and dragging it after him entered the shed—when he felt a hand against his cheek and jumped back with a cry of horror.

The hand which had stroked his cheek in the dark was cold as death.

For a moment Philip stood as though paralyzed, trembling all over. Then he pulled out his pocket flashlight and pressed the button.

The next moment he was flying out of the little building.

For what was it he had seen, hanging on a rope from a beam which went straight across the room?

With mouth distorted and tongue outstretched, with nose horribly swollen from the blow he had received that evening from Philip's foot, there before him had hung—the first president of Minorca!

CHAPTER 7

In Which It Is Shown That Those Who Escape Scylla Have Not Necessarily Settled Their Accounts With Charybdis

Without saying a word Philip threw himself into the boat and took the oars. Don Ramon sat on the cushion before him as silent as he, heedfully protecting the Grand Duchess' slender body with both his arms. He had seemed to notice neither the haste with which Mr. Collin had come rushing out of the low building nor the great speed with which he now rowed away from the shore. As far as Philip was concerned, his brain could think of but two things: the clammy hand which had stroked him there, in the darkness, and the poor distorted face which had suddenly stared down at him. He let the oars beat the water; the boat flew forward through the gray fog without his thinking of the direction it took; and a good ten minutes had passed before his excited state was replaced by a somewhat more normal frame of mind.

Then gradually his head grew clear of the fright; he let the oars rest and dried his forehead. The Grand Duke seemed as little to notice that the rowing had stopped as before he had noticed it had begun. "Your Highness!" said Philip.

Don Ramon did not move.

"Your Highness!" repeated Philip in a raised voice. "Has Your Highness any idea where the yacht lies?"

At last Don Ramon gave a start.

"The yacht," he mumbled, "of course, the yacht... No, Professor, really I haven't."

"We must call to them," said Philip.

He arose in the boat and put his hands to his mouth.

"Hullo, the *Stork*! Captain Dupont!"

There was no answer to his cry.

"Hullo, Captain Dupont! Hullo, the *Stork*!"

It was as still after the second shout as after the first. Philip called out again; the result was the same. No sound was heard and nothing could be seen in the fog.

Philip cast a look at the Grand Duke: this was a fine state of affairs! Would it turn out that Captain Dupont had sailed away, or had something happened to him on land? Suddenly an idea came into his head.

He drew out from his pocket one of the revolvers he had left from the evening's adventure. Holding it straight up in the air, he fired a shot, then another.

The effect was instantaneous, but of an entirely different sort than he had expected.

Before the faint echo from the revolver shots had even

died away, the fog around them was cleaved by a milk-white ribbon of light, which began to sweep forward and back over the water. A searchlight! Then came a shout in a strange language, a moment's pause, and then a dull shot. The next moment the ribbon of light had found their boat and with eyes dazzled by the glare they tried to discover where it came from. The boat, left to itself, began to drift. Philip quickly seized the oars and began to row trying to avoid the rays of light. He had hardly taken three strokes before another shot whistled over their heads and a voice called out in fairly good Spanish:

"Stop where you are, unless you want to be sunk! Who are you and what do you mean by shooting that way!"

"Shooting?" cried back Philip indignantly, "who is doing the most shooting, you or I? I have a yacht lying in the harbor and am trying to signal the captain."

"You are lying," cried the voice above them. "This isn't any harbor. Row over here immediately and let me question you... Some damned rebel," Philip heard him add, evidently to another person. Philip and the Grand Duke stared at one another with the same query in their eyes; were they dreaming? Were they awake? A searchlight! A strange ship, probably a warship! The Grand Duke's lies seemed to be coming true in a manner which exceeded all expectations! While they were still looking at each other in amazement another shot whistled by and a ball splashed in the water hardly a yard away from them.

"Row, for God's sake, Professor," said Don Ramon.

"Why, this here is worse than a madman's dreams."

Without answering, Philip seized the oars and pulled the boat around to the direction from which the voice had come; his brain, which was far from unreceptive, declined to accept as real any more of these phenomena: it must be a dream. Suddenly he saw a gigantic shadow silhouetted in the fog above his head and he heard the same voice as before shout:

"Stop! Wait where you are!"

A few moments went by; then a boathook was stretched out from the smooth-plated sides of the vessel beside them; their boat was gently pulled to a gangway not far from the water line, and he saw two persons in uniform. The light was indistinct and he could not make out their appearance. One, who was much the taller and evidently the same who had cried out before, mumbled something in a strange language to his comrade; then he said in Spanish:

"It is lucky for you that you obeyed. . . A devilish looking lot you are! Are you rebels? Come on board and give a report of yourselves!'

"By what right do you demand it?" asked the Grand Duke indignantly.

"By right of might. Besides, as protector of law and order here."

"A fine protec. . ." began Don Ramon, but stopped as Philip touched him on the arm. "Will you please help me with this lady? She is sick."

"A lady! Holding a picnic at this time of day!" The

stranger in uniform added a few words, evidently an oath of astonishment, and Philip quickly gave a start, for he had recognized the language. Russian! By Zeus, Russian! Then interrupting him the tall man in uniform leaned over and with a carefulness greatly in contrast to his former abrupt manner helped Don Ramon and his charge onto the gangway, the Grand Duchess in a kind of stupor still clinging tightly to the Grand Duke. Don Ramon's manner became more gracious and he thanked him with a nod before, limping heavily, he began to ascend the small iron steps with his burden.

"Your friend is wounded, Señor?" the man in uniform asked Philip.

"Yes," answered Philip shortly. "May I ask if you intend to keep us on board long?"

"Until I have asked you some questions."

"Many?"

"That depends."

"In that case you will only be doing your duty as officer and gentleman if you see that the young lady has proper attention. She is sick; fever. Have you a doctor on board?"

"Yes. You are perfectly right. I will attend to it immediately."

Philip and the two men, evidently officers, hurried up the steps after the Grand Duke. Still bearing the Grand Duchess in his arms, Don Ramon followed the shorter of the two officers, to whom the other had given an order. A few minutes later the two men returned alone.

"It is an ill wind that blows nobody any good," mumbled Don Ramon in French to Philip. "Poor child, now at least she will be taken care of."

"You speak French?" asked the taller of the two officers hastily. "Don't worry. I wasn't listening, but I thought I recognized the language."

"Yes," answered the Grand Duke, now absolutely conciliated by his manner. "We speak French."

"Really! Excellent! Can you then tell me what is happening on land?" He nodded toward Minorca. "Is the revolution still going on? They are keeping mighty quiet."

"The revolution," said Don Ramon quietly, "came to an end to-night. That is why everything is so quiet."

"Came to an end to-night! *Mille diables!* How do you know that? Are you standing there, trying to play a joke on me?"

"By no means. The revolution came to an end to night and I know, because it was I and my friend here—I should say my friend and I—who stopped it."

"*Mille diables!* You must be crazy! You and your friend! Who the devil is your friend? And who are you?"

"My friend, Monsieur, is Professor Pelotard of Sweden, and I am the Grand Duke of Minorca!"

There lay perhaps more than an ounce of self-satisfaction and some desire to produce an effect in Don Ramon's voice as he said it; but the impression he sought through his answer was widely surpassed by the effect won in turn by his adversary.

Without a moment's hesitation he put his hand to his mouth; there came the sound of a sharp call from a whistle, and then as the tramp of approaching feet was heard he uttered the following surprising words:

"You are the Grand Duke of Minorca? That is excellent! Then I give you my word that within half an hour you shall hang at the yard-arm!"

Don Ramon and Philip each took a step back, and while they stared at each other, Philip was filled with the same feelings as earlier when he had been rowing through the fog: this is a dream, it is impossible, these words were never spoken! If you are the Grand Duke of Minorca then you shall hang at the yard-arm within half an hour! Truly, poor Don Ramon was beginning to form too close an acquaintance with this manner of death. . . but it was impossible, they had heard amiss, they were dreaming!. . . Then as quickly as had come this overpowering feeling of nightmare came the word which awakened Philip from it.

The tramp of feet quickly came nearer; in the uncertain light Philip saw another officer in the uniform of the Russian navy, and then followed words which explained the whole affair. The tall officer beside him, said in French, evidently with the object that they should understand:

"Barinsky, have Mr. Marcowitz awakened immediately, and tell him to come to my private cabin!"

Marcowitz! The name rang through Philip's head. The tall officer turned to him and the Grand Duke and said curtly:

"Come with me. It will be best for you if you do not make a fuss."

Without awaiting an answer, he started off. The Grand Duke, who had stood as though paralyzed at hearing the name mentioned by the taller officer, quickly moved his hand to the pocket where he carried his revolver and there came an expression of desperation in his eyes which Philip understood and respected; but before Don Ramon's hand had reached the fateful pocket he felt Philip's fingers close around his wrist; Philip pulled him forward in the direction the tall officer had taken and he heard the Professor's voice whisper in his ear:

"Quickly, Your Highness, quickly! Here is my pocketbook! Use it but not before the last minute; what you need you will find in there! And deny everything, but play your role well!"

Don Ramon, whose hand had still been trying to reach the pocket containing the little weapon, gave up the task, and with eyes staring in surprise, mechanically obeyed the order. Before he could ask even one of the questions trembling on his lips the tall officer turned around and cried:

"Well, are you coming? Hurry, if you know what is good for yourselves!"

Philip silenced the Grand Duke with a glance.

"We are coming as quickly as we can. You know his Highness is wounded!"

The tall officer mumbled something; the next moment Philip, the Grand Duke and he were standing in a sparsely furnished cabin; the light fell on the officer's face and Philip jumped, on the point of letting out a ringing Swedish oath!

Because. . .

But before he could complete his thoughts, the door to the cabin was pulled open and a fat stocky figure came rushing in. His face was a glowing red, his clothes had evidently been pulled on in the greatest haste, and from his half-open mouth came a heavy wheezy sound—half of satisfaction, half of excitement. He was followed by the officer they had seen before on deck. The pudgy man began to gesticulate wildly and shout in a dialect where the words tumbled over one another, until finally he was silenced by a gesture from the tall officer.

"Silence, Marcowitz," the latter cried. "Wait until we are ready for you!" He turned to the Grand Duke and said curtly: "Do you know this man?"

Don Ramon quickly looked at Philip who gave a hasty, encouraging nod. Don Ramon's features resumed their usual expression of quiet self-consciousness and he answered in as curt a tone as the tall officer:

"No. May I kindly be informed what is the meaning of this examination?"

"You'll find out immediately," said the tall officer in the same abrupt tone. "Before we continue I want to ask you once more if you still persist in your former statement. You are the Grand Duke of Minorca?"

"I am, and I am not accustomed to being cross-examined by a foreign officer in my own country."

"You are mistaken if you think you are in your own country. You are in Russia, since you are on board a Russian man-of-war, and it is I who am in command here. You do not know this man then?"

"No," answered the Grand Duke as coldly as before, casting a look of disdain at him. "I have never seen him before."

"Ah, he does not know me! He has never seen me before! By the living Gott, this a fine piece of business! And my three hundred thousand pesetas—he doesn't know them either, eh? He has never seen. . ."

"Silence, Marcowitz!" the tall officer thundered. "Wait, I have told you, until we are ready for you. You are in Russia, Marcowitz, not in France. You understand the difference?"

The moneylender looked at him with eyes filled with fear. A strand of his thin hair became out of place and fell over his face. The tall officer turned again to the Grand Duke:

"This fellow here," said he, and made a movement with his head toward Marcowitz, "came on board at Marseilles just as I had taken over command of the boat and begged for an audience. I absolutely refused until he, through my adjutant, told me a story of such an unbelievable nature that, out of regard for Russia's imperial house, I had to convince myself as to whether it was true or not. . . . A Grand Duchess of Russia, two years ago, was on the point of becoming engaged to the Grand Duke of Minorca but the engagement stranded on account of the opposition of her exalted father. The princess, who strangely enough had fallen in love with the Grand Duke mentioned, although she had never seen him, was of a high-strung, romantic nature. One fine day she secretly wrote him a letter which was full of those incautious expressions a young girl so often uses on such occasions... It should have been his duty to return the letter; he did not do so. His affairs had been in a bad state ever since his accession to the throne and... now comes Marcowitz' story. His affairs were in such a desperate state that he turned to this Marcowitz, whose address he had received from a third party and—pawned the young princess's letter with Marcowitz, who carries on a business of that sort... He pawned it for three hundred thousand pesetas which he should have paid back this year just at this time. The revolution broke out on Minorca. The telegraph cables were cut and Marcowitz could not find out what had happened to the Grand Duke. He suspected the revolution was a plot to swindle the Grand Duke's creditors, and he feared he would lose his three hundred thousand. He went to Marseilles, where he tried in vain to get over to Minorca. He found out that I was in the city, sought me out and related his story. Out of regard for Russia's imperial house, I took him on board and we started for Minorca, where strangely enough, immediately after our arrival, we have a visit from the Grand Duke, who maintains that he has just quelled the revolution ... Have I expressed myself plainly? If such is the case what answer have you to give?"

Don Ramon, who seemingly unmoved had listened to

the tall officer's story, again cast a look quick as lightning at Philip. Philip alone read the agony with which it was filled; again he gave a hasty confirming nod and Don Roman said coldly:

"Before I answer, I beg leave to ask one question: is it customary for an officer in the Russian navy to immediately believe the stories which a man of Mr. Marcowitz' acknowledged profession tells him?"

The tall officer blushed slightly and replied somewhat more politely:

"Your Highness can be convinced that such is not the case. If Marcowitz had related his story without showing proof, I would immediately have put him in irons or set him in front of a firing squad."

"But he related nothing without proof," shrieked the little man. "He related nothing without proof! Marcowitz doesn't lie, no, not he! Your Highness denies" (he bowed with ironical servility to Don Ramon) "that Your Highness knows me. Well, will Your Highness also deny that Your Highness knows this?"

With a quick movement, he took some sheets of paper from his pocket, unfolded them and stuck them under Don Ramon's nose. To the Grand Duke everything seemed to go round and his eyes for the third time sought those of Philip Collin; then he turned to the papers which Marcowitz held before him and started as though waking from a dream. Did he see aright? Those papers. . . those papers! Why, they were nothing but clumsy forgeries. There was hardly a trace of similarity with the handwriting in that unfortunate letter from her! As though to convince himself he was awake, he again cast a look at Mr. Collin. He saw the latter's eyebrows lift themselves and his lips quickly form a word. Presently he understood what the word was!

P-o-c-k-e-t-b-o-o-k!

With feverish haste he pulled out the pocketbook which he had received from Philip; he opened it; and in another second his eyes were almost jumping out of their sockets at what they saw lying nearest at hand in the Professor's little pocketbook. The letter!. . . Her letter! That little letter, so light in weight, which for the last month, ever since his conscience had awakened from its stupor, had borne down on that same conscience with the weight of a block of granite! Was it possible? Or was everything simply a dream—a wonderful dream? After a while, which to him seemed like an eternity, he pulled the letter from the pocketbook, threw Marcowitz' forgeries aside and with flashing eyes turned to the tall officer:

"Will you be kind enough to tell me what this is?"

The tall man took the letter which the Grand Duke held out to him and looked at it. Then he mumbled:

"That may be a letter from my. . . from the princess in question. But Marcowitz also has a letter in her handwriting—and other papers signed by the Grand Duke of Minorca."

"Marcowitz! You take the word of a common usurer rather than that of Don Ramon of Minorca! Truly, an officer in. . ."

"Don't grow excited! I hold Mr. Marcowitz in as high esteem as you, but it strikes me as almost unbelievable that he would dare to fabricate such a story. . . He knows of course what he is risking. . ."

The tall officer looked at Marcowitz without completing the meaning to his sentence. The little man had turned yellow at the sight of the Grand Duke's letter. At the tall officer's words he began to tremble like an aspen leaf and a stream of words burst from his lips.

"But I swear. . . He is deceiving Your Highness. . . ah, it is an outrage! It is my letter which is the *echte*, the genuine letter. His is a forgery!. . . He wishes to deceive, to deceive!"

His voice kept rising to a piercing shriek until the tall officer, whom he had called Your Highness, stopped him through a certain little gesture of his hand—a movement of his index finger around his throat.

"Marcowitz," said he, "silence! Remember you are on board an imperial Russian battleship and not in a pawnshop. If you have done what is right, what is right will be done by you—and if you have done what is wrong, I pity you, Marcowitz!"

Knitting his brows, the tall officer looked for a minute first at him, then at the Grand Duke with an expression of deep thought on his face. Finally he turned to Don Ramon:

"You must forgive me that I am still at a loss to know what to believe. I do not know you; I do not know Marcowitz, consequently I am nonpartisan. As I said,

Marcowitz' story is so strange. . . he knows so well what he risks if it is not true, that. . ."

Before the tall officer could finish his sentence, to his amazement he heard someone say:

"If Your Highness wishes to determine immediately what is true and what is not true in this affair, I can be of instant help to Your Highness!"

He quickly looked from the Grand Duke to the speaker and saw to his surprise that it was the Grand Duke's friend, the so-called Professor. He raised his eyebrows questioningly; the Professor continued: "Nothing as a matter of fact, is simpler than to ascertain which letter is genuine. The lady who wrote the letter, you know, is on board."

"The lady who wrote the letter is on board! What do you mean?" roared the tall officer.

"I mean that the lady who came on board with his Highness and me and who a short time ago was entrusted to the care of your ship's doctor is the one who wrote the letter in question. In other words. . ."

"In other words? Speak up!"

"In other words, the Grand Duchess Olga Nikolaievna of Russia!"

If a bomb had suddenly exploded in the cabin where the two officers, Marcowitz, the Grand Duke and Philip stood, no greater consternation could have arisen than from Philip's words. Both officers drew themselves up and seized their swords as though to strike Mr. Collin down on the spot for his audacity, while Marcowitz stood rigid as a corpse. At last the spell was broken. The tall officer gave Philip a terrible look and shrieked, rather than cried, an order in Russian to his brother officer. The latter disappeared; and during a silence which was more eloquent than many volumes, the tall officer watched every movement of Mr. Collin as though to see that he should not escape after his audacious statement. A good ten minutes passed during which time Philip evaded the Grand Duke's glances; then at last slow steps were heard outside and the door to the cabin was opened.

CHAPTER 8

IN WHICH MR. COLLIN ATTENDS THE MOST ILLUSTRIOUS WEDDING OF HIS LIFE

The cabin door opened with a jerk and somebody rushed over the threshold; someone who without a moment's hesitation, without looking to the right or left, rushed straight over to the tall officer, threw her arms around him, kissed him and began to gush forth great streams of caressing Russian. It was the supposed Madame Pelotard, marvellously recuperated from her feverish swoon; behind her came the thick-set officer who had been sent to fetch her. He closed the door behind him and remained standing as silent spectator of the scene being enacted before him.

It is difficult to say which face in that little cabin at the moment expressed the greatest degree of amazement, suspicion and consternation; one thing is certain, it was not that of Mr. Philip Collin. Philip remained in his former position with a faint smile playing around his black-mustached upper lip and with a little gleam in the corner of his eye. It is not impossible that at the moment, deep down in his heart, he felt rather proud of himself; that he felt like some new, crafty Ulysses, or as the real messenger of Fate to the Balearic Islands. Fate and he had guided everything to where it now was, in sight of a fair and prosperous solution, satisfactory to all parties—with the exception of Mr. Semjon Marcowitz! He let his eyes wander from one to the other of those present and his self-satisfaction grew. There stood Semjon Marcowitz, his fat swollen face pale as chalk, his glances wandering from the Grand Duchess to the papers which lay on the table before the tall officer; there stood the tall officer in question with eyebrows raised high over his forehead, one moment pulling at his gigantic mustache, the next awkwardly caressing the supposed Madame Pelotard; and last of all, there stood Don Ramon XX of Minorca, Count of Bethlehem, but lately saved from being hanged by his faithful subjects and now threatened with the same ceremony by the tall officer. His looks devoured both the man who shortly before declared himself willing to be his executioner, and the woman whom he held in his arms, or more correctly, who held him in her arms. The poor Grand Duke's whole manner gave expression to but one single word: incomprehensible! At last Philip could not withstand his desire to laugh. Don Ramon, who heard his suppressed giggle, gave him a quick, indignant look; without paying the least attention to it, Philip leaned forward:

"Is it possible that Your Highness does not know the tall

officer who is receiving such gracious treatment from my former wife?"

Don Ramon shook his head without the expression in his eyes becoming milder.

"In that case I will no longer conceal from Your Highness that any and all jealous looks in that direction are unnecessary. His name is Peter Nikolaievich, Grand Duke of Russia, and the lady, who at present is embracing him, my former wife, is his sister!"

"His sister! Your wife! And you know him!" cried the Grand Duke all in the same breath. But before he could ask even one more question he was interrupted by a thundering, "Stop!"

"No consultations before this matter here is settled!" shouted the tall officer. "This man here" (pointing at Philip) "has shown that he speaks the truth. We will attend to his case later. First we have the case of the Grand Duke of Minorca—whether he or Mr. Marcowitz is to be hung."

At the Russian Grand Duke's words, Semjon Marcowitz's tongue let loose for the first time in half an hour.

"To be hung! I!" shrieked the little man at the top of his voice. "I am an honest man, an honest man! He is the one who has swindled us all, he, he! He should be hung, Your Highness, not I! He should be hu-hu-hu. . . "

"Silence, Marcowitz, or you'll get into instant trouble," cried Grand Duke Peter, stamping on the floor. "Here justice shall be dealt out, and nothing else. If what you have done is right, then what is right will be done by you."

During this time a strange scene had been taking place. For the first time since her entrance the Grand Duchess seemed to become aware of Don Ramon's presence. Her blue eyes opened wide with surprise and she stared from him to Marcowitz and from the latter to Philip. The message by which the other officer had brought her there in such haste had evidently made her forget everything else; now her memory awakened. What did it all mean? Who was the little fat man? Why did her brother talk in such a manner to Don Ramon? Before she was able to bring out a word her brother, after giving the inferior officer an order in Russian (evidently to keep an eye on Philip and Don Ramon), hastily began to speak to her in her own language. Although neither Philip nor the Grand Duke understood a word of what he said or the short exclamations with which she continually interrupted him, yet they could follow it all as plainly as though each were listening to his own mother tongue. First Grand Duke Peter said something with a gesture toward Semjon Marcowitz; then as he lowered his voice and glanced at the letters on the table a deep blush came over the Grand Duchess' face; as he continued his voice became more and more animated and he nodded now toward Marcowitz, now toward Don Ramon; her eyes grew larger and larger and began to gleam with a dangerous light. Suddenly, as he was continuing, she abruptly interrupted him in French:

"Never! I will listen no longer! What sort of a disgusting

story is this anyway? How can you—how can you put belief in that one there!"

She did not need to make her words clearer through a gesture in order to start Mr. Marcowitz trembling.

Her brother shrugged his shoulders.

"I could not. . . I could not help investigating his story," he answered, but his voice involuntarily sounded somewhat embarrassed. "Will you please tell me which of these letters is genuine, then we will immediately put an end to this affair, as well as to the guilty party."

She gave him a look, almost of scorn, then took up the two letters from the table. There was a deathly silence in the cabin and all, with the exception of Don Ramon, watched her intently. But they were not kept long in suspense.

"Which is genuine!" she cried with the same scorn in her voice. "Do I have to tell you that? Is this here anything but a clumsy forgery? And could it come from anyone but that fellow there?"

She cast a glance of Olympic disdain at Mr. Marcowitz, threw his letter from her and with the other letter pressed to her heart beamingly smiled at Don Ramon. Poor Don Ramon! As certainly as she believed this to be a moment of the highest triumph for him, so certainly did he at the same moment suffer all the pangs of hell, and his attempts to play his role to the end were close to stranding. Perhaps they would have stranded if a last unexpected event had not occurred.

Mr. Semjon Marcowitz had stood rigid as a statue

for a good quarter of a minute after the Grand Duchess had passed sentence. His eyes glowed in their encircling craters of furrows and wrinkles, and his hands opened and closed mechanically. Suddenly a hoarse cry of rage burst forth from his throat, and the next second with a spring as though he were a mad dog, he flew at the Grand Duchess. A knife gleamed in his right hand; it was lifted on high and a threefold cry of horror arose from the Grand Duke, Don Ramon and the shorter officer. It was lifted. . . but it never sank into the breast it was intended to reach. Before the others were able to shake off their paralyzing fear, a shot rang out; Semjon Marcowitz' face was distorted by a grin which bared his teeth, and with a heavy thud his body fell past the Grand Duchess onto the floor at her brother's feet. The knife which had not left his hand, even in death, sank deep into the floor an inch from the Grand Duke.

"My last shot!" said Philip Collin quietly. "It is lucky I had one left."

There was silence for fully a minute while all, their eyes still wide open with excitement, stared at him. Then Grand Duke Peter said slowly:

"It was lucky that you had one left. You have saved my sister's life."

Philip bowed.

"No one is happier than I," said he. "Only one thing could increase my happiness."

"What is that?"

"To again save her brother's life."

Grand Duke Peter stared at him. At last he said:

"Again? What do you mean? Have you saved my life? Do you know me?"

"Ah, Your Highness, do not misunderstand me. I have been royally rewarded for what I did.[4] But since the words happened to escape me—I swear it was unwittingly—I do know Your Highness."

"Since when? And when did you save my life?" The Grand Duke scowled.

"A year and two months ago, Your Highness. Has Your Highness forgotten a January night in Hamburg when a Herr Wörtz and a Herr Pelotard paid a visit to the beer hall of a certain Herr Schiemann. . ."

Philip stopped without completing his sentence. The Grand Duke's face lightened like the sky after a thunder shower and to the others' surprise he burst into a roar of laughter.

"You—ah, you! You have a strange faculty of showing up where one least expects it! What on earth have you been doing since I saw you last in Hamburg?"

"A little of everything," said Philip politely. "I have had my usual little adventures, but it was not in Hamburg Your Highness saw me last."

"Really? Where on earth then?"

"At the Gare de Lyon in Paris, five days ago. Your Highness stood at the door of the waiting room and kept

---

4. Recounted in the short story 'Becoming a Landlord,' available for free at https://shop.kabatypress.com/b/7g8N9.

watch of the evening train to Marseilles. Your Highness did not recognize me, and I did not have an opportunity to draw Your Highness' attention. . . I was namely at that moment busy running away with Your Highness' sister."

Mr. Collin got no further. A roar arose from Grand Duke Peter's throat.

"You, it was you who!. . . And you dare!. . ."

"Your Highness, I did it without knowing what I did, but I don't regret it. So much I'll admit."

"Ah, you do not regret it! Ah! Wait, my friend Pelotard, it will not be long before. . ."

"I will only regret it," continued Philip more quietly than ever, "if the Grand Duchess Olga herself regrets it— ask her if she does, Your Highness!"

The Grand Duchess, who since Marcowitz' attempt on her life had stood immovable, dumbly following the short exchange of words between Philip and her brother, hastily drew herself up. All signs of fear had disappeared from her countenance, her eyes beamed and with the Grand Duke's letter pressed to her heart, she cried:

"No, I regret nothing!"

Her glance met her brother's, firm and without hesitation, then she again looked at Don Ramon, who stood there as before, crushed by the events of the last hour.

"I regret nothing of all I have done," she repeated, "for I have seen and learned to know two men!"

For a moment she glanced at Philip; then her eyes again turned to Don Ramon.

Philip smiled. Grand Duke Peter stood there dumbfounded. Don Ramon's chest suddenly heaved a deep sigh.

"Ah, princess, do not be all too sure of that. I know that you have seen and learned to know one man" (he nodded to Philip), "but two. . ."

He stopped and his face bore such an expression of despondency that nobody could misunderstand it. Before the conversation could proceed any further, however, her brother scowlingly interposed.

"How long have you been travelling alone with these gentlemen?" he asked curtly.

It was her turn to appear embarrassed.

"Fi-five days," she murmured. "Three with the Grand Duke."

Grand Duke Peter grew silent. Then he quickly turned to the shorter officer who with the patience of an Oriental, was still standing at the door.

"Barinsky," said he in French, "please awaken Father Sergei, have the chapel put in order and on the way arrange for a guard of honor. All lights are to be turned on and the imperial salute fired in a quarter of an hour."

The officer saluted without saying a word and was on the point of leaving when Grand Duke Peter added:

"Inform Father Sergei that a wedding will take place."

A wedding! Philip Collin gave a start, overwhelmed with the greatest feelings of triumph he had ever experienced. A wedding! Truly Grand Duke Peter did not let the grass grow under his feet in arranging a marriage between two royal parties! He did not even consult them as to their views or their wishes! Let Father Sergei be awakened, arrange a salute—and no protests! There was some advantage in living in an autocratic country. . . but would the Grand Duke of Minorca agree to it? It did not seem as though he would.

For hardly had the last words passed Grand Duke Peter's lips before Don Ramon arose pale with anger. "Is—is this a joke?" he succeeded in stammering. "Will you immediately recall your messenger! This is—this is outrageous!"

Grand Duke Peter was not at a loss for an answer.

"My dear friend," said he coldly, "there is nothing outrageous in this. For two years you have carried about with you a letter from my sister which you should have returned when the plans for an engagement came to naught. . ."

Don Ramon grew pale.

"For three days you have been travelling with her and probably under very unconventional conditions. . ."

"Without any of us being aware of the fact," Don Ramon managed to wedge in.

"That doesn't matter. At last you arrive in the middle of the night on board of this Russian vessel with her in your arms. If you are a gentleman, there is only one way in which you can make amends for everything."

"There are two ways," murmured Don Ramon, pale as death. "I have my revolver."

"That means you prefer death to my sister?. . ."

Grand Duke Peter had hardly uttered the words before

his sister arose as pale as Don Ramon.

"Peter. . . stop!. . . not even you have any right to force me into this hateful. . . he does not love me. . . he would rather d-die. . ."

Her voice broke, but her words had an effect which nothing else could have had. Suddenly, with a cry full of longing, love and, in spite of all, sorrow, Don Ramon was on his knees at her side, and with his eyes unsteadily lifted to hers, he murmured:

"Princess—Olga—Do not misunderstand me! Do not misunderstand me after all the beautiful thoughts you had of me, before you had ever seen me. . . I love you. . . I worship you. . . I desire nothing else on earth but you. . . but. . ."

"But what?" There were tears in her voice.

"But performing this marriage ceremony without asking you. . . I did not know whether you. . . whether you wanted it. . ."

"Did not know it!" She looked at him with her blue eyes so full of tender reproach that all his resistance was suddenly overcome. He jumped up and Philip and Grand Duke Peter quickly turned away, driven by the same impulse.

But in spite of all Philip could not resist asking a question which burned on his tongue.

"Your Highness," he mumbled, low enough not to disturb the pair behind him, "excuse me, but what will the Czar say to this?"

Grand Duke Peter suddenly smiled like a street urchin and Philip was vividly reminded of Herr Wörtz of Altona and certain adventures one January night in Hamburg.

"His Majesty the Emperor," said the Grand Duke, "can deny me nothing now that I have settled down. You see, I have joined the navy like my father and have become a new man. And my little sister deserves being happy. Don't you think she will be happy with your friend Don Ramon?"

"I certainly do," said Philip. "The Grand Duke has gone through varied experiences, and he has profited by them. She will be very happy and. . ."

"And?"

"And he will be well tied to her apron-strings."

The Grand Duke burst into laughter.

"You are a great one," said he. "On my soul, I believe you are right. . . And now get ready to witness the wedding ceremony. Have you ever attended such an illustrious wedding before, you who have done so many things?"

"Never," said Philip, and looked at his watch. "And to tell the truth, never one held at such a late hour, either."

Half an hour later, after the religious ceremonies were happily over, Mr. Philip Collin stood in the midst of a noisy group of Russian naval officers whose only wish evidently was to fill him up with champagne in the shortest time possible. The story of the night's events had spread like wildfire. Grand Duke Peter had given an order, short but to the point:

"Talk all you want to-night, but any talking to-morrow, and there'll be a hanging at the yard-arm."

As a result gossip ran wild in the officers' mess, and

while the champagne corks kept popping in time with the imperial salute outside, Mr. Philip Collin, the only one accessible among the heroes of the night, unceasingly had to tell the same things over and over again, interrupted only by a new bottle of champagne being offered him every minute. There was a buzzing of Russian and French, healths were drunk and cheers were given. Suddenly the circle around Philip parted and a gigantic man with a blue-eyed young lady on his arm limpingly forced his way forward to Mr. Collin. He wore a none too immaculate suit, and his ear was bandaged.

The Grand Duke's eyes glistened. As his glass touched Philip's, he said:

"Well, Professor, what did I tell you? You will have to leave Minorca without your wi. . . alone!"

She who had just become Grand Duchess of Minorca, to the surprise of all, blushed like a rose and Philip hastened to reply:

"Your Highness is rather hurrying matters. I am not thinking of leaving Minorca yet."

The Grand Duke gave a nod and motioned to a servant to fill the glasses. Then he turned to the officers around him and said:

"Gentlemen, you do not know me. But you do know Princess Olga and you have heard something about our adventures. To the man whom you see here before you thanks are due that they have turned out as they have—I admit it with a heart full of gratitude. He has brought everything to a happy issue, and he has saved both our lives. I propose three cheers to the most fearless friend I have ever had—Professor Pelotard of Sweden!"

The murmuring which had stopped during his talk suddenly broke out like a storm; there was a thundering of cheers and when Mr. Collin, half smothered by the champagne offered him, regained his breath, it was just in time to prevent them hoisting him on their shoulders.

Half an hour later the Grand Duke and Grand Duchess Olga retired but before they left the officers' mess they again came to Philip.

The Grand Duke looked at him thoughtfully for a moment and then said:

"You knew who I was, you knew who the Grand Duchess was, who her brother was, who Semjon Marcowitz was. You seem to have been the one guiding hand in all our adventures. Tell me, you man of strange fortune, do you perhaps know as well who carried out the coup in Minorcan bonds? The Grand Duchess and I have just been talking together about it."

Mr. Collin smiled politely and in his most suave voice said:

"Why, certainly, I can tell you. It was I!"

BOOK FOUR

The Kingdom, The Power and The Glory

THE FIRST AND LAST CHAPTER

In Which Mr. Collin Leaves Minorca

It was shortly after nine o'clock next morning when Philip Collin awakened in a cabin which at first he had difficulty in recognizing. The echoing sound of heavy shots outside after a few minutes told him where he was.

He was on board the Russian battleship Czar Alexander, where a remarkable marriage had been celebrated the night before and he was there as the specially invited guest of Grand Duke Peter Nikolaievich of Russia.

With a jump and whistle Philip was out of bed, his toilette made in the twinkling of an eye—his clothes bore little witness that he had attended the most illustrious wedding of his life!—and ten minutes after he had awakened he was up on deck.

The sun was streaming down, the wind singing and the morning sky arched a deep blue and endlessly high over Minorca. Philip's brain felt as though it had passed through a cleansing shower—partly of champagne, partly of some other rejuvenating fluid.

With a smile a Russian naval officer, a friend from the champagne orgy of the night before, rushed forward.

"I was just on my way to your cabin, Professor. His Highness requests the pleasure of your company at a morning glass of beer!"

A laugh escaped Philip which he in vain tried to suppress; he suddenly remembered a late afternoon beer party at a little bar near the Gänsemarkt in Hamburg! Truly Grand Duke Peter had not changed all his habits!

He found his host already indulging in the aforementioned morning beer which in a highly un-naval manner had been placed on top of the compass on the upper officers' bridge. His Highness received him with a grunt of satisfaction and a seductive gesture toward the refreshments spread out before him.

"A mighty fine morning!" he remarked. "But such a thirst, such a terrible thirst! No matter how long I live I'll never be able to drink champagne. How did you sleep? Have a nip of something!"

"Thanks," said Philip bowing. "It will really taste fine. And caviar—I tip my hat to you, sir!"

"Caviar, yes, and I am willing to wager it is the best you have had in your whole life—unless perhaps you are acquainted with the Ruler of all the Russias also?"

"I have not had the pleasure yet," answered Philip. "But now after tasting his caviar I will not rest until I have done so!"

"Here is some of his vodka," added Grand Duke Peter.

"Please tell me what you think of that. Does it meet with your approbation?"

Philip's answer was to piously close his eyes while he let the imperial liquid slowly trickle down his throat. He needed no word from the Grand Duke to tell him that he had never drunk and probably never would drink its like again. He tossed off a glass of beer, another schnapps, and finished three caviar sandwiches, to his Highness' evident satisfaction.

Then he drew a sigh of contentment and lit a cigarette.

The Grand Duke suddenly seemed to remember something.

"By the way! They have been inquiring for you by signal from the new boat."

"For me? From the new boat?"

"Yes, the one which came in an hour ago—an English yacht, the *Petrel,* with a Jew on board. It is lying there inside the harbor."

Philip stared toward the harbor—for the first time he noticed how far out the Czar Alexander lay—to the place where a white yacht had anchored with the English flag flying at its masthead. Then with a puzzled look on his face he turned to his host.

"A Jew?"

"Yes, Isaacs, or some such name."

"Isaacs! Is Mr. Isaacs here too? I'll be bound, the whole world seems to be coming to Minorca. What does he want!"

"He asked whether by any chance we had seen anything

of you. He seemed very much worried. On board of your yacht they thought you had been killed or captured by the rebels. He asked me to help set you free."

"I can well imagine Captain Dupont has been frightened half out of his wits," murmured Philip, "all his guests disappearing that way."

"I told him you were safe on board here. The Jew then asked whether we would send you over to him. I answered you would have your morning glass of beer first. It seemed as though the Jew didn't understand."

Philip began to laugh.

"Did he answer at all?"

"Yes, and he seemed on the point of saying something disagreeable about you, but then thought better of it. I dare say he was afraid of my guns."

"Most likely," said Philip. "He is the one who made them, if I am not mistaken."

"Made what? The guns?"

"Yes. He owns a controlling interest in the firm of Vickers and Maxim."

The Grand Duke gave a whistle.

"That's a devilish sort of Jew. Then he is rich?"

"You might say so," said Philip drily. "A week ago he bought up the whole government indebtedness of Minorca—on my advice. As you know, there was a revolution and as they repudiated the state's debts, Mr. Isaacs lost one and a quarter million pounds. I do not believe it bothers him any, although he would most certainly affirm the opposite on principle. And now if Your Highness will allow me, I will go and talk the matter over with him!"

"Go?" said Grand Duke Peter, whose eyes had filled with amazement as he listened. "Invite him over here for a glass of beer, then you can argue with him to your heart's content. Breakfast will be served in an hour. Bought the whole government indebtedness on your advice! You're the devil himself!"

Philip laughingly bowed.

"Your Highness is too liberal! Will Your Highness give the order?"

The Grand Duke cried something in Russian to his adjutant, who had silently been waiting in one corner of the bridge. After a moment the signal flags began to dance from the Czar Alexander 's mast and very shortly afterwards a boat pushed off from the white yacht in the harbor. After ten minutes rowing it came alongside the colossal Russian war vessel and an elegantly dressed gentleman with a black Mephistophelean beard and an extremely serious air about him mounted to the deck, three steps at a time.

"Where is the Professor?" Philip heard him cry. "Professor Pelotard. They signalled that I should come over. Is he under arrest here?"

"Under arrest," answered one of the officers with a laugh. "The Professor is up above on the officers' bridge. This way, sir."

Philip heard the sound of hasty footsteps on the stairs, and then Mr. Isaacs stood on the officers' bridge. With a smile on his face, Philip stepped over to greet him.

"Good morning, Mr. Isaacs! How are you? How on earth does it happen that you are here?"

Mr. Isaacs looked at him with eyes which were not beaming over with good humor.

"I have come here to try and save one million three hundred thousand pounds," he answered coldly. "Does it surprise you? If Parliament had not prevented it, you may be sure I would have come before. One million three hundred thousand pounds lost on account of you! A nice bit of business, a plaguy fine bit of business! And you here indulging in a morning glass of beer!"

"Why, Mr. Isaacs, you mustn't grudge me that in a hot climate. But now let me present you to his Imperial Highness."

Mr. Isaacs took two steps back and looked at Philip as though he were crazy.

"Yes, his Imperial Highness, Grand Duke Peter of Russia, who has been kind enough to offer me a morning drink and to invite you here!"

Mr. Isaacs' hat flew off quick as lightning before the Grand Duke, who gave a friendly nod in return.

"You make our cannon?" said he. "May I offer you something? Vodka or caviar—help yourself!"

Mr. Isaacs, for the moment forgetting his Vickers and Maxim shares and everything else excepting Minorca, stared first at him, then at Philip, now evidently firmly convinced that he was on board a floating madhouse. Then, probably recalling some frightful stories of life in Russia and the eccentric actions of its Grand Dukes when not obeyed, he hurriedly took a caviar sandwich, gulped down the glass of vodka which Philip gave him, and quickly looked over to his yacht.

"I think I must be leaving," he murmured. "Absolutely mad. A fine bit of business."

The Grand Duke, who had been watching him with a most serious air, said:

"Will you give me the pleasure of having breakfast on board? I will leave you to your friend the Professor, so you can settle your differences during the time before breakfast. We sit down in an hour. . . No excuses, please!"

His heavy eyebrows knitted together slightly, and after a longing look at his yacht Mr. Isaacs hastily bowed and accepted.

But the Grand Duke was hardly out of hearing distance before his feelings broke loose.

"Now, listen here, Professor, what in the devil is this anyway!. . . You entice me into an affair to the tune of one million three hundred thousand, the next day there is a revolution, you telegraph you are going to Minorca to see whether everything is lost, and when I get here I find you on board a battleship, drinking with a. . ." he stopped quickly " . . . with a person who you say is a Russian Grand Duke. What did he mean about my making his cannon?"

"Vickers and Maxim," said Philip. "Don't you own the controlling interest? I told him so at least."

Mr. Isaacs was silent for a moment, enlightened as to that point; then he continued as violently as before:

"But what in the devil do you mean by running away from your yacht? The Captain is half crazy worrying about you—and here you are quietly drinking beer. Why don't you get him to bombard Minorca and force the rebels to pay us? If you at least did that! But instead, you are. . ."

It was impossible for Philip to control himself any longer. To Mr. Isaacs' inexpressible disgust he burst into peals of laughter; then he said:

"I cannot help it, Mr. Isaacs, but if you had been in my shoes you would most assuredly have had some beer too. In the first place, Grand Duke Peter is an old friend of mine."

"An old friend of yours? Well, I'll be. . ."

"An old friend of mine," repeated Philip. "I made his acquaintance in a beer hall in Hamburg. Therefore I could not refuse to have a glass with him on board his ship. Secondly—" he paused for a moment in order to enjoy the expression on Mr. Isaacs' face— "secondly, I had to celebrate the happy event of last night."

"The happy event of last night? That you ran away from your yacht and let the Captain wander around Port Mahon for seven hours looking for you!"

"Not so much that," Philip explained, "as the fact that, during the night the revolution was happily terminated in five hours by the Grand Duke of Minorca and me together."

"The Grand Duke. . . you. . . together. . . terminated. . ." Mr. Isaacs could hardly speak.

"Of course, and then the Grand Duke made a match with a dowry of some scores of millions of rubles and is my eternally grateful friend, especially as it is my former wife he married."

It was too much for Mr. Isaacs. Forgetful of his fear of the Russian Grand Duke, of his loss, of everything except getting out of reach of the Professor, who probably would become violent at any moment, he let out a hoarse cry and started to rush down the steps which led to the ship's deck. Shaking with laughter, Philip succeeded in blocking his way. While Mr. Isaacs' glances flew over the deck in search of a belaying pin or some other weapon, Philip succeeded in stammering:

"Why, Mr. Isaacs! Don't be afraid—you know there is usually method in my madness! Every word I have told you is gospel truth, although it sounds like a fairy tale. Let me tell you about it peacefully and quietly and then you can let me know whether or not you begrudge me my little morning Pilsener!"

Mr. Isaacs looked at him, still far from convinced of his harmlessness; then after carefully putting the compass table between himself and Philip he said curtly:

"Tell me your story!"

And Mr. Collin, now and then laughing at the expression on his listener's face, began to relate—a story which lasted forty minutes and which in the beginning was listened to by the big financier with distrust, then with breathless eagerness and at last with a steady fusillade of many a: "By Jove!" and "You must be lying!" Finally he was convinced and leaving his place of refuge came over to Philip with hand outstretched.

"Forgive me, Professor," said he. "You deserve a keg of Pilsener every morning of your life—you are a great man, a great man, and I am your humble follower. The revolution suppressed, the Grand Duke saved by you, his wife saved by you, and some scores of millions as dowry. By Jove! It came near being a Waterloo—you are better than Napoleon: you turned it into an Austerlitz!"

"Mr. Isaacs, Mr. Isaacs, you mustn't exaggerate! It was more luck than my efforts, and if it came to that—what would one and a quarter million more or less mean to you?"

Mr. Isaacs' face darkened for a moment.

"That's just like you," said he. "You have always behaved in a careless manner with my money. But I will forgive you this time. And it is a devilish queer thing how luck always turns right side up for you!"

An officer suddenly stood before them, bowing and saluting.

"His Highness bids me welcome you to breakfast, gentlemen!"

Mr. Isaacs cast a hasty look at the caviar sandwiches and vodka on the compass table.

"Do you think there will be any more like that down below?" he whispered to Philip. " 'Pon my soul, it was the best I have ever tasted, in spite of the fright I was in while I was having it."

"There should be more," said Philip, "if I judge his Highness Grand Duke Peter rightly! And I am not surprised you appreciate his wares, Mr. Isaacs—it isn't every day you eat the Czar of Russia's caviar and drink his Imperial Majesty's vodka!"

As breakfast was finished—and it neither ended too quickly or with its guests in too low spirits—Philip who, in a further corner of the room, had been talking over with Mr. Isaacs what should be done next, felt a tap on his shoulder. It was Don Ramon with his bride.

"Professor," said he, "there is something we want to talk over with you."

"And I can guess what it is," Philip replied. "The matter of the Grand Duchy of Minorca's indebtedness, am I right?"

"You are. Will you now please explain everything to us. You will pardon us, Mr. Isaacs?"

Philip smiled.

"Your Highness, it really does not matter if Mr. Isaacs listens. As a matter of fact, he should listen. It was with his money that I carried out the coup."

The Grand Duke gave a laugh.

"You took care not to risk your own money in such a dubious enterprise?"

"On the contrary, the enterprise was of the best and I risked what I could, but the principal part of the money came from Mr. Isaacs."

"Tell us all about it, please."

And Mr. Collin, whose tongue had never or seldom

before been so occupied in either drinking, eating or talking as during the last twelve hours, began to tell—a story which this time was not interrupted by Mr. Isaacs, who listened with a proud smile on his face.

When he had finished Grand Duchess Olga turned to him and for the first time took part in the conversation.

"You told me in Marseilles, before you knew me that those who made the coup on the exchange did so to make money. You were the one who did it. Will you now tell me how much you thought you would make?"

Philip squirmed. Suddenly with her blue eyes looking at him, the whole coup on the exchange and the money he had thought of making from it seemed distasteful, almost sordid. After a couple of seconds hesitation. he said hastily:

"I don't know. . . Please ask Mr. Isaacs!"

The Grand Duchess turned to the big financier with that quiet, businesslike air which so often showed itself in her (Philip suddenly remembered their little settlement of accounts in Marseilles.)

"Mr. Isaacs, perhaps you will give me some information on the subject?"

The big financier began to explain as he stroked his black pointed beard.

"My friend the Professor," said he, "had worked out a list of what the former owners of the bonds earned. I believe his figures varied between thirty-nine and six per cent. Let us say an average of fifteen or sixteen. But. . ."

She interrupted him.

"And what was the whole amount you laid out for your coup, capital, interest and commissions?"

Mr. Isaacs looked at her somewhat in surprise: capital, interest, commissions: this was an unusual young lady!

"One million three hundred thousand pounds was my contribution," said he. "The Professor put in fifty thousand. That includes the commissions. The interest, if we should count that, would be about fifteen hundred."

She listened attentively; then came her next question, which was uttered in the same quiet manner as before:

"What price would you ask in selling the bonds now, immediately?"

The matador of the exchange stared at her and repeated as though uncomprehendingly:

"Now, immediately. . ."

"Yes," she said impatiently, "now, immediately. What price would you ask?"

There was a pause for some half a minute, before Mr. Isaacs seemed to understand this was meant in earnest; then with a glance at Philip he said:

"If anyone offered me, let us say, two millions. . ."

"Two millions," she interrupted hastily. "Excellent."

And before anybody could say a word she quickly sat down at the table, drew out a checkbook from a little embroidered handbag, then a fountain-pen, and while all, excepting the Grand Duke, watched her with eyes of consternation, she hastily filled out a little slip of paper.

She calmly handed it to the great financier.

"Mr. Isaacs, please, this is your check. May I ask you to give me an acknowledgment that you have accepted it and that the Grand Duke of Minorca's state indebtedness is paid, with the exception of fifty thousand pounds?"

Mr. Isaacs stared at her as though at a ghost, then at the check. It was drawn on the Credit Lyonnais in Paris and on the middle line where the letters hardly found space his eyes read the words: To Ernest Isaacs or order, fifty million (50,000,000) francs. The largest draft he had ever seen. . . A draft worthy of what it settled—the century-old debts of the Grand Duchy of Minorca. . . Then he looked shyly at her and murmured:

"With the exception of fifty thousand pounds?"

"The Professor's amount," she answered quietly. "We have a special account with him—Don Ramon and I."

At these words Philip at last aroused himself from the astonishment with which her words and actions had overwhelmed him.

"Your Highness," said he, "I have risked fifty thousand pounds—I have no objection to receiving them again, but not a penny more! When I made the coup on the exchange I made it against strangers; unless you wish to deprive me of the right of considering you my friends, you must not even talk of any money settlement."

She looked at him and took out a little folded paper.

"Then you refuse to accept this?"

Philip opened the little piece of paper. It was a check on the Credit Lyonnais of the same sort as that which Mr.

Isaacs had just received, and in its upper corner the figures read five million francs.

Philip quietly folded the little piece of paper together and turned to the table where a candle stood for lighting cigarettes. He carried it to the flame and let it change to ashes while Mr. Isaacs looked on with gaping mouth. Then the Grand Duke said:

"You force me to write out a new check—that is not kind of you!"

"I hope it is not enough to rob me of your friendship," Philip answered. "One million two hundred fifty thousand francs is the right amount, if I am not mistaken."

She sat down at the table again, and a moment later handed him the check. Philip put it in his pocket while Don Ramon smilingly said:

"This is the advantage of having a determined and energetic wife—I have simply been forbidden to say a word in this affair. Housekeeping is to begin without debts. I am already beginning to feel the apron-strings about me, Professor!"

"Your Highness," said Philip, "I know exactly how it feels!"

And while the Grand Duchess blushingly looked at him, he added:

"May I ask Your Highness one thing?"

"Gladly," said she, "what is it?"

"Why did you never call your present husband by his right name? Raoul, Roland, Ronald—you called him everything excepting Ramon!"

She blushed still deeper and took hold of the Grand Duke's arm.

"You are not as shrewd as usual," said she. "Naturally, because I wanted to hear his name!"

In the afternoon Philip and Mr. Isaacs with the grand-ducal pair, Grand Duke Peter and old Señor Paqueno paid a visit on land. Squads of Russian sailors patrolled the streets where the people, still scared and frightened, stood in clusters under the garlands and flagstaffs which Don Ramon had hastily given orders to erect in celebration of his entry with the Grand Duchess. Horsemen rode around proclaiming the Grand Duke's marriage; not a word was mentioned of the revolution, but instead the proclamations made a different announcement: from that day forth all taxes on Minorca were reduced to one-tenth of what they had been before, and if possible would be reduced still further.

"Your Highness need fear no further revolutions," said Philip. "Minorca is looking forward to a brilliant future!"

"Thanks to you," replied Don Ramon with a long look at him. "And still you have not told me about the most astonishing of all astonishing things: the letter. . . How. . ."

"Your Highness," interrupted Philip, "we will leave that story untold. It does not suit the day. Let it be buried with Semjon Marcowitz and the seven others who have been laid in their nameless graves!"

"You are right," murmured the Grand Duke with a

slight shudder. "You are right! It does not suit the day."

Up in the old palace garden, where the rusty fountains for the first time in ever so long, and somewhat asthmatically, gushed forth their cascades, and where the wild Easter lilies sprang from the ground like hundreds of yellow flames of gas, Mr. Isaacs wandered around with old Señor Paqueno. Together they had gone through some of the account books belonging to the Duchy of Minorca, and the big financier's mind was still full of what he had seen there.

"It is wonderful," said he, "wonderful. Inconceivable! For thirty-four years, you say? Inconceivable! With such creditors, such resources and such a reputation! Tell me. . ."

He stopped for a moment, then continued:

"Tell me—and your salary?"

"My salary, Señor!" Old Paqueno gave a slight laugh, too happy to be offended. "My salary has been my prince's affection and the right to be counted as his friend."

"And. . . nothing else?" Mr. Isaacs' voice was full of doubt and suspicion.

"And nothing else, Señor. It was more than enough for me."

Mr. Isaacs looked at him again.

"Let's say five thousand. . . I mean: if you would care to take a position with me—of course it isn't a princely one, but—with let us say, five thousand pounds a year. . . to begin with. . . I have several companies in bad—less successful shape, and. . ."

Old Paqueno laughed again.

"Ah, Señor, it is too late," said he. "Neither five nor ten thousand pounds would tempt me now."

Mr. Isaacs brow darkened.

"Ah, I understand. There is some competitor! Of course, some competitor of mine has already spoken to you?"

Old Paqueno laid a little withered hand on his shoulder.

"There is a competitor, Señor," said he, "but a competitor of another sort than you mean. A little monastery, Señor, a little Jesuit monastery in Barcelona. It is there I am going, after my gracious master gets accustomed to his new conditions. To a little cell in the Brotherhood of the Sacred Heart in Barcelona, Señor."

Mr. Isaacs stared at him without understanding, stared for at least five minutes. Then he recalled Mr. Collin's behavior with the check and shrugged his shoulders. There were things which he really could not understand!

Early in the evening of that same day Mr. Isaacs and Philip Collin partook of a farewell dinner on board the Czar Alexander, where to Mr. Isaacs' joy, neither the imperial caviar nor vodka was lacking. Then the *Petrel* was brought close alongside the colossal gray battleship and in a few seconds Philip and the great financier were rowed over to the great financier's boat in an imperial Russian skiff. Captain Dupont, dismissed by Philip that afternoon, was already standing out to sea with the *Stork*. It was beginning to grow dusk; the palms in the west outlined themselves in purple contours against the horizon and the evening sky glowed like a fading rose leaf over old Minorca. From the deck of the Czar Alexander Grand Duke Peter, Don Ramon and the Grand Duchess waved to Mr. Isaacs and Philip, while the *Petrel* slowly glided out over the evening-tinted Mediterranean.

Mr. Collin leaned over the railing and cried: "I'm coming back to Minorca next year with Captain Dupont's boat! And I hope by then its namesake will already have paid a visit, and that the succession to the throne is assured through Don Ramon XXI!"

THE END

A Note From The Publisher

We hope you enjoyed The Grand Duke's Last Chance, by the first internationally famous Swedish crime writer, Frank Heller! This book was originally titled The Grand Duke's Finances but this Kabaty Press edition was retitled to reflect better the contents. It's been filmed in 1924 (silent movie with English title cards) and again in 1934 (sound remake, only in German) under the previous title, and you can find both versions on YouTube.

Heller clearly enjoyed adding references to Mr Collin's other adventures into this book, and we have made a number of the stories referred to available for free download on https://shop.kabatypress.com. While you're there, why not join our mailing list, and make sure you're always up to date about our upcoming releases?

The Scandinavian Mystery Classics Series

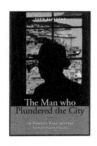

THE MAN WHO PLUNDERED THE CITY: AN ASBJØRN KRAG MYSTERY

Sven Elvestad
(trans. Frederick H Martens)

When a series of jewel thefts scandalise Christiania (now Oslo), detective Asbjørn Krag encounters a master criminal who has his measure—or does he? From the dark brickyards on the city's outskirts to the bright lights of the Grand Hotel, Krag must use all his skill to turn the tables on the gang and their mysterious leader.

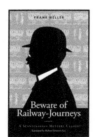

BEWARE OF RAILWAY-JOURNEYS: A SCANDINAVIAN MYSTERY CLASSIC

Frank Heller
(trans. Robert Emmons Lee)

When Allan Kragh impulsively follows a beautiful grey-eyed woman onto a train, he finds himself sharing a hotel with the Maharajah of Nasirabad and his fabled jewel collection. . . and a master criminal intent on stealing it.

> **COMING SOON**

THROUGH THREE ROOMS:
AN ASBJØRN KRAG MYSTERY
(Upcoming in March 2023)

Sven Elvestad
(trans. Lucy Moffat)

When a properous landowner turns overnight into a shivering wreck, he refuses to tell anyone what he fears - not even detective Asbjørn Krag. Krag must uncover the secrets of Kvamberg country house and its three mysterious rooms, as well as the stranger glimpsed in the snowy grounds.

Lightning Source UK Ltd.
Milton Keynes UK
UKHW041146160223
417122UK00007BA/853